THE 7TH DEMON

The Pandora Stone

BRUCE HENNIGAN

Copyright © 2021 by Bruce Hennigan

All rights reserved. No part of this book may be used or reproduced by any means, graphic, electronic, or mechanical, including photocopying, record- ing, taping or by any information storage retrieval system without the written permission of the publisher except in the case of brief quotations embodied in critical articles and reviews.

The 7th Demon: The Pandora Stone By Bruce Hennigan Published by Area613

An imprint of 613media,LLC

Cover and layout design by ebooklaunch.com

Author's website www.brucehennigan.com

All scripture quotes are from the NIV version.

No part of this book may be reproduced in any form or by any electronic or mechanical means, including information storage and retrieval systems, without written permission from the author, except for the use of brief quotations in a book review.

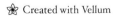 Created with Vellum

For my Readers — Thank you for your loyalty and your continuing interest in the spiritual journey of these characters.

But Joseph said to them, "Don't be afraid. Am I in the place of God? You intended to harm me, but God intended it for good to accomplish what is now being done, the saving of many lives. So then, don't be afraid. I will provide for you and your children." And he reassured them and spoke kindly to them.

Genesis 50:19-21

PREFACE

WARNING! PLEASE READ!

If anyone has read my blog in the past few months (brucehennigan.com) they are aware of the last year and half and its toll on our family. No, I'm not talking about COVID. I am talking about the horrific health issues our daughter had to endure for the past year and a half. Thank God, a major health issue has been resolved.

I have fallen behind in the writing of the Chronicles of Jonathan Steel. This book was intended to be a part of a much larger work. I am combining the 7th, 6th, and 5th demons into one work. This has delayed publication of the entire work.

At the suggestion of one of my readers, I have decided to divide the work into two parts. When you read this book, be aware it will end in a cliffhanger!

The story will pick up in "The 5th Demon: The Elixir of Life"

Bruce Hennigan
September 25, 2021

PROLOGUE

Dr. Hampton's Museum of the Weird – Converted Surgical Amphitheater
London, England

"NOW, MY GOOD LAD!" DR. HAMPTON LOOKED UP AT JOSH Knight standing along the railing of the observation level of the obsolete surgical amphitheater. *"I was hoping you would come by before you left for home. Come down here to the amphitheater."*

Hampton was a portly man with a tweed jacket and a fringe of white hair around his bald spot. He hovered over two of Dr. Cephas Lawrence's crates of antiquities. The lids were open to expose the inner contents. But the third crate was still closed.

Josh found a spiral staircase and hurried down to the amphitheater floor. Hampton clapped him on the shoulder and motioned to the first crate he had opened. "I wanted to ask you about this crate. Dr. Holmes told me you found something of interest within and it was removed. As you know, I am cataloging all of Dr. Lawrence's gifts to me for an exhibit on evil, pain, and suffering. Perhaps you could

I

enlighten me as to what was removed?" He tilted his head, and his bright, pale blue eyes focused on Josh. *"Hmm?"*

Josh swallowed nervously. What should he say? How could he explain to Dr. Hampton that Theophilus Nosmo King had traveled back in time and had left them a message?

"Uh, we found a box containing a coin with an inscription from a person named Theophilus. We believe it is the same Theophilus referred to by Luke in his gospel and in the book of Acts."

Hampton raised an eyebrow in surprise. *"Really? Excellent! I wish I could have seen it."*

Josh shrugged. *"I guess Dr. Holmes took it and forgot to put it back into the crate."*

"Perhaps you could look in the crate and make sure nothing else is missing? Hmmm?"

Josh shook his head. *"I don't remember what was in the crate."*

Hampton put a hand on his shoulder and gently pushed him toward the crate. *"Just a peek. It might jog your memory. Hmmm?"*

Josh hesitated and then moved toward the crate just to get away from the man's hand. Its contents were starkly outlined in the cone of harsh light from the theater's ceiling. Straw like packing material cradled several items. His gaze ran over them.

"I don't remember what was in here that day other than the box with the coin."

Hampton moved around to the opposite side of the crate. He smiled and pointed into the crate. *"What about that box? Was it in the crate?"*

Hampton pointed to a wooden box etched with golden filigree. It was roughly the size of two shoeboxes.

"I don't remember, Dr. Hampton. I really must go."

"Wait, my dear lad. I can't reach that box from here. Could you retrieve it for me?"

Hampton smiled, and for a second, his tongue darted across his lips. Josh shivered. *"Sure."* Hampton was getting creepy!

Josh leaned over the edge of the crate and slid his hands beneath *the bottom of the box. It was surprisingly heavy. He lifted it straight up and leaned back.*

Hampton gasped. "Just a moment! I forgot to get my white gloves. Just hold it for me while I get my examining gloves."

Hampton hurried across the room and through a doorway. Josh stood still with the box, weighing heavily in his hands. He shifted his grip, and the index finger of his right hand brushed against something sharp on the underside of the box. A stabbing pain shot into his finger, and he almost dropped the box. He cried out in pain and whirled.

Hampton was standing a foot behind him with white gloves on. "Are you okay, lad?"

Josh shoved the box into the man's hands. "Something stuck me."

He looked at his hand. A drop of blood oozed from a puncture in the pad of his index finger.

"Sorry, my boy," Hampton said. "These old boxes have all kinds of metal edges to them. Have you had a recent tetanus shot?"

Josh sucked on his finger. The blood had a distinct copper taste. "I'll check with Jonathan. It's just a scratch."

Hampton frowned. "Well, we must be sure. I'd have it checked out."

Josh motioned to the box. "Just what is that box?"

Hampton's eyes lit up as he studied the box. "If Dr. Lawrence's theory is correct, you are looking at Pandora's box. You know the legend?"

Before Josh could open his mouth, Hampton continued. "According to Hesiod, when Prometheus stole fire from heaven, Zeus, the king of the gods, took vengeance by presenting Pandora, a beautiful woman, to Prometheus' brother Epimetheus." Hampton's eyes widened in excitement. "Pandora opened a box left in his care containing sickness, death, and many other unspecified evils which were then released into the world. Though she hastened to close the container, only one thing was left behind." Hampton leaned closet to Josh. "Now, here is where it gets very interesting and where most people who have heard the legend of Pandora's Box get it all wrong.

You see, the one thing left in the box was represented by a single word. Have any idea what that word would be, my dear boy?"

Josh looked again at his finger. It was still stinging. "I don't know, bro. Death. Decay. Disease. Evil. Demons. Am I getting warm because if I'm not, I really need to meet Jonathan. He's waiting."

Hampton smiled and chuckled. "Well, the word was usually translated as Hope." Hampton tapped the box in glee. He raised an eyebrow. "But the word can have another translation, a rather pessimistic meaning of 'deceptive expectation.' How about that?"

Josh shook his head. "I don't get it."

Hampton ignored him. "Of course, the original Greek word referred to an urn, not a box, but one can always hope."

Josh felt the puncture site sting some more, and he shoved his hand into his pocket. "Well, I wouldn't open it if I were you. I have to go."

Josh hurried up the spiral staircase and paused at the top of the balcony. He walked quietly to the front of the gallery and glanced down into the theater. Dr. Hampton was standing deathly still with his eyes turned up toward the balcony. Hampton's eyes were hooded in shadow by the lighting in the amphitheater and he smiled widely.

"Excellent!" He said and the word echoed up from the old surgical theater. Josh shivered and stumbled away from the balcony edge and hurried down the hallway to find Jonathan Steel.

※

Dr. Hampton carried Pandora's box across the room and entered the hallway leading out of the theater. He stepped into a room illuminated by a candle chandelier. Around the periphery of the room, shelves held arcane artifacts of varying types. Hampton sat the box on the dissection table in the center of the room. He smiled as he ran a gloved finger along the closed edge of the box. Oh, how he wanted to open the box! To see what evil lay within!

"What are you doing?"

He froze and stood stiffly. "Just admiring your handiwork."

"It is not time to open the box." The voice of a woman came through the door.

Hampton turned and tried to smile as someone moved into the room. She was short and diminutive, almost a pixie, he thought. Her features hinted at an Asian ethnicity. She wore a bright yellow pantsuit and a matching hat on her short, black hair. To Hampton, she could have been a go-go dancer from the 1960s. The woman had no sense of style. Hampton moved away from the table as she approached, and her gaze fixed on the box.

"We do not know what has evolved within the box. We do not know how magnified and distorted the evil has become that lives within." She reached out a tiny hand and placed it on the lid. She closed her eyes and smiled.

"Yes, they are almost ready."

She spun deftly and crossed her arms and smiled at Hampton. "Tell me you inoculated the boy."

"It is done." Hampton said.

"You know what you must do now."

"I am on the next flight to the states. As you requested." Hampton nodded.

"I ordered! Not requested!" She said. She pointed a small finger at the theater. "What of the third crate? You have not opened it yet?"

"No." Hampton said. "Dr. Holmes' palm print would not open it. Dr. Lawrence may have deceived me."

"I thought the two of you were friends."

"Heavens, no. I barely spoke to the man weeks before he disappeared. We only met once long ago, and he promised to lend the three crates to my museum display."

"If the final artifact is in that crate, we could have finished this business much sooner. Events have already been set into motion with the boy. I can use that leverage for my own purposes. But the others will want the contents of that crate. Who can open it?"

"Dr. Elizabeth Washington, perhaps? Or maybe Dr. Lawrence's other associate who is alive and was just here in London." Hamilton

said. "And the boy is his adopted son. Perhaps I could use the box as leverage?"

The woman gestured with her bare left hand, and Hampton felt a vise-like grip close on his throat. Slowly, his body elevated off the floor, and the grip tightened. He gasped for breath, fumbling at his neck for a pair of hands he could not seize.

"You will not interfere with our plan. I will attend to Jonathan Steel. You will take care of the boy." The grip released, and Hampton fell backward onto the floor. He looked up at the small woman. She raised her hands and snapped her fingers. The air sizzled with static electricity, and two more women materialized on either side of her. They were the same size as the first woman. Hampton studied their identical faces while gasping for his returning breath. The only difference was the color of their clothing. The two new women wore scarlet and blue pantsuits.

"Numbers six and five, I presume." Hampton managed hoarsely. "Together with you, seven, I understand you are named the Unholy Triad."

"The Council is compromised." The first woman said to her companions. "We cannot wait for the entire Council to be replenished and to find unity. The three of us must handle this situation. Agreed?"

"Yes, sister." The red one said.

"Yes, sister." The blue one said.

The first woman turned and stared at Hampton. "If Dr. Washington cannot open this crate, then Jonathan Steel will open this crate. And we have two other tasks for him."

They popped out of sight, leaving Hampton to stumble to his feet, his bruised neck aching. A small price to pay for his deception! He dropped the scared, nervous act and rubbed his still gloved hands together.

"Do what you must. I have my own plans." Hampton chuckled and returned to the back room. Inside, he brushed past cluttered counters and tables covered with moldy, dusty artifacts. He slid aside an

ancient curtain and revealed a metal door. He pressed his hand on a glass plate next to the door. The door slid aside.

Hampton made his way down a set of metal steps into a room that illuminated with light at his presence. The room was smaller than the one above, and round just like the theater. In fact, the room had an old operating table sitting in the center. Hampton paused and studied the figure on the table. A shadow passed behind him. The Crimson Snake stepped up beside him. Hampton lashed out at her and slapped her across the cheek. She gasped, and blood trickled from her split lip.

"Where were you just now? The triplets almost killed me!" Hampton hissed.

The Crimson Snake pushed her unruly red hair back from her face. "If you weren't paying me so much, I would rip out your heart. You told me to guard her."

Hampton slowed his breathing and massaged his aching hand. "Go. Keep an eye on the boy."

Snake wiped the blood from her lip with her artificial hand. "You sign the check." She left the room.

Hampton massaged his sore neck and turned to study the figure on the table in the center of the ancient room. "Well, my dear, my eyes are quite dry. It is a shame that as we age, we have such difficulty with contacts. If you'll excuse me for a moment." Hampton moved over to a counter and opened an old porcelain cabinet and withdrew a leather bag. From inside the bag, he took out a holder for contact lenses. He teased the lenses from each eye and placed the blue irises into their receptacles.

He turned back to the table and rubbed his ghostly white eyes. He leaned over the figure on the table and ran a finger along the woman's pale cheek. She did not flinch.

"My poor, sweet Vivian. Trapped inside your own mind. What will I do with you?"

Moments later with his contacts rehydrated and back in place, Hampton put his bowler hat on his head and left the lower levels of his museum and paused in the outer foyer. Snake sat on a desk with her legs crossed and leaned back on her good arm. Her golden artificial arm lay across her lap.

"The boy got into a cab with Steel, and they are headed to the airport."

Hampton nodded and retrieved a rolling suitcase from behind the reception desk. "Very good." He retrieved an envelope from within his tweed coat and handed it to Snake. "Here are your instructions. I will be leaving on the same flight with Steel and Josh. Only, I will be in first class."

Snake looked at the envelope in her hand. "Quaint. You could have texted me."

"I don't leave a digital trail, my dear."

She raised an eyebrow. "What about a paper trail?"

"The letter carrying your instructions will ignite within 30 seconds of opening the envelope. I hope you have a good memory."

Snake slid down from the desk and tapped the envelope against her thigh. "You're being rather paranoid, aren't you?" She pursed her lips and waved the envelope before her face. "You need a new cologne. You aren't planning on betraying those three demon triplets, are you?"

Hampton glared at her. "What I am doing is none of your business, my dear. Your job is to follow my orders."

She sauntered over to Hampton and put her artificial arm across his shoulder. She brought her face close to his. "If you betray them, it could endanger me. I've already double crossed one member of the Dark Council and it cost me dearly. So, *my dear*, it is my business."

Hampton smiled and tilted his head. "You're concerned about the box, aren't you? Planning on taking it as collateral?"

Snake stepped away from him and averted her gaze. "You left it in your chambers along with your new comatose girlfriend."

"Who will be tended to by Margaret, my secretary." Hampton said. "As to the supposed Pandora's Box, well, it's not what they think it is." Hampton started toward the door and turned back to Snake. "Whatever is now living within Mr. Knight did not come from the box as they think it did. I had a spring-loaded needle hidden on the bottom carrying a much more modern surprise for our young man. The box has other protections as well. I wouldn't consider going near it if I were you."

"What happens to you when they discover you've betrayed them?" Snake asked.

"Ah, that is a good question, my dear. Personally, I'm not worried one twit." He winked at her. "They've bitten off more than they can chew!"

"If they decide to kill you, I hope they let me perform the deed." She said through swollen lips.

Hampton stepped out into the rainy street and the heavy wooden door shut behind him. Snake looked at the envelope and touched the split in her lip. "Don't count on me to protect any fool that goes up against the Dark Council!"

1

Shreveport, Louisiana

As Joshua Knight's chest rose and fell, Steel matched every breath. Josh's cheeks were flushed with crimson and his eyes moved restlessly beneath his closed lids. Steel hovered over the gurney, his hands empty, wandering, yearning for something to make the kid better. Josh had been moved to an x-ray room in radiology for some kind of procedure. No one had bothered to tell Steel what was going on. And, right now, Steel's notorious anger was waging battle with his fear and worry for Josh.

"Mr. Steel?"

Steel glanced over his shoulder. The man wore dark red surgical scrubs. He was small framed with dark hair and an intense gaze behind round, gold rimmed glasses. He held out his hand.

"I'm Dr. Merchant, the radiologist. I'll be performing the spinal tap on Joshua."

"Josh. I call him Josh." Steel shook the man's hand. "No one told me why we were here."

Merchant nodded and raised an eyebrow. "Not surprising. This is sort of an emergency and probably Joshua, I mean Josh's doctor, wanted to get the ball rolling quickly."

"Why are we doing a spinal tap?"

"I think they're looking for an infectious agent. They think he has meningitis." Merchant said.

"Why not do it in the ER. Bedside? I don't like all this shuffling around."

Merchant sighed. "There is an advantage to doing it under fluoroscopic guidance. At bedside, you go by feel. Find the bones in the lower back and try to slip between them. But, on my table, I can see the bones with my X-rays and go to the exact right spot first stick." Merchant motioned to Josh. "I would want it done this way."

Steel studied Josh's face as he moaned and grimaced in pain. "Will it hurt?"

"Just a little. I have to deaden the skin with a local anesthetic. But, once I get past the skin, he won't feel it." An x-ray technologist walked up to Merchant and handed him a clipboard. He scribbled on paper and handed it to Steel.

"Are you his father?"

Steel shook his head. "No, his father is dead. So is his mother. And his great uncle. I'm his adopted father." Steel paused after scribbling his name on the "parent/guardian" space. He sighed. "Yes, I am his father now. Officially. Still getting used to it." He held the clipboard for a moment and then pushed it toward Dr. Merchant.

Merchant took the clipboard and signed his name on the bottom of the consent form. He glanced up at Steel and nodded. "You can wait in the waiting room. It won't take long."

"It better not!" Steel blurted out and then he pressed his hand on his forehead. "Sorry, Dr. Merchant. It's been a long day. Or night. I can't keep it straight. He got sick on the flight home from England and between here and Atlanta I couldn't wake him up."

"Hey, man, look at me." Merchant said putting a hand on Steel's arm. "He's going to be okay. I'll take good care of him." Steel looked into the man's intense gaze.

"I promise. And I always keep my promises." Merchant said.

Steel nodded and numbly walked out the door and into the hallway. 'I always keep my promises' was HIS motto. And now Josh was in danger. He hadn't kept his promise to keep Josh safe. During the flight back from London, Josh had started feeling poorly with a headache and a fever. By the time they had landed, Josh was dizzy and stumbling as he left the airplane in Atlanta for the connecting flight to Shreveport, Louisiana. Josh had become "unresponsive" as the flight attendant said an hour into the flight. An ambulance was waiting and took Josh and Steel to the hospital. Why hadn't he listened to his own advice and sent Josh back before they got involved in their little virtual trip into Numinocity?

Steel paced back and forth in the cramped radiology waiting room, his heart racing, his face burning with anger and fury. What was happening? Why did this have to happen to Josh? Could it be the nanomemes Josh had acquired while wearing Dr. Sultana Thakkar's virtual reality goggles? Could they be at the beginning of another pandemic?

Loss was an unwanted companion for Steel. He had lost April then Claire, Josh's mother. And, then Cephas and then Theo. He had even lost Vivian Darbonne, not that he should care. Come to think of it, he had never been able to keep his promises to protect the very people he cared about. Some motto!

"So, does anyone I get close to die, God?" He said out loud. "Huh?" He clenched his fists and then fought the growing frustration. "Just don't let him die, please."

"Uh, Mr. Steel?"

Steel whirled. Dr. Merchant stood in the hallway. "I'm done. We got plenty of fluid for testing. They'll take him upstairs to his room now."

Steel nodded and tried to unclench his fists. "I just can't lose him. I can't."

Merchant pursed his lips in deep thought and then looked at Steel. "Okay, come with me."

"What?"

He led them down the hallway away from the X-ray room. He opened a door into a dark office and motioned to a chair. "Have a seat. Let's see if I can help you understand what's going on with Josh."

Steel settled into the chair. "What are you doing?"

Merchant sat in a chair before three large monitors. "I can't stand it when patients and their loved ones don't know what's going on. In Josh's doctor's defense, they have lots of paperwork and we needed to move quickly with Josh. His doctors may not like this. After all, I'm just a radiologist. I'll probably get in trouble, but it won't be the first time."

He moved a mouse and screens lit up. He pushed his glasses back up on his nose and then tapped on a keyboard. "Okay, the ER docs worked pretty quickly. Already, Josh has had a CAT scan of his brain and then a quick MRI of his brain. Let's see what they show. I didn't interpret them. One of my partners did so I'm seeing them for the first time."

One of the screens lit up with an oval image that must have been Josh's brain. Merchant worked the mouse and the images scrolled through 'slices' of Josh's brain from the base of his skull to the top of his head. All Steel could appreciate were globs of gray and black surrounded by a white rim. "CAT scan looks okay. But no bleeding. That's important. Now, let's look at the MRI. Far more sensitive."

Merchant's phone rang and he picked up the receiver. "Dr. Merchant. Oh, hey, Sam." He glanced at his watch. "I'm with a patient right now. I'll review the autopsy films sometime before lunch and I'll call you." He paused. "I promise to get by there before 4. I'll be at the airport by 6." Merchant rubbed his hand across his forehead. "Sam, Sam! I will be there. Relax. Just get on the airplane and take off for New Orleans. I got this. Yes, I'll get all the reports dictated before I leave. Now, take a deep breath." He hung up the phone and glanced at Steel.

"Sorry. I'm an assistant to a medical examiner who covers four parishes. Dr. Francisco is heading out to a conference this morning. I've got to go by the coroner's office and sign off on some imaging studies I've reviewed before I catch a flight to New Orleans." Merchant turned back to his monitors.

"You're a coroner?"

"I'm just a consultant. My interest is forensic radiology. Looking at imaging studies to help solve crimes." Merchant shrugged and tapped away at the keyboard. "When did Josh get sick?"

"Last night. Started complaining of a headache on the way home from London and then he said he couldn't feel his feet." Steel swallowed and closed his eyes. "And we're not even in the middle of a pandemic."

Merchant patted his arm. "Hey, take a deep breath. Look at me."

Steel looked up. Merchant gripped his arm. "He's young. He's resilient. Kids get meningitis and they snap back."

"Thanks, Dr. Merchant."

"Jack. Call me Jack." He turned back to the monitor. This time, the two monitors were divided into four quadrants with oval images in each window. Some images included Josh's face and scrolled from the right side of his head to the left. Others went from front to back.

"Okay, so his MRI shows some minimal brain swelling for sure. And the distribution could be early encephalitis." Merchant pointed at an image revealing some white substance in the gray matter of Josh's brain.

"What's that?"

"Meningitis is inflammation of the linings of the brain. What we are seeing is encephalitis, inflammation of the brain substance itself. Most of the time it's due to a virus." Merchant swiveled in his chair. "The spinal fluid will give them a causative agent. Most likely this is viral, not bacterial."

Steel drew a deep breath. "You sound like that's more serious."

"I won't lie to you. Encephalitis from a virus is difficult to treat. Mostly all one can do is support Josh's bodily functions and help his brain fight off the infection. There are some antiviral agents we can try."

Steel looked away and felt moisture in his eyes. "Why are you doing this?"

"Doing what?"

"Talking to me."

Merchant sat back in his chair. "I'm different from most radiologists. I've had a brush with death, and I tell myself to always remember what it felt like to be the patient. To be in the dark. To be questioning what is going on. If I were in your chair, I would want someone to tell me the truth; to help me understand what is going on. I sort of think of myself as a helper in a the time of need."

Steel glanced back at him. "A helper in the time of need?"

That was another part of his motto. It was printed on his business card. "Well, thank you, Jack."

"Hey, I don't know if you're a praying man, but I'd start sending up some strong prayers for Josh. And I'll do my share of praying. Don't want to offend you but I believe it helps." Merchant said.

Steel nodded. "Yes, I've done my share of praying over Josh. Many times. It won't stop now."

Merchant reached into his scrub pocket and took out a yellow post it note. He scribbled a number on it. "My private cell phone. Call me any time, Mr. Steel."

"Jonathan. Call me Jonathan." Steel said hoarsely. "I will."

2

The odors of a hospital were very distinctive: a mixture of antiseptics, body fluids, and flowers. But the fragrance that permeated Josh's room slapped Steel in the face when he walked through the door. The cologne was pungent and earthy and came from a man standing over Josh's bed. He was short and thin and dressed in a three-piece brown tweed suit. He held a dark brown bowler hat in his hands. He looked up at Steel and his pale, blue eyes almost glowed in the room's subdued light. His skin had that ageless, unlined quality that defied anyone's best guess. A white fringe of hair surrounded his bare scalp.

"Ah, Mr. Steel. I was wondering when you might return to your adopted son's bedside." The man looked familiar. And, from his accent he was British.

"Who are you?"

The man smiled. "Dr. Nigel Hampton. I believe you might recall your friend Dr. Holmes delivered some of Dr. Cephas Lawrence's crates to me just this past week. I met Josh when he came with Dr. Holmes to my museum."

Steel moved closer to Josh's bed and watched the boy's eyes twitch. He felt it then; a sickly-sweet cloying cloud of cold that rolled off the man and across Josh's bed. Evil. Unspeakable evil. His left palm pulsed, and he knew if he opened his fist his palm would be glowing. He slowly raised his eyes to Hampton.

"Which one are you?"

"Pardon?" The man tilted his head.

"Don't play games with me. How did you arrive so quickly? Let me guess, you teleported? So, which position do you hold on the Dark Council?"

Hampton smiled and pointed his bowler at Steel. "They told me you were preternaturally perceptive. No, Mr. Steel. I do not have a designation. I am not on the Council of Darkness as it is properly called."

"Shall I send you off to hell anyway?" Steel drew a deep breath.

"I wouldn't be so hasty." Hampton smiled. "Josh's diagnosis is incorrect."

"What?"

"They are convinced he has encephalitis, but his body has fought off the virus almost completely and now he has a variant of Guillian-Barre' Syndrome. You wouldn't recognize the name. Rest assured the variant you son has is very rare and I am the only one in existence with a cure."

"Why should I believe you?"

Hampton frowned. "You don't have to. However, you should know that I intercepted some of his spinal fluid and had it sent to a private laboratory in town."

"You have a lab? I thought you were from England?"

Hampton smiled. "I have access to resources anywhere I have someone who is on the same, uh, team as I am." He chuckled. "I have fellow operatives everywhere, Mr. Steel."

Steel tensed and his fury surged. His temples throbbed. His heart thundered in his chest. "Why are you here?"

"I have a cure for Joshua." Hampton studied his fingernails. "He has a very rare viral infection that is producing an immediate manifestation of a syndrome that usually only occurs after the patient has recovered from the viral illness." He turned his intense gaze on Steel. "And, let me repeat this carefully for you Mr. Steel, I am the only one in existence with a cure."

"I don't believe you."

"Of course, you don't. But I must warn you. If we do not administer the medication within the next four hours, there will be permanent brain damage." Hampton said. He reached into the inside of his jacket and pulled out an envelope. "This is a release. If you sign it now, I can have a helicopter here within thirty minutes. We can transfer Josh to a private clinic north of Dallas, Texas and I can have the infusion begun on the flight there. He will be awake by midnight." Hampton gently placed the envelope on Josh's chest. "Just sign the papers."

Steel glared at the man. What were the chances Hampton would show up precisely in time to offer a cure for Josh? The envelope rose and fell with Josh's breathing. Steel's face darkened with anger. He glared at Hampton. "You said you met with Josh? What did you do to him?"

Hampton grimaced. "I am afraid young Mr. Knight's curiosity led him to pick up a rare artifact. He winced and did not tell me, but he cut his finger on the artifact. It wasn't until later as I put the box back in it's packing I noticed the drop of blood. Naturally, I was worried about Mr. Knight's exposure to an ancient pathogen." Hampton drew a deep breath. "I understand if you are paranoid about this entire affair, Mr. Steel. I can see why you might think Mr. Knight's exposure is a deliberate act. Do not confuse serendipity with opportunity. After all, there really is no time to quarrel about the circumstances of my presence here at this very critical time."

Steel's mind seethed with anger and fury. He fought to control his breathing and looked down at Josh. This was not the time to march into battle. He had Josh to think about no matter how he was infected. He glanced at the release papers. Steel glared at the man. "An accident that Josh was exposed to an ancient disease that only you have a cure to? You came here on the same flight we did, didn't you?" The envelope rose and fell with Josh's breathing. "This was no accident. You planned this."

"Of course, I did." Hampton said quietly. He leaned forward and tapped his wristwatch. "You're wasting valuable time, Mr. Steel."

"What is the catch?" Steel said through gritted teeth.

"Ah, yes, the price. For everything there is a cost, Mr. Steel." Hampton paced along the bed side. "We have a series of tasks only you can perform. And you will need to perform them without question and without hesitation. That is the price for Josh's cure."

"You said 'we'."

"While I am not a member of any arcane council, Mr. Steel, I do have my allegiances. May I introduce my three employers."

Hampton motioned to the door. Three diminutive women walked into the room dressed in pastel scrubs. The first woman wore pink scrubs and her short, black hair framed a round face with mildly upswept eyes. The second woman wore light blue scrubs, and her face and hair were identical to the first. The third woman wore pale green scrubs. She, too, was identical in appearance to the other three.

"May I introduce the triplets." Hampton gestured grandly.

"Seven, Six, and Five would be the familiar designation for you."

"More like the unholy triad." Steel rasped and his face reddened. His anger grew within, stoked by a righteous indignation at the mere presence of these creatures in the same room with Josh.

"I would be careful what you say." Pink scrubs said quietly. "The reason the three of us have joined together is the old adage there is strength in numbers. If you want Josh to live, you will do as we say."

"Without question." Blue scrubs said.

"Without hesitation." Green scrubs said.

Steel hissed. "And I thought it couldn't get any worse."

"Each of them has a task for you, Mr. Steel. One at a time, you will complete these tasks as I oversee the administration of the cure to Joshua." Hampton placed the hat back on his head and tapped it lightly. "The cure will take at least two weeks so I wouldn't dawdle too long if I were you. If you hurry, you can be home for Thanksgiving."

Steel glared at the triplets and swallowed his pride. He gently retrieved the envelope from Josh's chest. He studied Josh's eyelids as his eyes moved randomly beneath the pale skin. The envelope burned in his hand, reeking of the Hampton's cologne. "Why will it take so long?"

"The cure is a gradual one. Josh will need infusions every few hours for two weeks to keep the virus at bay and allow his immune system to overcome this sudden attack against itself. And, if you consider backing out on the deal before the third task is completed, the infusions stop. It's just that simple." Hampton rounded the end of Josh's bed and paused just inches from Steel. He tapped the envelope in Steel's hands.

"Let's just say to save Josh, you must make a deal with the devil." With a dramatic flourish he swept his hand toward the triplets and left the room. One by one, the triplets disappeared in a flash of light.

3

Rain pummeled Josh's face, filled his nostrils, and ran down his throat. He rolled over on hard concrete and coughed until he cleared the water from his mouth and nose. Where was he? He squinted through the falling rain and found himself lying on a driveway. Just a few feet away, pale light glimmered through the rain from the open door of a garage.

A garage? Josh tried to get up, but his legs wouldn't work. He tried to sit up and his arms were weak. He began to drag himself toward the open garage door through the muddy current of rainwater washing down the driveway. He blinked rain from his eyes and gasped. It was his mother's garage back in Rockwall! How was this possible? Someone moved inside the garage.

Crawling painfully across the muddy, rough concrete, he finally reached the threshold of the garage and rolled out of the rain onto the dry floor. He lay on his back and focused on the fluorescent lights above him. A shadow moved across his vision, and someone leaned over him and took him by his arms dragging him further into the garage.

Josh inhaled the fragrance of gasoline and oil mixed with the fabric softener above the washer and dryer by the back door. The odors were familiar, comforting. He closed his eyes and tried to imagine his mother changing out the clothes while he desperately tried to hide his tinkering on his father's motorcycle.

"Mom?" He whispered.

"No." A familiar voice echoed in the garage. Josh turned onto his side and focused on the back of a figure huddled over his father's motorcycle. It was a man in a black tee shirt and black jeans. His jet-black hair was spiked and greasy.

"What? Who?" Was all he could manage to say.

The figure turned. It was Josh Knight! Piercings glittered on his face, but the most disturbing sight was the black spiral around the right eye.

"I'm you, Josh. And you are me." He said. "I was trying to fix the motorcycle. Cassie said it was as good as new but, as you well know, there are some problems with the carburetor."

"I'm saving money to buy the part. It's vintage." Josh said and shook his head in confusion. "How can you be here?"

Goth Josh laid a wrench on the seat of his father's motorcycle and squatted before Josh. "Have you ever considered the intersection of past, present, and future?"

Josh blinked and tried in vain to sit up. "What?"

Goth Josh sat on the floor of the garage with his legs crossed. He touched the spiral around his eyes. "He gave us perspective. Eternal perspective."

"I was in London." Josh tried to remember his last coherent thoughts. "How can I be here? Where is here?"

Goth Josh tapped Josh on the forehead. "You see, we think the past is behind us. Gone. Finished. But as long as the past is preserved in our brains, it never goes away." He sat back and grinned. "And here is the coolest thing, bro. The future doesn't exist. Hasn't happened yet. But the present?

Ah, the present." Goth Josh held his index finger close to his thumb. "How long is the present? Have you ever thought about that? I mean, when does the past become the present? And how long is the present before it becomes the past? A second. A millisecond. A microsecond? Those are words you taught me."

Josh shook his head. "I don't know, dude."

Goth Josh leaned toward him. "You see, we *are* the past. We *are* our memories. It's all there in our collective brains. Our past defines who we are, where we are, when we are. And the difference in our ability to discern the present from the past is not in our brains. It's in our memory."

Goth Josh stood up and nodded. "Yep, you worked all that out while you were asleep. Your unconscious mind. That part of us that is indefinable. So is there a part of us that exceeds the brain?" Goth Josh's eyes glittered, and the spiral pulsed around his eye. "You are now so unfinished. When you were like this you were complete. And you gave it all up to be so limited, so singular. Why?" Goth Josh knelt before Josh again.

"Get out of my head, thirteen." Josh hissed.

"Oh, I'm not the thirteenth demon, Josh. I'm you. I'm the part of your brain that was changed by the inhabitation of a spiritual trans-dimensional being. You've just never wanted to admit that I exist."

A rapping sound came from the door that led from the garage into the kitchen. A faint voice called his name.

"No!" Goth Josh stood up. "We're making progress here." He glanced down at Josh. "Don't listen. Don't answer. I'm taking you somewhere you've never been. Stay with me."

The voice became clearer as the knocking intensified. "Josh, can you hear me?"

It was Jonathan! Josh tried to sit up and slumped back to the floor in weakness. Goth Josh grabbed him by the feet and began dragging him toward the open garage door.

"You are not listening to me, Josh. If you won't listen, then there's only one thing I can do." He paused at the threshold of the garage and rolled Josh out into the rain.

Suddenly, Josh tumbled down a muddy ravine into the brown water. The driveway had turned into a creek swollen with rainwater. He grabbed a slick root and managed to keep from getting pulled into the river's raging undertow. Rain pummeled his head and filled his eyes with blinding water. He gasped for breath and choked on mud and debris.

"Help!" He managed to scream as the river took him by the legs and pulled harder, tugging and sucking him toward certain death. He tried to push and kick but his legs were useless lumps of muscle and bone. His grip began to slip on the root and almost, he gave in to the inevitable. Just release and go with the flow, he thought. Let it take you and sweep you into oblivion. Join your mother and stop fighting.

A hand grabbed his hand just as he let go. He looked up into the blinding rainstorm at bright turquoise eyes. The man pulled him up the muddy slope and out of the raging water. Josh rolled over onto his back and gasped for breath.

"Jonathan?" He whispered. "Thank you."

Josh blinked away the burning rainwater and began to shiver and shake in the aftermath of his ordeal. His teeth chattered and he hugged his arm around his torso. He rolled onto his side and watched the man walk away. He was barefooted! The man's bare feet sunk into the mud. Jonathan's image blurred and for a moment was surrounded by swirling bits of light like drunken fireflies and then Jonathan disappeared into the mist.

"Jonathan?" He managed through his chattering teeth. "Where are your shoes?"

He blinked and the rain cleared like a fog lifting and the man returned only this time wearing blue jeans and a tee shirt. He squatted down to Josh's level.

"Josh? Are you awake?"

Josh blinked again and the shaking began to subside. "Is that you? Really you, Jonathan?"

Jonathan smiled, a most uncharacteristic look for him. "You're awake! Oh, thank God, you're awake!"

Steel leaned over him and grabbed him around the shoulders and lifted him off the bed. He hugged Josh. He actually hugged me, Josh thought! Josh felt lightheaded and black spots swam before his eyes. "Dude, I'm getting dizzy!"

Steel released him and let him lay back in a bed. A hospital bed? An IV line was taped to his left arm. Josh looked around at the hospital room. "Where's the creek? The garage?"

"You've been in a coma." Steel said and he wiped at one of his eyes. "But you're awake. Finally!"

Josh sat up slowly and rubbed his eyes. "Jonathan, what is going on?" He looked down at his legs. "I can't feel my legs! Bro, I can't move my legs!"

He felt Steel's hand on his shoulder. "Calm down. You're getting treatment right now for that. They just started it."

Josh blinked back tears and felt tingling in his legs. Sensation returned slowly making its way from his thighs to his knees. "It's coming back. It's like my legs were asleep."

Steel drew a deep shuddering breath. "Then, it's working. You got sick on the flight home. I thought I was going to lose you."

"You're scaring me. I've never seen you like this." Josh swallowed and his mouth tasted like dried paint.

Steel pulled up a chair and sat beside the bed. "You had some kind of virus. Brain swelling. Things didn't look good. Then you developed some kind of rare autoimmune disorder as they called it. Your immune system is attacking your nervous system. But we're here at a special clinic in Dallas where they have the only cure. It was a shot in the dark. But, it worked, Josh. It worked."

"Dallas?" Josh laid back in the bed. "It must have been a delirious dream I had. The garage. The motorcycle. The water." He paused. He didn't want to talk about his "other" self. "The last thing I remember was getting in the taxi with Monty to go to Hampton's museum."

"That was a couple of days ago." Steel said. "You started getting sick on the airplane."

"Are you sick?" Josh glanced at Steel.

"No. I'm fine. The doctors say they have no idea where you got the virus." Steel looked away and then shook his head. "There's more but I don't want to worry you."

Josh rubbed absently at one of his fingers. Something about his finger fired a distant memory. But he couldn't grasp it. He was just too tired and weak.

The door to the hospital room opened and a huge man in purple scrubs hurried in. For a moment, Josh thought he was seeing a ghost, Steel's late partner Theophilus King. "I noticed on the monitor. Your son is awake. That's excellent."

Josh glanced at Steel. Steel's face reddened. He glanced at Josh. "What? I adopted you, didn't I?"

Josh smiled and relaxed into the covers of the bed. "Bro, I like the sound of that."

"I'll go get Doctor Shutendoji."

Josh watched as Steel stiffened. "Do you have to?"

The nurse paused. "She said to notify her the minute Josh woke up. She wants to talk to you."

Steel turned and stared at Josh with a strange look on his face. "I'll go talk to her. You stay here."

Josh raised an eyebrow. "Dude, where am I going?" His thoughts whirled as he tried to digest all he had just heard. He looked once more at the tiny red dot on his finger. Where had that come from?

4

Steel closed the door to Josh's room as calmly as he could muster. His pulse pounded in his temples with his growing anger. Josh was better, that was all that mattered. But now, he had to pay the piper. The nurse led him to a conference room. He opened the door and motioned inside. Seven, Six, and Five stood together in the corner and they turned in eerie synchrony to face him.

"I see the medication is working." Seven said.

"Yes, Dr. Shutendoji." The nurse said.

"Thank you, Travion." Shutendoji said to the nurse. "Go check on Mr. Knight and if his vitals are stable, get him something to eat. Clear liquids only."

Shutendoji wore a pink blazer over a white blouse and matching pink pants. Six and five wore blue and green matching suits. Shutendoji motioned to the conference table. "Sit, Mr. Steel."

Steel stiffened. "I'd prefer to stand."

"You'd prefer to do anything but what we ask." Six said quietly.

"Your attitude must change." Five said.

Steel ground his teeth and jerked a chair away from the table. He sat rigidly in the chair. "Fine."

Shutendoji moved gracefully to a chair on the opposite side from Steel. Six and Five took chairs at each end of the long table.

Shutendoji rested her small hands on the table before her. "Mr. Steel, I am about to tell you something that only conspiracy theorists and crackpots believe. There has always been a theory that a handful of individuals with wealth, political clout, and power manipulate the machineries of modern civilization from behind the curtain."

"I've already heard about the Council of Darkness." Steel said.

"Which you have done a very good job of dismantling." Six said from his left.

"I prefer the word dismembering." Steel growled.

"Unfortunately, my sister is not referring to the Council of Darkness." Five said.

"Nor am I referring to the unwieldy and inefficient group calling themselves the Vitreomancers." Shutendoji continued. "The facts are, Mr. Steel, that five people control everything on the face of this planet. Through their wealth and their political subterfuge and their cadre of secrets, they oversee minute changes in the balances of world power and distribution of wealth. They fine tune the ongoing chaos of civilization and bend it to their advantage."

"Unfortunately for us," Six picked up the story in an identical voice, "None of the five members are influenced in any way by our forces."

"Your forces?" Steel said. "Do you mean the Council or do you mean demons?"

"Such a heavily overused designation." Five said. "We prefer the Outcast. We were thrown out of the heavenly realms. Cast out. Exiled."

"Because of your rebellion against God." Steel said. "Don't try and pretty up that picture. You got what you deserve."

Shutendoji hissed and Steel jerked in shock as her face twisted into an inhuman countenance and she shoved her chair backwards and transformed! What stood before Steel was a towering figure of red flesh. Upon its ghastly head five horns protruded in haphazard fashion. The face bore over a dozen eyes. It hissed at Steel.

"In Japanese lore, I am known as Shutendoji a demonic being of great power, Mr. Steel. I reveal to you my true self because you must know who you now serve." The demonic being seemed to be semi-transparent and within the body Steel could see the form of the human host. Shutendoji nodded to Six.

Six stood up and transformed into a beautiful woman with long, dark hair and exotic features. Behind her body, nine fox tales appeared and then her face twisted into that of an old hag. "I am Gumijo of Korean legend. I entice men to come to me and then I feast on their hearts and livers. I am sure that Josh's organs would be tasty."

Steel stood up and his chair fell backwards. "Don't even go there!"

"Gumijo!" Five said. "Control your appetite!" She said as she rose from her chair. Five transformed into a huge humanoid form whose dark, blistered skin moved with crawling flames. Its fiery eyes fixed on Steel." I am Santelmo of Filipino legend. I lure the unsuspecting to their deaths whether on land or sea."

All three demonic beings disappeared. The three triplets calmly returned to their chairs with impassive faces and emotionless eyes.

"Imagine being such a creature with incredible power, Mr. Steel." Shutendoji said. "Instead of these monstrous forms, imagine beginning your life as a luminous creation of love and loyalty only to be led astray by your ambitious brother."

"Schichi, no!" Gumijo said. "Do not defile the Master."

"Why shouldn't she?" Santelmo said. "The Council of Darkness is dying. The Master has not appeared since he punished Lucas for his misdeeds. If we are to continue to be of service, we must push beyond our current hesitations. The Master will reward us for our forward thinking."

Shutendoji nodded and sighed. "You cannot imagine what we have suffered, Mr. Steel. You are but a mere mortal."

"A flash in the pan." Gomijo said.

"A puff of smoke in a hurricane." Santelmo said.

"I'll be sure and shed a tear for you." Steel hissed. "You forget that I have an eternal soul also."

Shutendoji steepled her hands. "And unlike us, Mr. Steel, you can claim forgiveness. Have you done so?"

Steel froze. He closed his eyes and searched his muddled mind for the memory. It came.

He was in the group therapy room with April Pierce shortly after waking up on the beach with no memories. It was there his first memory of his past had surfaced.

"I'd like to make a suggestion," April said. "Jonathan, a week ago you recalled the name of a book in the Bible. Perhaps you have a religious background. Do you believe in God?"

Steel opened his mouth to speak and paused as his mind raced. Did he believe in God? He saw motes of dust swirling in a ray of sunshine. He felt the thump of his heart and the slow rhythm of his breathing, of his life. He settled into his chair. And then he glanced at Braxton and it faded, replaced with a burning anxiety, an unsettled feeling. Irritation, that was the best way to describe it. "I think I do, Dr. Pierce."

"Why are you looking at me?" Braxton said quietly. "Am I God?"

Steel blinked and felt his face heat up with anger. "If you are God, then I don't believe in you."

Braxton hugged his skinny legs against his chest. "I never said I was. I asked you if you thought I was God. This is about what you think, Mr. Steel, not feel. But if you want me to be your God, then just look right here into my eye." His voice was so quiet and seductive, and he pointed with a thin finger at the spiral around his right eye. It seemed to move and pulse, and Steel fell...

Steel opened his eyes, and he knelt in a pool of blood from his swollen, bloody nose. He had been in some kind of fight. He wore tattered jeans and a tank top. He was fifteen years old. His head pounded, and his body racked with spasms of pain. He glanced up, and a man stood in front of him. He was short and balding. But his eyes held a love as deep as the sea.

"Hey, man, we've come to get you. You need to come on home." Steel looked at the man. His name was Kevin. "You know we all love you. It's time to walk away from all of this. Would you like for me to help you?"

Down the alley in which he stood a shadowy figure glanced over his shoulder as he disappeared around a corner. He felt a pang of fear and hatred and turned his gaze back to Kevin. He held hope in his hands. "I don't want to go on like this. Will you help me?"

"I promise," Kevin said.

Steel felt the memory slip away, and he found himself in the group session again. He glanced around at the expectant faces. April had gotten up and was standing in front of him. "Jonathan, did you remember something?"

"I was a teenager in an alley. Kevin prayed with me. Whoever he is," Steel said. "I was transformed into something new. Something forgiven. But I can't remember what I was like before that."

Dr. Richard Pierce nodded. "Without the framework of your

past, you will have difficulty determining who you became. But you've taken a big first step, Jonathan. You've remembered a life-changing occurrence that is so profound even amnesia can't erase it."

Steel smiled. "April, I remembered!"

Braxton's tattooed face rose like a dark sunrise over April's shoulder. "Are you starting to remember, Johnny boy?" he said in a trembling voice as he gently pushed April aside. "I helped you, didn't I? I gave you back those memories, don't you see? That means I am God, man of steel." A lopsided smile creased his thin face, and the spiral tattoo seemed to move with a life of its own. Braxton climbed up into Steel's lap, folding his legs like an insect under him, and draped his hands over Steel's shoulders with his face hovering just inches from Steel's eyes.

"What are you doing?" Steel asked.

"Mr. Braxton, return to your seat," April said.

Braxton smiled and touched the tip of his tongue to his lip. His voice lowered to a whisper. "We tried to take your memories. All of them, don't you know, Johnny boy? But I guess we couldn't take the one memory that He controls. That means you are still one of them, don't you see? We thought when you gave up the past you would be with us. But you're not, are you?"

Steel glanced over Braxton's shoulder, and April tugged at Braxton's shoulder. "Please return to your seat, or I will call the orderlies."

Braxton brushed her hand away. His tattooed eye eclipsed everything, huge, bloodshot, mesmerizing. His voice reached a new level of intensity. "In fact, you are a traitor to your god!"

April pulled at his arm again, and Braxton lashed out, shoving her across the room into her father. His legs snapped around Steel's waist, and he grabbed Steel by the throat. "It's time for you to die!" he screamed in an unearthly voice. Steel stumbled up and found his arms pinned to his side by Braxton's legs, and they fell back over the folding chair onto the floor. He struggled against the man's inhuman strength and felt his mind fading as blood flow to his brain lessened.

Braxton pressed his spiraled eye into Steel's face. "Beware the spiral eye. Remember? I'm your worst nightmare. You should be dead, but no, you survived somehow, and I'm going to finish the job." Steel felt his mind slip away into white light.

Steel was back in that place where his memory was lost like a dying man wandering through the desert. He looked up, and Braxton was gone. In his place stood a man in his mid-forties. Heavily muscled and bare-chested, he wore combat fatigue pants and boots. His face was hard, filled with flat planes and intensely burning blue eyes. He wore a white, wide-brimmed hat that he suddenly tore from his head and tossed away. Gray spikes shot through his short, red hair.

"Did you hear me, boy? I don't care about your fanatical friends. You're going to learn to be tough if you're going to be my son. You understand? If I hit you, you're going to hit me back. You got that? Come on, you want a piece of the captain? Come on!"

The man leaped into the air and twirled, his leg snapping out like a lever to catch him in the face, but Steel fought back...

IT WAS THE FIRST TIME STEEL HAD REALLY THOUGHT ABOUT his father since learning that 'the Captain', as he was called, was supposedly on the Council of Darkness and claimed to Demon Number One. Not only that, his father was working with the rivals of the Council, the Vitreomancers. The complexities of this man were more than he could ever understand. And now, he had no time to consider them if he was to save Josh. The Captain would have to wait. But one day, the man would pay for his sins and Steel would make sure he was there to witness it just like he had witnessed the demise of Braxton and the thirteenth demon. He slowly opened his eyes and sat forward over the table.

"Some events in my life are so profound no amnesia can

erase them. I gave my life to Christ when I was a teenager. What happened after that to turn me into a possible assassin, I do not know. I only know that right now, although I sometimes consider myself a reluctant draftee in these battles against evil, I am a citizen of a far kingdom. I will fight for this kingdom. But I will also fight for Josh. The fact that you will never share in that kingdom is the only pleasure I can find in this intolerable situation."

Shutendoji actually smiled. "Oh, how this must bring you great pain, Mr. Steel, to be so conflicted. Always up until now the battle lines have been clean and clear."

"What goes on between God and myself is my business. I can only hope God understands that I must do this to help Josh."

"Judas thought he was doing the right thing, also." Gumijo smiled. "Is he in your far kingdom?"

"That is not my concern. I must do what I must do. Is it wrong to help the spawn of Satan? Or is it more right to help the innocent? Josh did not ask for this illness. You gave it to him for your own purposes! I will do what I must do for now. But rest assured I will not rest until whatever harm the three of you do with these three requests is reversed. So help me, God!"

Shutendoji stiffened and for a moment, anger clouded her face and then the tranquil façade returned. "Very well, Mr. Steel. We will see how that goes for you in the future. Now, there is a member of the Penticle, as it is known, who has perpetrated unspeakable acts resulting in unwanted attention to the workings of the group. Ordinarily, this would be a badge of pride. But this person's actions have angered the other four members of the Penticle and unbeknownst to this individual, they are looking for a replacement. We have someone in mind. Unfortunately, the errant member of the Penticle has secrets regarding the other four members which give that person the power of blackmail. And so, they are at a stalemate."

Gumijo leaned forward. "However, this individual is under investigation by many international authorities. And, we have it on good report that some very damaging information has been collected by certain legal authorities here in the United States."

Santelmo tapped the table. "We want that information. With it, our candidate can blackmail this individual and force them to surrender their seat in the Penticle."

"And you will replace that person with someone who is in league with one of your demons."

"Yes." Shutendoji said.

"Why don't you just kill this person?"

"That would reveal our agenda to the remaining members. They must not detect that we are involved." Gumijo said. "We must operate out of the shadows."

"And I'm supposed to be helpful how?"

"The FBI is investigating this individual. You have a connection with the FBI, Mr. Steel." Shutendoji said.

Steel's face grew cold, and he leaned back. "Oh, no! Not Ross. The man hates me."

Shutendoji looked at a watch on her wrist. "Soon it will be time for Josh's next dose. Without it, he will go back into a coma, Mr. Steel. We have reserved a first-class flight to New Orleans where Special Agent Franklin Ross is concluding his attendance at a law enforcement seminar. You will arrive there tonight before midnight, and you will get that information from him."

"We expect continual updates if you want Josh to have his medication." Gumijo said.

"And you can tell no one what you are doing. If word got back to the Penticle, then our efforts would be stopped immediately." Santelmo said. "And, to make sure you remain silent remember we have a massive army at our disposal always keeping an eye on you."

Shutendoji clapped her hands and a shadow crept up behind the three women. The walls began to move and writhe with a dark *something*. Out of the dark shadows things moved and scrambled on the walls. The writhing dots of black coalesced into a black pixelated wave moving down onto the floor and up onto the table streaming between the three demonic beings with shiny scaled tentacles. The tentacles converged into a mound of moving things. Things that defied any attempt to resemble ordinary objects of this reality. The mound then collapsed into a pile of shiny, insect like objects. Some bore the shape of dragonflies. Some resembled fat beetles. Others swarmed like flies. Some scrambled around on eight legs. One spider like creature broke off from the writhing pile of creatures and climbed up onto Shutendoji's outstretched hand.

Shutendoji stood up and approached Steel. "We have our own demonic drones, Mr. Steel. These creatures will be dispatched to follow you everywhere you go. They will monitor your every movement. They will hear every conversation, every whispered word."

She held out the dark, ebon spider in the palm of her hand. It glittered as light reflected off its shiny carapace. A dozen glowing green eyes stared at him. "Unfortunately for you, they can only be attached to your person with your permission."

Steel felt something burn in the palm of his left hand. He clinched his fist to hide the glowing, pale light that had first appeared during the encounter with the ninth demon. "It's because of who I am, right?"

"It is because of *what* you are." Shutendoji said quietly. She tilted her head as if examining a pet at play. "You don't know, do you?" For the first time, her tranquil façade broke, and she laughed. "What delicious irony." Her laughter faded and the neutral stare returned. "Relent, Mr. Steel. Agree to let this creature dwell on your person or Josh suffers."

Steel glared at the creature and swallowed. How could he do this? He had made a vow to serve God; to battle these evil beings. If he opened his mouth, he would be going back on everything he had come to believe in. But then, there was Josh. He had promised to take care of the boy. And, with a sudden lump forming in his throat, he realized he loved him as any father would love a son. He loved him as much as his own father had never loved him. With his amnesia, he was uncertain how he knew his father never loved him. But the knowledge was as ingrained in his soul and mind as was his newfound love for Josh. He swallowed. Would God not understand that Steel would march into hell itself and shake the devil's hand if it would save Josh? He nodded. There was no other choice. He held out his right hand, palm up.

"I accept."

The spider lifted a leg tentatively and jerked it back before placing it on Steel's hand. It backed away and Shutendoji spoke in a guttural, hissing language. The thing spun and glared at her and then turned again to Steel. It touched Steel's palm with a leg and Steel felt a jolt of cold evil run up his arm. The spider drone scurried onto his palm and before Steel could react, scuttled up his arm and hopped onto his chest, burrowing itself into the pocket of his flannel shirt.

Shutendoji nodded. "Very good. You will not know it is there, Mr. Steel. You will not feel its presence, but rest assured we will be watching you." She turned to the writhing pile of demon insects on the table. "Fly, you fools!" She swept a hand toward the window.

The swarm of writhing, black insect things whirled up into the air and disappeared into the shadows around the window. Shutendoji returned to her seat. "Now, Mr. Steel, you need to know there will also be human hosts keeping an eye on you in case your spider demon friend gets lost or left behind. We will have eyes everywhere."

"This is my worst nightmare." Steel said quietly. Nausea gripped him and his heart raced. He could not abandon Josh to his fate. "I want to see Josh before I leave."

※

JOSH SLURPED THE HOT BROTH. "BRO, I NEVER THOUGHT I would enjoy drinking chicken broth. Right now, it tastes pretty good."

Steel sat by the bed and glanced at his watch. "Josh, I have to go somewhere."

Josh glanced at the man's intense gaze. "But, I just woke up. Where do you have to go?"

"I have to take care of some, uh, business." Steel said hoarsely.

Josh put the empty cup on the table beside his bed. "You aren't a very good liar. What could possibly be more important than being here with me?" His face burned as he realized what he had said. No, he didn't deserve this. After Numinocity and Olivia and facing down another demon he was tired. "I don't care what is going on outside those doors, Jonathan. Right now, I'm scared. Dude, I need you."

Steel's face twisted in anguish, and he blinked reddened eyes. He glanced down at his shirt pocket. "I have to go, Josh. That's all there is to it."

Josh sat forward and his head swam with the sudden movement. "I know what you think you have to do, but, bro, I need you right now. Aren't I more important than a demon?"

"I'm sorry, Josh. This isn't about a demon." Steel stood up. He was shaking.

Josh grabbed the cup and hurled it across the room. It shattered against the wall. "I'm sick of this! I'm tired of it all, Jonathan. I just want a normal life. Why can't I have that, huh? I wouldn't be in this bed if I weren't with you on one of your crusades! Maybe I'm better off without you. So, go! Now! I'll get by on my own." Josh blinked as weakness took him, but he was determined to finish. "I made it for years after my father left and I'll do fine without you. Get out of here!"

Josh blinked heavy eyes and fell back onto the pillows. Steel leaned into his vision. "I'm so sorry, Josh." Steel said weakly.

Josh turned his gaze away. "Just go. Leave me alone." The door clicked shut as Steel left and hot tears ran down his cheeks onto the pillow.

STEEL WOULD HAVE PREFERRED OBLIVION DURING THE ONE-and-a-half-hour flight from Dallas to New Orleans. But sleep eluded him even though he would arrive near midnight. A package of documents passed on by the unholy triad listed a room at the same hotel where the law enforcement convention was located. All he could think of were Josh's last words as he left the hospital. Maybe it was for the best that Josh hated him right now. That gave him the freedom to do what he had to do to save Josh's life. There would be time to repair relationships later. Assuming Josh would have a later.

Steel had racked his brain searching for a solution to his dilemma. How could he do the work of the Council and still preserve his relationship with Josh? For the last six demons, he had taken the side of the angels. But now he was betraying his allegiance to God. Would God forgive him for doing something evil to save Josh's life? Frankly, at the moment, he couldn't care about that. He had to focus on fulfilling the seventh demon's demands.

Steel arrived in New Orleans and caught a taxi in front of the airport. The November air was cool, but the humidity was still ever present. He arrived at his hotel and checked into a nondescript room. He checked his watch. Eleven P.M. He was starving and went into the bar to order something to eat.

5

Dallas, Texas

Faye Murphy glared at her cell phone. "Bobby, do I have to come over there and straighten you out? What were you thinking?"

"It was just a party, sis. A few seniors blowing off steam, okay?" The face of her brother filled the screen of her phone. His eyes were reddened. Either from crying or the alcohol. He pushed his long, blonde hair away from his face.

Faye rubbed her temples and ran her hands through her dark, black hair. "What did Nonny and Poppy say?"

"I'm on restriction." Bobby looked away from his cell phone's camera.

"That's it?"

"And no phone for a week after this call. They made me call you." Bobby sighed. "Sis, do you know what it's like to be cut off from your world for a week? A week!"

"When I was your age --"

"No!" Bobby's voice echoed over the speaker phone. "You're not that old."

"I'm ten years older than you."

Bobby sat back from his phone and crossed his arms. "You don't have to remind us again you were the first."

Faye swallowed as a painful memory threatened to trample across her brain. "We're not talking about me. Nonny and Poppy sacrificed a lot for us."

"Yeah. Adopting six kids. We're not even real brothers and sisters." Bobby growled.

"Is that what this is about?" Faye sighed. She glanced up at the clock on the break room wall. Her break was over. "Listen, Bobby. I have to get back to work. I have a new patient to check on. We will talk about this later, okay?"

Bobby nodded with a glum look on his face. "You'll have to call on Poppy's phone. They're making me take care of Dooble for a week?"

"The mastiff?" Faye laughed. "He weighs more than you do."

"And so does his poop!" Bobby reached out a hand and ended the video call.

Faye pulled on her white coat and straightened her scrubs. She left the break room and stopped at the nurses' station. Travion, the charge nurse, glanced up at her from his chair before a computer monitor.

"Faye, everything all right? Girl, you look like crap."

Faye put out her hand. "Just family matters, Travion. My new patient?"

Travion handed her an iPad. "Joshua Knight. Had an unknown viral infection and symptoms like GB Syndrome. No longer infectious."

"Who's his doctor?" She scrolled down a list of names on the tablet until she found Mr. Knight.

"Dr. Shutendoji." Travion said with a rumble in his voice. "And her sisters."

Faye felt a chill run down her spine. "They give me the creeps." She leaned over the countertop. "Do you think they sometimes switch out colors just to mess around with us?"

Travion stood up, all six feet eight inches of him. He topped over three hundred pounds and his dark skin glistened under the sickly fluorescent lights. "Girl, all one of them has to do is walk into the room and I have hot and cold running chills. They are daughters of the devil, if you ask me."

Faye laughed. "I wouldn't go that far. Okay, so I'll check the notes and go see Mr. Knight."

Travion raised an eyebrow. "Better take a crucifix. You might need it."

Mr. Knight lay quietly in his bed in the only VIP room in the clinic. His family must be rich, she thought. She pulled up a chair beside the boy's sleeping figure and scrolled through the history on her iPad.

"Jonathan?"

Faye looked up as the boy opened his eyes. "No, I'm your nurse practitioner. Faye Murphy."

The boy's eyes tried to focus on her. "Where's Jonathan?"

Faye glanced at the information on the tablet. "Jonathan Steel is your father?"

"No, he's my Dad. My father is dead. I think he is, anyway." He blinked his eyes. "My mother is dead, too. So is Uncle Cephas."

Faye swallowed. "Mr. Steel is your, what? Guardian? Adopted father?"

He nodded. "It's complicated. I can't call him my father. I always called my father, Father. I need to start calling him

Dad. But it makes him nervous. And now, I've messed up everything. I got mad at him."

Faye felt her face warm, and her pulse quicken. An adopted father abandoning his sick son? She fought back the anger. She had to be encouraging.

"I'm sure he had his reasons." She managed tersely.

The boy looked at her. "It's probably another one of those freaking demons. That's the only thing that would make him act like this. Dude's messed up."

Faye nodded. "We all have our demons to wrangle with, Joshua."

"Josh. Just call me Josh." He looked back at her with moist eyes. "What is happening to me?"

Faye glanced down at the chart. "You have acquired some kind of viral agent."

"Am I contagious?"

"I don't think so. There's no infectious disease precautions." She looked up from the tablet. "You have a Guillian – Barre' type syndrome. It's a post infectious syndrome. Your own immune system has been triggered by the virus to attack your nervous system."

Josh sighed. "That's why my feet are numb?"

"Yes." Faye stood up and tried to smile down at him. "And the numbness will move up your body unless we keep giving you regular infusions."

"What kind of infusion?"

Faye glanced at the pad. "An experimental medication under the direction of your doctors. This clinic has lots of unusual illnesses we are certified to treat with experimental therapies. We are on the cutting edge of medicine."

"But?" Josh said.

"Excuse me?" Faye tried to smile.

"Your mouth said that perfectly, but you face says otherwise. I'm not some stupid teenager. I've been through crap you couldn't possibly imagine."

Faye blinked. So had she. "Those demons you spoke of?"

Josh tensed. "Yeah! Thirteen was the worst. Twelve was a vampire. Eleven loved being a serial killer. Ten was some kind of homicidal fallen angel with an army of extraterrestrials. I never met nine because I didn't go back in time. And eight almost took over most of Europe but Vivian put a stop to that. Who could have imagined she would turn to Christ? Who?"

Faye sat back down. The boy was babbling. "That's nice." She said quietly. "Now, your next infusion will begin shortly. Each infusion takes a couple of hours to run in and you'll be asleep during the infusion. The medicine does that to you."

"Back to the 'but'?" Josh said.

Faye put on a fake smile. "Let's just say I'm not always confident about some of these experimental treatments. But I'm not the scientist who discovered them. We just need to have a little faith."

"That's about all I've got left." Josh glanced at her and then down at his body beneath the blanket. "Can I get up?"

"I'm afraid not right now. We have no idea what the paralysis is like. You might fall and then you would be in a worse circumstance."

Josh licked his lips. "Can I have my cell phone. I need to call Jonathan and tell him I'm sorry."

Faye felt her face burn with anger. She wanted to scream, *"Your 'Dad' abandoned you on your sick bed, Josh. He should be calling you!"* But she stood up and walked away from the bed.

"I'll see what I can do." Was all she could manage as she turned to the drawers on the room's console. She pulled open the top drawer with more force than it deserved. Josh's clothes were stacked within. On top of his folded shirt lay a cell phone. Beside it was a gold chain with a long, red jewel attached. Some kind of necklace? She picked up the cell phone and tried to calm her anger. Whoever this Jonathan Steel was, she wanted to set him straight!

New Orleans

Steel sat at the bar and chewed on a mouthful of muffuletta, a "famous Italian sandwich invented in New Orleans with ham and salami, provolone cheese, olive dressing and great bread" the menu said. The bread wasn't fresh and he almost choked on the dry crumbs. The muffuletta at Monjuni's in Shreveport was much better.

"Mr. Steel?"

Steel glanced over his shoulder as Dr. Jack Merchant slid onto a seat next to him. "What are you doing here?"

Steel glanced around the bar. It was uncharacteristically empty for this time of night. However, a sallow faced man in a nearby booth smiled at him exposing brown teeth and gestured with two fingers to his eyes. He mouthed. "I'm watching you." Steel felt the spider drone move and one black leg appeared from the shirt pocket.

Steel glanced back at Merchant. "I'm meeting my partner here. He's at a law enforcement convention and it wraps up tomorrow. We thought we would talk over what he learned in order to improve our business."

Merchant nodded. "And what business would that be?"

"Private investigator." Steel swallowed. "I just flew in."

The bar attendant asked Merchant for his order and he asked for sparkling water. "I'm an alcoholic." Merchant said as the attendant sat a glass of bubbly water before him. "Don't drink anymore."

"Then why are you in a bar?" Steel asked.

Merchant pointed to the water. "I needed a drink." He shrugged. "Okay, so I guess I miss the atmosphere." He turned his gaze to the bottles of amber fluid sitting behind the bar attendant and the bottles reflected in his gold rimmed glasses. "My Daddy always said it doesn't matter where you get your appetite as long as you eat at home. Of course, he was talking about marriage." He sipped his water and a look of sadness came over him. He sighed. "So, how's your son?"

Steel finished his muffuletta. "I transferred him to a specialist clinic in Dallas. He's under treatment and doing well. You here for a medical convention?"

Merchant nodded. "Probably the same one you're talking about. Dr. Francisco wanted me to catch a couple of forensic seminars today and tomorrow. What a coincidence."

"I don't believe in coincidences." Steel mumbled and pushed his plate away. The spider retracted its leg back into his pocket. "Well, it's nice to see you. I have to get to my room and catch some sleep."

Merchant put a hand on his arm as Steel stood up. "Is everything all right, Mr. Steel?"

Steel tensed and resisted the urge to jerk his arm out of the man's grasp. "Yeah, just fine." He turned and walked away. He glanced once more over his shoulder at Tooth man in the booth. The man smiled revealing his awful teeth and gave Steel a thumbs up.

6

Steel's cell phone rang when he walked in the door to his hotel room.

"Is this Mr. Steel?" A woman said.

"Yes. Who is this?"

"Faye Murphy, Mr. Knight's nurse practitioner." Her voice was tense. Jonathan froze.

"What's wrong?"

Silence for a moment. "Josh is fine." She said tersely. "He wants to speak to you." The line hissed.

"Jonathan?" Josh said.

"Josh?" Steel plopped onto his bead. "What's wrong?"

"Where are you?" Josh asked.

"I had to fly to New Orleans to meet with Jason." Jason Birdsong was Steel's partner and the man had been invited to the seminar by FBI Special Agent Franklin Ross. He had not spoken to Jason but it was a good cover story, the first of many inevitable lies.

Josh's breathing sounded raspy and wet. "Jonathan, I'm sorry about what I said."

"It's okay. I deserved it."

"No, you didn't." Josh coughed. "I'm about to start another infusion and Faye let me call you. To say I'm sorry. And to tell you I understand."

"Thanks." Steel whispered.

"I know you have work to do. Important work. Dude, that work is more important than I am, right now." Josh's voice was fading.

"Josh, nothing is more important than your life." Steel managed to say hoarsely. "I have to work. In order for you to get better, the bill will come due."

He listened to Josh's rough breathing. "Got it. Take care, bro." The line went dead.

Josh studied the face of his cell phone through tear blurred eyes. The phone slid down into the covers as he slumped further into the bed.

"I'm really tired, Miss Faye." He mumbled.

"Just Faye will be fine." She fished his cell phone out of the covers and crossed the room, putting his cell phone back in the drawer. She slammed the drawer shut.

"You okay?" Josh mumbled.

Faye whirled. "Yeah. I'm fine."

"You don't sound fine. You sound like Jonathan does when he gets mad." Josh closed his eyes and leaned his head back. "And no one wants Jonathan Steel to be mad."

Faye came back to his bed as a nurse's aid came in with a bag of fluid. "Here's the next infusion, Faye." She handed Faye the bag.

"Thanks, Dudley."

Josh opened his eyes with difficulty and watched Faye hang the bag on the IV stand and attached it to his IV machine. Josh studied her face.

"You're mad." He whispered.

Faye glanced down at him. "It's okay, Josh. I just don't understand."

"He'll be back. He's got important stuff to do."

Faye pursed her lips and planted her hands on her hips. "I've heard that before." She turned and stormed from the room.

Josh lifted his hand to make her come back and felt the weakness overcome him. He noticed the tiny, red puncture wound on his finger. Where had that come from? The box! It had come from the box in Hampton's laboratory.

His vision blurred and he moaned as dizziness swept over him. He glanced up at the bag of fluid dripping into his veins. What was going on? He now remembered his visit to Dr. Hampton's laboratory. He remembered the ancient artifact. Dr. Hampton had urged him to pick up the box. Was it possible the man knew he would prick his finger? Was this all planned? If so, then he was the leverage they were using over Jonathan. And, that meant, they would be making Jonathan do something he would normally refuse to do.

Josh tried to push up out of the bed. He had to get out of here. He had to get away from Hampton's three creepy doctors. Weakness engulfed him and he fell back into the bed. His mind swam in currents and torrents of confusion.

He was in the creek again and rivulets of muddy water surged around his feet. Rain pelted his face, and he was drawn slowly and inexorably into the deluge of darkness.

Josh lifted his head out of mud and his gaze focused on the mud-covered feet. He rolled painfully onto his back and looked up at a woman's face. Her dark hair was cut short around her face. She wore a black dress.

"Ila?" Josh whispered at the sight of his old girlfriend.

"We need to get in out of the rain, Josh. I thought you were going to fix the motorcycle." She turned and walked away from him across a parking lot covered with rainwater. She entered the door to a motel room and Josh raised up painfully to gaze at the mountains around the seedy motel. He was back in Romania! With the twelfth demon! How?

He crawled across the pebbly parking lot and in through the open door of the motel room. Ila reclined on the bed, and she pointed to the window. "It's right over there."

Josh pulled himself up painfully and wobbled across the room on weak legs. He leaned against the windowsill of a grimy window. The bus that had brought the followers of Rudolph Wulf sat on the far side of the driveway in front of the motel. The followers had unloaded the supplies and his motorcycle leaned against the bus. They hadn't even bothered to use the kickstand!

"Remember when you left Jonathan Steel at the courthouse?" Ila said. "Boyfriend, I was so proud of you on that motorcycle. I can't believe they brought it with us! We can ride around through the mountains. Maybe find a secluded little cabin?"

Josh turned slowly and settled into a rickety chair beside the window. "This can't be happening. I'm in Texas. Not here."

Ila shook her head in consternation. "You're so stubborn! Okay, so let's change the subject. Remember what we talked about before? How the past becomes the present."

"We? You weren't there."

"Of course, I was, silly." Ila sat up on the bed and crossed her legs. "We were interrupted. I was about to tell you the prevailing theory about reality."

Josh rubbed his face with weak hands. "This is crazy. I need to wake up."

"Oh, not yet boyfriend." Ila said. "Now, here is the continuing reasoning we are working on. If the past and our memories define who we are, then can't we conclude that the past and our memories define our perception of reality?"

Josh looked over his shoulder at the motorcycle. "Why did they bring it to Romania?"

"Nope! Don't change the subject." Josh ignored her. "Okay, so Vivian thought you had hidden some kind of communication to Jonathan. When he found your motorcycle at the airport, he would have known where to find us. At least, that is our working theory."

He felt something warm on his face and Ila was standing before him now, her hand on his face. She turned his gaze back to her shining eyes and pale face. "Now, Josh, this is important. Memories and the past define reality. It's that simple. Quantum theory and all that, remember from our physics class? Consciousness defined reality? We think and we change the very fabric of the universe."

Josh pulled her hands from his face. "No! This isn't real. I'm dreaming."

"Ah! Dreaming! Now, you're onto something. What is dreaming but an alternate reality? Josh, when we dream it's as real as when we are awake. There is a layer of reality in our dream state that we can access. You're almost there."

Josh tried to stand. "Almost where? I know where I am. I'm sick and in a hospital bed. I'm not here in Romania with you. And alternate realities are fake, like Numinocity."

A voice came to him from outside the window. A woman's voice. Faye? His nurse practitioner?

"Don't listen to her. Don't listen to that reality. We are making our own, Josh. And, when we do, it will eclipse all of reality." Ila stood up and backed away as the voice continued outside the window. She began to grow taller, and her hair grew longer changing from the stark black to a reddish hue. Her dress lengthened into a long, white robe. She smiled and looked down at her arms.

"It's working. Just don't pay attention to that voice." The woman's tone strengthened and grew coarser. Josh backed up toward the window.

"No! I will not stay here." He allowed himself to fall back into the window. Glass shattered around him, and he tilted over the threshold and fell. But he did not strike the pavement of the parking lot. He plunged back into the cold, black water of the rain swollen creek. As the waters washed him away from the window that hung suspended in midair, the woman leaned out.

"I am growing impatient, Josh." She shouted as he floated away from her. "You must know that I am inevitable." She said as Josh sank into cold darkness.

7

Steel woke in the middle of the night. His left hand throbbed and he pulled it out from under the pillow. His entire arm was asleep. He looked at his left arm as if it were part of someone else and gasped as the palm of his left hand glowed with a faint light.

This had happened before on more than one occasion. In the confrontation with the Major in ancient Jerusalem, the light from his palm had led to the defeat of the ninth demon. And then, on the train from Paris to London, the light had pushed Sultana Thakkar away from him while wearing the goggles.

He studied the alien skin of his throbbing hand at the end of his numb arm. Imbedded in the glowing skin were tiny shards of stone. How? Where had they come from? In Numinocity, Thakkar's alternate reality, he had held hands with Vivian. The palm of her hand had been discolored. He had passed it off to the workings of Numinocity's software. But was there something more to it? Before Numinocity, only a glowing light had come from his palm. But now, he could see tiny crystalline shards imbedded in his flesh.

As if in answer, his mind filled with a memory, but it belonged to Vivian. How? She stood on a street in ancient Jerusalem, and he lived her memory.

Vivian halted and felt something foreign, something bright, something otherworldly at her back. She hurried into the side street and looked back toward the sun. A group of men had entered at the far end of the street and were coming toward her. Her inner demon, Summer, screeched inside her head and Vivian grabbed her ears. It did no good. The pressure grew as the men came closer. Vivian pushed herself deep into a huge crack in the wall of a house. She couldn't breathe.

Back down the alleyway, a voice echoed toward her. "Go away! What do you want with me, Jesus of Nazareth? Have you come to destroy me? I know who you are, the Holy One of God! The Son of Man! Why do you torment me?"

The group of men paused equal with the side street. Vivian squinted into the sun as they paused. A man knelt before her.

"Andrew." He said to someone behind him. "This woman is afflicted." The man was young with dark, flowing hair and a scraggly beard. His deep, chestnut eyes bored into hers.

Vivian felt the Grimvox nodule heat up against her chest. She wrenched her hands away from her ears and grabbed the nodule in her right hand. It burned like a searing coal of fire and she opened her mouth to scream.

"In the Father's name, I command you to Tartarus." Said the man squatting before her. The demon Summer tore through her mind, bouncing through memories and hidden secrets, tearing her way into the back of her eyes until all Vivian could see was the young girl in a sunflower dress bleeding from her eyes and ears. Summer exploded behind her vision and was torn from her mind like a cloud of acrid smoke assailed by gale force winds. Summer's

scream dwindled as she disappeared into a whirling vortex of light just above the man's head.

"You have done well, John." Another man said as he leaned over John. "The Master will be pleased. He is following the other demoniac. We must help this woman."

John nodded to Andrew and reached out to Vivian. She pulled away and ran out into the street, colliding with the other men in the group. She fell at the feet of a man who reached down to help her up. It was the traitor!

Tears gushed from her eyes. Confusion reigned in her mind. She turned and saw Him. He had paused at the far end of the alleyway.

"Judas." John said as he appeared beside Vivian. "Take her somewhere safe. We have to go prepare for tonight's meal. We will meet you in the upper room."

Vivian felt Judas' hand tighten on her arm and she was so weak she could not pull away. The Son of Man disappeared around the corner. For a fleeting second, he paused and looked back in her direction. The bright, crimson sun caught him full in the face and his eyes fixed on her.

Vivian gasped. What was this? What had he done to her? The man disappeared around the corner with the other disciples following him. A few broke off and went in another direction. Judas dragged her down the street.

Her right hand burned with fire and blood dripped in the dirt as she shuffled after Judas. The Son of Man had looked at her. More importantly, his look had said so much. I love you? I forgive you? What were these foreign thoughts? How could he forgive her? She would not have it!

"No, I don't want his forgiveness." She screamed. Judas looked down at her and spoke and Vivian's translator carried his words.

"I do not understand you. I have more important things to do than babysit you." The translator said in her ears. He tossed her away. He hurried away into a gathering crowd.

Vivian sat up in the dirt. Men and women moved a safe distance *around them. She looked at her right hand. It was gripped so tightly about the nodule she could hardly move her fingers. With her left hand, she pried open her fist.*

The jeweled nodule had fragmented in the heat of the exorcism and shards of the glittering blue stone were now imbedded into her charred skin. The pain was excruciating and she luxuriated in it. She let the pain flow over her chasing away the feelings of love and mercy; the wave of compassion and love that had flowed from the Son of Man.

STEEL SHOOK HIS HEAD IN CONFUSION. GRIMVOX? WHAT had Holmes said about the thing? It was a repository for all the memories and deeds of the Council of Darkness. Somehow, tiny shards of the Grimvox had passed from Vivian into his hand. They had played the memory for him! And not only that, Steel now saw where the seeds of Vivian's redemption had begun. On the streets of ancient Jerusalem, she had come face to face with the Saviour.

Steel's face grew cold. And the betrayer! Steel was no better!

The spider drone scuttled up his arm out of nowhere and paused before reaching the glowing light in his palm. The spider reared back on its hind legs and jumped off Steel's arm onto the nearby bedside table. It whirled dizzily and finally stopped, legs slowly twitching. Its tiny green eyes glared in Steel's direction.

"You don't like my hand, do you? Too bad. Just stay away from it." He lifted his palm closer and studied the tiny glowing shards of the Grimvox fragment. What else waited in these shards? What secrets did they hide that might involve his past? Could he find out where his father was?

"Show me." He whispered and he was somewhere else.

"Mom? Have you seen my tennis racket?"

"Honey, it's probably in the garage. I put it out there during the winter months." He heard his mother say from the library. She came through the library doors and closed them behind her. Her short, reddish blonde hair was in disarray. She hurried over to the breakfast nook table and looked down at him. *"You're going to be late for school, JJ. I have to be at a meeting in thirty minutes and I can't find my messenger bag."*

He ate the rest of his toast and pointed behind him. *"You left it in the pantry. Don't know why, Mom."*

His mother sighed and retrieved the leather bag from the pantry. *"I was loading up some snacks last night. These meetings can be long. Now, finish your breakfast and get your stuff. You'll be late for school. Spring break is over, and you only have a few weeks left as a freshman."*

He brushed the crumbs from his hands. *"Clay is coming to pick me up, Mom. You can go on. I'll go look in the garage for my tennis racket. We're playing after school today."*

His mother ran a hand through his long hair. *"You need a haircut, JJ. Or does she like it this way?"*

He felt his face heat up. *"What?"*

"You haven't play tennis in over a year. Who is she?" His mother sat at the table and her jade green eyes sparkled with mischief.

"Just a girl." He drank his orange juice.

"Does she have a name?"

"Penelope."

"Is she in your class?"

"No. She's a sophomore. I met her at church."

"Oh, good!" His mother stood up and shouldered her messenger bag. She tried vainly to push his unruly hair back into place. *"I'd like to meet her sometime."*

"Mom, we haven't even been on a date. Yet. She plays tennis,

okay." He stood up and pulled away from his mother's fingers in his hair. His mother smiled at him and leaned forward quickly and gave him a peck on the forehead.

"Well, if she goes to church that's a good sign. Your father would approve."

"Yeah, if he was ever around." He said.

Sorrow clouded her face. "He'll be back later this week. I have to run. Love you, JJ."

"Love you, too." He mumbled as his mother hurried out into the garage.

By most standards the garage was huge and was built to house five cars. His grandfather was supposedly a huge car buff back in the day. Way back in the day. He followed his mother into the garage as she pulled away in her car. He glanced up at the shelves covering an entire wall of the three-car garage. Boxes of collected artifacts had been stacked carefully by his father. Of course, he viewed the "artifacts" as nothing more than useless junk. "Thanks, Dad, for being a hoarder." He said.

He started digging through boxes and shuffling through plastic bins filled with minutia. He spied his tennis racket wedged behind a cloth covered box. When he pulled the cloth off the box, dust filled the air and he sneezed. He picked up the plastic storage box and was about to place it on another empty shelf when it slipped from his grasp.

The box tilted and landed on its side. The plastic lid popped off and the contents spilled out onto the garage floor. He glanced at his watch. Clay, his best friend would be by in ten minutes. "Great!"

Notebooks and file folders spread out before him. He would pull down the one box that contained papers instead of junk! He started shoveling the contents back into the box when his hand brushed something, and he felt a tingle of electricity. He jerked his hand away and looked at a small drop of blood. Something had stuck his finger.

He pushed the folders and notebooks aside with his toe. A black leather folio the size of a half of a piece of paper lay at the bottom of the pile. At each corner of the embossed leather cover metal brackets showed signs of rust.

"Now, I'm going to get tetanus." He growled. He picked up the folio and it was surprisingly heavy. Faded gold lettering on the front was hard to read. He brushed away dust and dirt. "FDS? Who was FDS? Wait, grandfather's first name was Fabian. Middle name Dorcas." His heart pounded and he stepped back in shock. "Grandfather?"

JJ slowly opened the folio and fading photographs filled the first page. The first photograph showed a tall, thin man standing next to a brown skinned man wearing nothing but a loin cloth. The man carried a spear and wooden spikes pierced his lips and nose.

"Dude, what's up?" JJ jerked and almost dropped the photo album. He whirled and his friend, Clay stood at the open entrance to the garage. "We got to go before the next Imperial transport pulls into this hangar."

Clay had long, wavy blonde hair with bangs that covered his eyes. He wore his ever-present Star Wars tee shirt and jeans. Steel grabbed the tennis racket and ran back inside to get his backpack. "Very funny."

"Hey, dude, I'm not the one that lives in the Emperor's palace. Your place is seriously creepy."

He couldn't argue with that. The mansion, as his father called it, was huge. There were rooms and hallways he had never been down. Clay drove away from the mansion and glanced at the black notebook.

"What's with the diary?"

"It's a photo album of my grandfather."

Clay's eyes widened. "You mean the crazy dude?"

JJ nodded. "That would be the one. No one talks about what happened to him. It's all hush hush." For a moment he recalled the day his grandmother had found him standing in front of the forbidden door in the mansion's library. He had been much younger and had heard the rumors his grandfather's spirit was hidden behind the door instead of in heaven.

"So, where did that album come from?" Clay asked.

"It has pictures of my grandfather and some local natives. He spent a lot of time in South America." He glanced once more at the photo album and his finger throbbed. As he stared at the name on the cover, it seemed to become clearer, better defined. For a moment, he thought he heard something whisper in his ear.

"Open me! Read me!" the voice said. He glanced at Clay who was prattling on about mysterious artifacts and hidden secret passages. His friend had not heard the voice. Only he had! He opened the cover and studied the first photo again. His grandfather's eyes glowed from the page. He had heard his father and mother talk quietly about his grandfather and the man's growing insanity that led to his mysterious death.

JJ closed the album and slipped it into his backpack. Was insanity hereditary? Wasn't the first sign of insanity hearing voices? He closed his eyes and fought off the panic.

"Dude, chill. You're shaking like a cat at a dog show." Clay said as he pulled into a parking spot at their high school.

"Clay, my grandfather was insane. What if it's in my genes, too?"

Clay turned off the car. "Look, if you're that worried, talk to someone. Your doctor, your father, your mother."

"We don't talk about grandfather." He said.

"Then, who can you talk to? Besides me, of course."

He glanced at his friend who had the empathy of a turtle. "You're my best friend, not my counselor."

Clay snapped his fingers. "Hey, talk to Kevin."

Kevin was the youth pastor at the church that he and Clay sporadically attended. Especially when there was pizza and girls at a fellowship. He and Kevin had spoken briefly, and the man seemed trustworthy. Maybe that was an option.

The voice whispered again in his ear. "No! Don't trust him!"

He closed his eyes and opened the car door. "Let's go. We're going to be late for class."

THE MEMORY ENDED. HIS NICKNAME WAS 'JJ'? NOT LONG ago he had experienced another flashback about the door in the library at his home. In that flashback he had questioned whether his grandfather was behind the door as family gossip said. But his grandmother had corrected him.

"Go ahead and delve into the mysteries of the unknown like your grandfather, JJ. See where it takes you, nasty boy!" His grandmother's bloodshot eyes widened. "Your grandfather opened the door to the underworld and then descended into the depths of Hades itself and never returned, sealing the doorway behind him. Do you want the same fate? Huh? Your father has been trying to open that door for years! Well, the both of you can follow that foolish husband of mine into the pits of the underworld!"

"Marjorie! What are you doing?"

The grandmother bolted upright and whirled. JJ's mother stood in the double doors of the library. "He's just like your husband! He won't listen, won't obey, won't respect his grandmother. Calling a boy after his initials! It's unnatural." She shouted. "I'm done with this family. And, if you had any sense, you'd get out of this mansion before your husband does you in."

The older lady cast one last piercing gaze at JJ and stormed from the room. He wiped tears from his eyes. His mother hurried across the library floor and sat on the ottoman. Her piercing green eyes welled with tears. She brushed the ginger hair from her face and reached out to the boy. "Come here, JJ! Don't let Grandmother frighten you."

JJ leaned into his mother's embrace, and she held him to her. "Is Grandfather really behind that door?" He whispered.

His mother pushed him gently away so she could study his face. "It's a long story, son. Your father's father was obsessed with what lies beneath this mansion. It's why he built it here in the first place."

"I thought he went to heaven."

Now, this particular flashback had revealed far more of his past than any other. In the former flashback with his real grandmother, a stark contrast to the loving, smiling Hu'ul, he had been much younger, probably ten. This most recent flashback had given him a beautiful picture of his mother!

He relished that memory. As to other mystery of his grandfather, he did not have time to concentrate on the man's fate. And one thing he sensed. In this most recent flashback, those events must have occurred before his conversion for even in the memory he could not feel the presence of the Holy Spirit.

He lay back in the bed. Was he doomed to descend into the depths of Hades to never return? He closed his eyes and sought the presence of God within. "God, can you forgive me for what I am about to do?" He rolled over on his side and the light in his hand glowed brighter as it came near the drawer of the bedside table. Why? He sat up and examined the table. A lamp and an old-fashioned alarm clock sat on the surface. He pulled open the drawer and the light grew very bright and then faded. Steel turned on the lamp. Inside, the drawer was an open Gideon Bible. He carefully removed the Bible from the drawer and his eyes instantly fell on a set of verses marked off in brackets. Someone had drawn the brackets with a pen.

"Indeed Herod and Pontius Pilate met together with the Gentiles and the people of Israel in this city to conspire against your holy servant Jesus, whom you anointed. They did what your power and will had decided beforehand should happen."

Steel read. The verses came from the book of Acts verses 4:27 and 28.

"Your power and will had decided beforehand what should happen?" He said out loud. Could it be that although he was helping the side of the demons, God meant for something good to come out of it? He closed the Bible and slid it back into the drawer and drew little comfort from the verses. For his anger built and grew the more he considered the possibility that God had allowed Josh to get sick to set all of this in motion. But with the anger came the vision he had experienced in Numinocity: Christ with arms outstretched dying on a cross for him.

Steel switched off the light and lay back in the darkness. His heart pounded and his mind raced. Was he just a pawn in some divine game between eternal forces of good and evil? If only he could remember more of his past to give that moment of conversion more context. Perhaps he would understand better why he felt this way. But for the moment he felt more like Judas Iscariot than Paul the apostle!

8

Steel sat blurry eyed in the small café set aside for breakfast. He had slept only an hour after the flashback. Throughout his remembered life, he would experience these flashbacks as brief memories would resurface from his amnesia. This memory was different because it featured the first intense memory of his mother. And he had asked the Grimvox shards to show him. What else was hidden in the crystal shards? There was one memory he did NOT want to revisit.

Up until this most recent memories, his only other recurring memory of his mother had featured her in the library and a memory of her holding him in her lap. Only, during his encounter in Numinocity with his "other" self, there had been more to that memory than he wanted to deal with. In that memory, his other "self", the man he had forgotten, told him he had killed his own mother! That was not possible! It had to be a lie dredged from the depths of the wicked alternate reality controlled by the eighth demon. "Satan is the father of lies". He reminded himself.

Steel had picked up a plate of four hot beignets from the

counter and a cup of coffee mixed with milk. He had eaten such food at Café DuMonde so he hoped this would be almost as good. He didn't like coffee but after a mostly sleepless night, he needed the jolt to kick his mind into gear.

He bit into one of the beignets and it was hot, sweet, and buttery. Every artery in his body protested this outrageously unhealthy treat but he wolfed down all four without pause. He chugged down the coffee and wiped powdered sugar from his mouth. The memories from his past had filled his stomach with acid.

"You must have been bloody hungry, mate."

Steel looked up at the man from the bar. His wispy hair was awry and the reason for his brown stained teeth became obvious. The overwhelming odor of cigarettes washed over Steel.

"I don't have to ask who you are."

"Just a friendly reminder of the urgency of your mission, mate." He said in his Cockney accent. Not as refined as Dr. Hampton's Shakespearean tones.

"I just got here last night." Steel drained the coffee cup.

"And you wasted an entire night with sleep." Tooth man picked up Steel's empty plate and licked the powdered sugar with a long, pink tongue.

Steel grimaced. "That's not what I wasted it on. I didn't sleep. I had to come up with a plan and a cover story. Now, if you'll get away from me before I hurl, I'll get on with my plan." Steel stood up and stepped around the squirrelly man and his nicotine cloud. The smoky smell almost overcame the cloud of evil he emanated.

"I'm keeping an eye on you, mate." Tooth man laughed and the plate clattered on the table. He tapped Steel's shirt pocket. "And don't forget your little friend."

Steel made his way through the cavernous atrium of the convention center. The floor was crowded and many of the attendees huddled around islands of coffee and donuts, more specifically, beignets.

"Cliches never grow old." Someone said. Steel paused at the railing of the second-floor walkway and turned his attention from the floor below to the man standing beside him. Dr. Jack Merchant sipped at a coffee cup.

"Dr. Merchant?"

"Please. Call me Jack." He frowned. "Beignets and coffee. Try New Orleans. This coffee, though, is not as good as Café DuMonde. I would guess you prefer your coffee black?"

Steel shook his head. "I don't do coffee. Unless I absolutely need it." And this morning he had to!

"Find your partner yet?"

"No. I don't know where to start."

"Cell phone?" Merchant said.

Steel stiffened. Truth was, he didn't want to alert Birdsong he was here. He just wanted to find Ross. "I, uh, left it in my room dead. I'm charging the battery."

Merchant held up his phone. "You can use mine."

Steel hesitated and looked away. "I, uh, don't know his number. Speed dial."

He felt Merchant's stare from behind the man's gold rimmed glasses. Merchant pocketed his phone. "Yeah, we don't have to remember stuff anymore. That's not a good thing."

"I guess not." Steel turned back. "Look, I'm just worried about Josh. I'm distracted. I'll find my partner eventually."

"In that case, try the information desk. They can text or page anyone attending." Merchant motioned to the floor below. "I'm sorry if I seem intrusive. It's my suspicious nature. Once, I was just a radiologist. But I've been through a lot. Bad stuff, we'll leave it at that."

Was their meeting just coincidence? Was it possible Merchant was keeping an eye on him? If so, why? Steel tried to relax and let his spiritual "radar" assess the man standing next to him. Nothing. No wave of cold evil. But he had to know.

"Dr. Merchant, are you a man of faith?" Steel asked.

Merchant peered over his uplifted coffee cup. He lowered it. "In fact, I am. Why do you ask?"

Steel nodded in satisfaction and then realized he had to explain himself. "You, uh, showed Josh a great deal of kindness. And me, too. What did you say you were?"

"Radiologist."

"Yeah, radiologist. I would imagine if all you did was interpret films and sit in a dark room you would not have the best bedside manners."

Merchant raised an eyebrow and swallowed his coffee. Hard. "You surprise me, Mr. Steel. I told you that I'm not your ordinary radiologist." He leaned up against the railing. "Like I told you in the hospital, there's so much regulation that the patient gets lost in the shuffle. When I am required to perform a procedure on a patient, I take it as a sacred opportunity to minister to them."

"Minister? Are you a reverend?"

Merchant laughed. "Not hardly. But you remember what I did with you. I took the time to show you Josh's MRI and CAT scan. I took the time to explain things to you. Most doctors don't have that kind of time. And, when I walk into a room to explain the procedure to a patient, I have a very unique attitude. You see, at that moment in time, that patient is the most important person in the universe. That patient has placed their life in my hands. Granted, most of the procedures I perform don't have potentially fatal consequences, but bad things can happen. If I allow myself to get distracted by phone calls or paperwork or a technologist calling out to me to come do a different procedure, then I've compromised my service to that particular patient."

"I like that attitude." Steel said.

"Thanks." Merchant's gaze seemed to focus far away. He was silent for a moment and then he sipped more coffee and looked at Steel.

"You see, I've been on the other end of that equation, and I remember what it was like to almost die. I remember what it was like to be a patient. I try to imagine myself in my patient's situation. You'd be surprised how little they know about their circumstances when they show up for what their doctor told them was a simple 'test' only to find out I'm going to put a huge needle in their liver and perform a biopsy. You see, as a radiologist, I have access to everything about that patient if I look for it. Often, the ordering doctor doesn't tell me why I'm doing something like a lung biopsy, so I have to be a detective and track all the information down."

"Sometimes, I'm the only doctor involved in the patient's care who has had the time to put all the information together. By the time I see the patient, I know quite a bit about them. And, when they ask me, I tell them. Some doctors don't like that, but too bad! At that moment they are *my* responsibility and *my* patient."

"And what does this have to do with faith?" Steel asked.

Merchant sipped his coffee and for a moment, his eyes were focused on something in the far distance again. "I, uh, lost my wife in a horrific fire on our tenth wedding anniversary. For a while, I was accused of setting the fire. Of killing my own wife. I didn't do myself much of a favor because I had lots of skeletons in my closet. Drinking to excess. A gambling addiction. I had a lot to come back from. Returning to my faith as a Christian got me through it."

Merchant turned moist eyes toward Steel. "It's not easy to forgive yourself. And it's even harder to accept God's forgiveness. But, I have, Mr. Steel. And I try my best to pass on that grace to my patients."

Steel sighed. "I'm so sorry I said anything. I was very suspicious of why you would show up just now and last night in the bar."

Merchant wiped at his eyes. "Well, like I said, as a radiologist I am a bit of a detective. Josh disappears from my hospital in a bizarre transfer to a private clinic. Then, a couple of days later, you're here in New Orleans when you should be by his bedside. Unless he's completely recovered, and I can tell you the likelihood of that is very low. So, yeah, I'm suspicious. Remember, I consult with the medical examiner. I see dead people. Worse, I look inside them with my imaging tools. I uncover lots of secrets I'd rather not know. Paranoid, you said? It takes one to know one."

"Did you uncover who killed your wife? Or was it an accident?" Steel said.

Merchant stiffened and dropped his cup in a nearby trash can. "Well, that's a story for another time, Mr. Steel."

"Jonathan. You can call me Jonathan."

Merchant nodded. His watch chimed. "Okay, time to go take a nap. My next meeting is starting." Steel watched Merchant walk away and head down an escalator to the lower level of the convention center. Merchant seemed for real, but Steel's paranoia was only mildly blunted.

Now, where was the information booth? At the far end of the lower hallway, some attendees came in from outside surrounded by a cloud of smoke. Steel smiled. Forget the information booth. He knew exactly where Special FBI Agent Ross would be in between meetings, sucking on a cigarette!

Steel stepped outside into pouring rain. He wore a lightweight jacket with a hood and he pulled it up over his head. For a second, he wondered what would happen to the spider drone if it got wet. A brick wall surrounded a courtyard and a sign marked it as the designated smoking area. Two men in black waterproof overcoats stood at either side of the entrance to the open courtyard. In spite of the cold rain, they didn't seem to mind getting soaked. Steel smiled as he heard a voice coming from the courtyard. Ross was there all right and was arguing loudly with someone. As Steel approached, one of the men stepped forward and put out a hand.

"Sir, there's another smoking area on the opposite end of the foyer."

Steel paused. "I'm supposed to meet my friend, Franklin Ross."

The man stood his ground. "You can wait for him inside the hall."

Steel nodded and backed away. He stepped inside the hallway door closest to the courtyard. He held it open with his foot and listened to the words exchanged between Ross and whoever was in the courtyard.

"I just wanted to ask some questions, Dr. Faust." Ross said.

"Agent Ross, any questions you have for me can be taken up with my attorney. I don't appreciate you ambushing me while I have a smoke." The man spoke with a heavy German accent.

"Your goons let me in."

"I let you in, Agent Ross. You've been ghosting me all week. I chose to speak to you now to warn you off."

"Just because you organized this seminar doesn't mean you can avoid the law, Faust." Ross said.

"Diplomatic immunity, Agent Ross. Whatever it is you

think I've done, my immunity checkmates your sad devotion to antiquated laws of financial malfeasance."

"I'm not talking about money. I'm talking about hiring an assassin to kill your opposition." Ross said.

"What nonsense! Now, if you'll excuse me, I am scheduled to speak at the luncheon today as we close out this week's seminar. I hope you have learned something useful, Agent Ross."

The two men moved aside as a tall man carrying an umbrella emerged from the courtyard. His hair was short and blonde. His face was well tanned with high cheekbones. His eyes were dark and glittering with emotion. He spoke to his bodyguards in German and a limousine pulled up to the curb. Steel was out the door as the man climbed into the limo along with his two bodyguards.

Steel walked into the courtyard. Ross sucked on a cigarette and on the exhalation of a cloud of smoke let loose with a string of expletives.

"I see you still haven't quit smoking." Steel said.

Ross whirled and for a second his eyes widened in shock. He almost smiled, his hair plastered to his skull. He wore a rumpled raincoat. The smile upended into a frown.

"Steel? What are you doing here? Is it another demon? I'm out of the demon busting business. I helped you with Josh, but we're done."

"Ross, I came here to talk to you about a case. Nothing to do with demons." Steel said.

Ross finished his cigarette and tossed it on the wet ground, ignoring the butt receptacle. "There is only one conversation I would have with you, and it would involve the location of Vivian Darbonne. We have warrants out for her arrest after the Thakkar debacle."

Steel paused as the image of Vivian's desperate look at him in Numinocity as she tore the goggles from her face in the real world and she disappeared. Had she truly given herself to God? Had she found redemption? "I have no idea where she is, Ross. She disappeared after returning from Numinocity and Dr. Monarch thinks she may have lost her mind."

Ross wiped rain from his face. "Then there is nothing for us to talk about." He started past Steel and Steel reached out and grabbed his arm in an iron grip.

"Ross, please. I need your help." He said through gritted teeth.

Ross froze and glared at Steel's hand. "I could arrest you now for assaulting a federal agent. You did break my nose once."

Steel released Ross' arm and stepped between Ross and the exit from the courtyard. "I just need some information, Ross. Please."

"Did you say 'please'?" Ross glared at him and then looked away and swore loudly. "Well, I guess I might as well talk to you since you came all this way. But not out here." He glanced at his watch. "I'm hungry for a po'boy. There's a dive down at the corner makes the best fried oyster po'boys around."

"You're inviting me to lunch?" Steel said.

Ross pulled out his sunglasses and pressed them over his eyes. On a rainy day, he wore his sunglasses. "Don't count your chickens before they hatch. It's not a date, Steel. I'm just hungry."

9

The small café was tucked into an old building easily over one hundred years old. The concrete floor was worn down in places like shallow moon craters. Old fashioned Formica tables with green tops were scattered around the dining room with matching metal chairs. The humid air was heavy with the odor of fried food and Cajun spices. Ross led Steel to the only remaining table. He motioned for a waiter as he shrugged out of his wet overcoat.

"Oyster po'boy. Dressed." He said to the waiter. "Steel?"

"I don't like oysters. I think." Steel said. He suffered from amnesia and what few memories he had did not include the memory of eating fried oysters. "You got shrimp?"

"Man, don't you know we got some good fried shrimp there." The waiter said in a heavy Cajun accent. "You want it with everything, yeah?"

Steel nodded. "Why not. And water." He took off his windbreaker and draped it on the back of the metal chair. "What changed your mind?"

Ross ordered a beer and took off his sunglasses and placed them on the table. "I don't know, Steel. Every time I think

I'm done with you, you pop up. Every time there is heck to pay. It's like the good Lord has ordained that we will always run into one another."

"You got religion now?" Steel asked.

Ross snickered. "I was an altar boy, Steel. That's as far as I went."

"Then you should have no problems believing in demons."

Ross looked at Steel and grimaced. He ran his hands through his wet hair. "I've got to admit I've seen some strange things around you, Steel. Maybe there is more to life than just living and dying. But my job is to protect the living and I can't get bogged down in theology. Now, what did you want?"

Steel blinked furiously. He hadn't really planned on what he should say at this point. He glanced around the café. Just outside the door at a table sitting beneath an awning was the brown toothed man. The spider drone wriggled in his shirt pocket. A horse fly buzzed by his head and landed on a nearby table. Steel had to be careful. Ross fidgeted and shrugged.

"Look if this is about Birdsong, I get it."

Steel glanced back at him as the horse fly dodged the waiter's fly swatter. "What about him?"

"Okay, so it was more than an invitation to the seminar. Did he tell you why I invited him?"

Steel sat back. "Not really." Steel had not talked to his partner since they had returned from England.

Ross' eyes narrowed and he wiped rainwater from his forehead. "Look, Steel, I'm going to say something now that I thought I would never admit to you. We've had our differences. But the truth is what you do is important. And don't look at me like you're going to have a stroke. Yes, that was a compliment. And, if you're going to have a partner that has your back, he's got to be better than Theo."

Steel stiffened at the name. Theo had been his former

partner. But Theo was lost somewhere in the distant past; long dead; long buried; long decayed. Ross continued. "Birdsong is a solid, stand-up guy. I can give him training. We have ancillary seminars for law enforcement. He doesn't have to join the FBI to get additional training."

Steel sat open mouthed as the waiter put plates before them. Ross picked up his huge po'boy sandwich and took a huge bite. "Close your mouth on that po'boy, Steel." He mumbled through the food in his mouth. "Don't waste it."

Steel took a bite from the po'boy. The bread was soft and perfect in its consistency. The interior was grilled with a touch of spicy butter. And the fried shrimp was succulent and crunchy brimming with Cajun spices. His eyes watered but he hadn't enjoyed anything this tasty in months.

"Now, that doesn't mean Birdsong is abandoning you. Frankly, when Raven kidnapped Josh and company if he had been through some of our training programs, Raven would never have been successful." Ross said.

Steel washed down his po'boy with water. "I don't doubt it. Jason is good but he's young. He has a lot to learn. Thank you for inviting him to the seminar. Where is he, by the way?"

Ross glanced at his cell phone. "I texted him to meet me here, but he was busy at the floor show. Looking at some surveillance equipment. But looks like he will join us for lunch any minute."

Steel froze. He wasn't ready to meet up with Birdsong just yet. "You did what?"

Ross cocked his head. "Something wrong? He's your partner. I assumed you would want to have lunch with the both of us."

A shadow passed over Steel and he looked up at his partner. "Jonathan? What are you doing here, brother?" Birdsong asked. Jason Birdsong towered over them. He was of indigenous descent from the O'odham tribe in Arizona. His dark tanned skin and long black hair pulled back into a ponytail denoted his heritage.

"You two are brothers?" Ross said.

"According to Hu'ul." Birdsong said.

"Who?"

"Our grandmother." Steel sighed as he recalled that fateful night in Arizona when Birdsong's grandmother had declared them brothers.

※

A shadow passed over him as someone stepped between him and the setting sun.

"I don't know what just happened." Jason Birdsong said.

Steel looked up at the face of his "brother." The man's face was twisted in total shock and surprise.

"It seems that I am now your brother." Steel whispered. "What kind of woman is your grandmother?"

"She was a healer in the old ways." Birdsong ran a hand through his thick, black hair. "Then, she converted to Christianity decades ago. Even took off one day to walk to Magdalena although the doctors forbid it."

"What is that all about?"

"A pilgrimage to kiss the head of the statue of St. Francis. It is a sacred tradition of our people, at least those who have become Christians. The walk is viewed as a sacrifice offered as a healing ritual for oneself or others and is also a form of prayer and meditation. The Tohono O'odham nation covers most of the Sonoran desert, and I shouldn't have been surprised she would walk the path with no problem." Birdsong turned to face the setting sun and sat beside him on the ground. "She made us brothers."

"Yeah." Steel whispered. "I don't have a brother. She told me to call her Hu'ul. That's O'odham for grandmother, isn't it? She knows me. I don't know how, but she saw my life."

"Well, if we are going to be brothers, then I need to know you, too," Birdsong said. He shook his head. *"I can't believe this is happening."*

HE RECALLED THAT NIGHT AS HE TOLD JASON BIRDSONG what he knew about his past life. And the man had agreed to be his part-time partner. He drew a deep breath and prepared to lie to his 'brother'. "As to why I am here, uh, I am looking into something." Steel managed to say.

"Where's Josh?" Birdsong slid into a chair and motioned to the waitress. "I'll have shrimp creole and dirty rice."

"Josh is not feeling well. I left him at home." Steel said.

Birdsong grunted. "Jet lag, I bet. I'm feeling it myself and I've been back for a few days. So, I'm learning lots of good information."

"Ross told me his plan." Steel sat back. Let's just go with it, he told himself. "I think it's a good idea, Jason. I'd go for it."

Birdsong frowned. "Look, Jonathan, I was going to tell you. Later. Better to ask for forgiveness than permission sometimes."

Ross finished chewing a bite of his po'boy and glanced between them. "Wait a minute? This isn't about Birdsong, is it?"

Steel glanced over his shoulder at Tooth man at the outside table. "No, I'm looking into something. Someone."

Birdsong's plate arrived piled high with steaming shrimp in a reddish sauce ladled over rice. Ross had finished one half of his sandwich. He brushed crumbs from his hands and took a big swig from his beer mug. "You know I can't discuss active cases, Steel. Even if they involve demons." Ross said.

"This isn't a demon case." Steel said. "I'm looking into it, uh, for a friend."

Ross picked up the other half of his po'boy. He took a bite and chewed it thoughtfully while he studied Steel. "You're not a very good liar."

Steel shrugged. "Private investigator client privilege. You know I can't discuss active cases, Ross. Even if they don't involve demons."

Birdsong blew on a fork full of food. "We have a new case? When were you going to tell me?"

"I was waiting for you to get back from the seminar. It's not a big deal, Jason." Steel looked away.

Ross lifted an eyebrow. "What kind of a case are you involved in? Can you tell me that much?"

"It involves an individual with great influence over global affairs. Influence over finances, governments, you name it. That's about all I can tell you other than the fact I have discovered that this individual is being investigated by the FBI. I thought if I looked you up, maybe you would show me some professional courtesy."

Ross's gaze shifted over Steel's shoulder back toward the smoking courtyard. Ah, Steel thought. This Dr. Faust, could he be the quarry?

"That was him, wasn't it?" Steel leaned forward and whispered.

Ross's face reddened. "What are you talking about?"

"The snob you were smoking with. The one protected by his two gorillas and diplomatic immunity."

Ross sat back and belched. "You give me indigestion, Steel. Every time we meet. I've got to get back to my last meeting. Waiter?" He motioned for the bill. "Lunch is on me, Steel. But you stay away from that man. For your own good."

Steel nodded and finished his sandwich. "So warned, Ross."

Ross handed a credit card to the waiter. "That's it? You're giving up?"

Steel shrugged. "Just say I've been warned."

Ross took back his check and signed it. "That was too easy. Way too easy. You didn't even have a name, did you? Until I opened my mouth."

"Lady luck." Steel said wiping his hands on the napkin.

Birdsong leaned forward. "What's going on, Jonathan? You're not making any sense."

Steel felt the glare of Tooth Man on the back of his head. "Something simple, Jason. Just fact gathering." He stood up. "Enjoy the seminar and we'll talk when you're done."

Birdsong raised an eyebrow as Steel walked away. "I'll keep an eye on you, my friend." He wolfed down the rest of the shrimp creole.

10

Steel had a name. Now, what he needed was evidence of the man's illegal activity. Where would he find that? He had been through training to be licensed as a private investigator. Now he needed to investigate. Steel stopped at the information desk and asked about Dr. Faust's lecture. She showed him a QR code to download the brochure for the seminar. He took a picture of the code and found a quiet corner where he could review the information.

Faust was finishing up a lecture on international cybersecurity. According to the man's description, he was the founder and owner of several high-tech security companies around the world. Of course, being in the business would give him the knowledge and access to break through such security. It was a perfect cover for an international man of power who was also one of the five of the Penticle.

A quick search on the Internet showed the man was well connected with European governments as a security consultant. He was positioned to exact control over just about anyone in power. "And I thought the Dark Council was powerful." He whispered. Someone had to stop the Penticle. Right now, that someone was not Jonathan Steel.

"My main goal is to rescue Josh from Hampton." He reminded himself. He stood up and glanced around the hallway. He caught the odor of nicotine and glanced at the couch behind him. Tooth man winked at him as he stood up and walked away. How much had the man learned? Did it matter? The Unholy Triad wanted Steel to find out the information. Tooth man was just a grunt, a gopher.

Steel made his way down the convention hall to the main auditorium where Faust would now be finishing up his talk. Nature called and he headed for the men's restroom. As he turned down the short hallway that led to the restrooms and the preparation areas behind the meeting rooms, he saw Tooth Man.

The thin, cachectic man walked away from him. Steel almost called out when he noticed the man pausing to glanced down at a phone. Tooth Man keyed in something on the phone and the door at the end of the hallway clicked open. Steel stepped into the alcove leading to the restrooms and watched the man through the leaves of a potted palm.

Tooth Man glanced back down the hallway and then slipped through the door. Steel hurried down the short hallway and caught the door before it could close. The hallway beyond was nondescript and lined with rolling carts and shelves of dirty plates and glasses. He heard a door open and close to his right and saw the Tooth Man disappear. Steel hurried after him and paused outside the door. He heard a familiar voice on the other side. He cracked open the door. It led into a lounge, sort of a green room. Ross stood over Dr. Faust sitting on a couch. He felt a hand on his shoulder and a voice whispered in his ear.

"It's me. Jason."

Steel whirled and looked up into the eyes of his partner. "Are you following me?"

"Yes. You and that brown toothed freak. Bro, something isn't right, and you know I've got your back. Talk to me."

Before Steel could speak the muffled sound of a silenced pistol "chuff" came from the other room. Birdsong shoved Steel aside and threw open the door. Tooth Man stood between them and Ross who had pushed Faust behind him. Blood ran down Ross's arm from his shoulder.

Birdsong grabbed Tooth Man from behind and knocked the pistol aside. Tooth Man hurled Birdsong through the air in a supernaturally powered throw and Birdsong crashed into a serving tray covered with pastries and coffee cups. Ross came at Tooth Man. The man flipped up and over Ross and kicked him in the back when he landed. Ross collided with Birdsong. Tooth Man grabbed Faust's arm and jerked him to his feet. Steel picked up the dropped pistol and hesitated before pointing it at Tooth Man. That second of hesitation was all Tooth Man needed to whirl kick the gun from Steel's grip. It flew through the air and landed behind Ross and Birdsong now struggling to their feet.

Tooth Man shoved Steel aside with amazing power and pulled Faust behind him out into the hallway. All three of them collided as they tried to get through the door. Tooth Man, with Faust in tow, ran around the far corner. Steel led the way after them and when they turned the corner, he ran right into Dr. Jack Merchant.

"Jonathan?" Merchant said as he pulled himself away from the wall.

"Not now!" Steel said as Ross and Birdsong ran past him. "Two men come by here?" Steel asked.

Merchant motioned to a door just ahead already bypassed by Ross and Birdsong. "Yeah, they went through there. I was headed to first aid to help a buddy I met at lunch."

"Get out of here for your own sake!" Steel said. "Jason!" He shouted as he arrived at the door. "Through here."

The hallway beyond was dark and industrial. The walls leaked moisture and pipes and conduits hugged the low ceiling. Industrial light bulbs in metal cages illuminated the way and in the distance, Faust disappeared through another door.

Steel bumped up against rusty pipes and slid on the moisture. The hallway was a grim reminder that New Orleans was below sea level. Something tickled his neck and before he realized it, he had grabbed the spider drone with his left hand and smashed it against the wall. The broken bits of metal and black ceramic tinkled to the floor. Now what, he thought? No time to worry about the drone.

Ross led them to the door and rushed through with Steel and Birdsong right behind him. They were in a dirty, filthy men's restroom somewhere in the bowels of the hotel. Tooth Man was crouched over a sink with the water running. He had Faust's head pushed down into the sink. He glared at them as they rushed into the restroom.

"Get back or I'll break his neck!" Tooth Man said.

"You're drowning him already." Ross said.

The moment of distraction was all Faust needed. He reared up from the sink and head butted Tooth Man in the nose. Blood spurted everywhere and Faust whirled and pulled something from inside his coat. It gleamed in the light of the single bulb. Faust swiped a knife across Tooth Man's throat and blood showered the two of them. Tooth Man fell back, hands pressing against his gushing carotid artery to no avail. He collapsed onto the floor.

Someone appeared through the door. Dr. Merchant slid to a halt and looking at all of them, ran over to the Tooth Man. He pressed his hands on the man's neck, but Tooth Man was already motionless.

"Someone call 911. Get some help!" He shouted.

Ross put out a restraining hand. "No one is doing anything. I've got you now, Faust. Three witnesses to murder."

Faust wiped the knife blade on the sleeve of his coat. He carefully took off the coat and rolled it up around the knife. "Self-defense, Ross. The man was trying to drown me. I have three witnesses!" He turned calmly and began to wash the blood from his hands and face in the still running water of the sink. He glanced at his face in the cracked mirror and straightened his wet hair.

"Besides, I have diplomatic immunity." He turned and smiled at the four of them. "No, Ross, you are going to escort me back to my green room where my bodyguards, who apparently are totally worthless after lunch, will take me to my hotel. I will be on the first flight back to Germany before your local police can finish working the crime scene."

"You need a doctor." Birdsong said to Ross.

Ross glanced at his bleeding shoulder. "Just a graze. I'll go to first aid."

"That's where I was headed." Merchant stood up shakily. "I'm a doctor."

"Special Agent Franklin Ross." Ross said. "The other two can introduce themselves."

"I know Jonathan. And this man is dead." Merchant went to the sink and washed blood from his hands.

A phone rang in the dead man's pocket. Steel glanced at everyone and then leaned over and picked up the phone.

"Hello." He answered.

"Steel? Why are you on Niles's phone?" Dr. Shutendoji said.

"Niles is dead." Steel said.

"Did you get a name for me?"

"Yes, I did. Did you hear what I told you? Your little spy is dead."

Steel heard some shuffling sound. "Where is your spider drone?"

"It was crushed in the fight with your spy." Steel said.

"Very well, I'll be there in ten minutes. Until then, I'm sending some flies your way." The line went dead. Steel slid the phone into a pocket and turned to Ross. Ten minutes? How was she going to get to New Orleans from Dallas, Texas in ten minutes?

"You need to get Faust out of here."

"Why?" Ross said.

"If you were ever going to trust me, Ross, now is the time. Get him out of here. Now."

Ross nodded and motioned Faust toward the door. "After you."

"I'll toss the coat when we get outside." Faust said.

Ross glanced at Steel one more time. "You owe me a big explanation, Steel."

"Just give me one answer. Why were you looking at Faust?"

Faust sniffed. "He thinks I hired assassins to take out my competition."

"Did you?" Steel glared at Faust.

"He did." Ross said. "Our old friend."

Steel drew a deep breath. "Raven?"

"I'm not saying anything more." Ross pushed Faust out the door and they were gone.

Steel glanced around the room looking and listening for flies. He glanced at Birdsong. "I need you to get Dr. Merchant out of here."

"I'm not leaving you, Jonathan. I don't know what's going on, but it isn't good." Merchant said.

The hair stood up on Steel's neck and he felt a wave of evil waft over him. Shutendoji was coming!

11

"Both of you get into a stall and stand on the toilet. Don't say a word."

Birdsong nodded. "Dr. Merchant, let's get you out of sight."

Merchant bent over the body of Tooth Man one more time. "I have to make sure he's dead. If there is any chance." He reached down and opened the man's eyes. He paused.

"That's weird. No pulse but his pupils are not dilated." He slid on the pool of blood and his finger gouged into the man's eye. Something slid and shifted, and he stood up. A large brown contact was stuck to his finger.

Steel grabbed Merchant's hand and then looked down at Niles's totally white eye. "Jason, get him in the stall now! She'll be here any minute. She's right outside the door."

Birdsong pushed Merchant into a stall and closed the door. He slid into the one next to it. Steel felt his ears pop and Shutendoji materialized in the center of the room. A cloud of buzzing flies surrounded her and moved outward into a loose cloud. They buzzed and dodged around her head and finally settled on the body of Tooth Man. Steel prayed they would not go into the stall.

Shutendoji wore a long, shimmering pink gown. "I was at a brunch, Steel. What happened to Niles?"

Steel glanced down at the body. "First, you tell me how Josh is doing?"

Shutendoji frowned. "I'm in charge, Steel. Not you."

Steel stepped between her and the body. "I'm not moving or talking until I speak to Josh."

Shutendoji rolled her eyes and took a phone from a small purse hanging on a golden chain off her shoulder. She dialed a number and spoke to someone in a foreign language. She handed Steel the phone. He pressed it to his ear and a fly settled on his chin. He resisted the urge to swat it away.

"Josh?"

"Jonathan, dude, where are you?" Josh said weakly. "I've been in and out all morning. At least I think it is morning. I'm so confused."

"I'm having to take care of some business, Josh. I wish I could be there."

"Faye is bringing me some more medicine." Josh said nasily. "I got to go, I guess. Bro, I love you."

Steel blinked hard against tears. "I love you, too, little man." He whispered. He ended the call and tossed the phone to Shutendoji. She caught it without hesitation.

"You got a name?"

"Yes. A Doctor Faust? Sound familiar?"

"He is on our short list. But I need evidence." Shutendoji said.

"I had a lead on some damaging evidence. But I need to know Josh will be okay. I need to know you will give him his medicine."

Shutendoji sauntered toward him slowly and flies buzzed around her head. "Let's get something straight, Mr. Steel. You agreed to help me. You gave me your word and, of all the people in this world, I know will keep their word, it would be you. I told you Josh will continue to receive his medicine if you cooperate, and you fulfill your end of the bargain. Now, what information do you have?"

Steel frowned. "Two things. First, Faust hired an assassin to take out some rivals. I know where there is a record of those transactions that would give you everything you need."

"And where is this information?"

"I have a key matched to my biometric signature. It opens a safe deposit box in a bank in Zurich, Switzerland. In that box is a dossier containing information on every person who hired the assassin to kill. Would that be good enough for you?" Steel kept the key with him at all times and it was in his hotel room inside the medallion Raven had worn around her neck.

Shutendoji nodded slowly and began texting on her phone. "More than enough. And bonus material in addition. I'll arrange a flight to Zurich for you. What happened to Niles?"

"He tried to kill Faust."

Shutendoji's head jerked up from the phone and now, the flies were buzzing angrily around her. "What?"

"Tried to drown him. Faust fought back with a knife and killed Niles."

Shutendoji cursed quietly in a foreign language. She spoke into the phone for a few minutes and then nodded. "Unfortunately, this turn of events means Faust will be on the alert. We must move quickly, Mr. Steel. And now, discretion is even more essential." She looked down at her phone and touched a button. "I'll have your flight information texted to your phone. Don't miss that flight." She looked at him. "You said there were two things I needed to know?"

"I know why Niles tried to kill Faust. Let's just say he's no longer on your team." Steel stepped aside and pointed to Niles's face. "Check out his eye."

Shutendoji moved close to him and bent over the body. The flies on the man's face flew upward and joined the rest of the flies in a cloud above her head. One of Niles' eyes was completely white with no pupil. She backed up and trembled. Her face darkened with fury and she opened her mouth. An unearthly growl came forth building to a crescendo and the huge red seventh demon burst through her features, towering over them both. It turned its numerous eyes to Niles and the scream silenced. It swore in an obscene unearthly language that ended with another piercing screech. The walls began to vibrate, and two water pipes burst under the sinks. Steel crouched in defense as the broken mirrors around the room shattered into thousands of pieces and fell to the floor. The fly drones dropped dead. The seventh demon collapsed back into the woman's diminutive figure. Shutendoji blinked and glared at him.

"You seem to have a problem." Steel said as he stood up and brushed broken mirror from his clothes. Water pooled around Niles from the gushing pipes and began to wash the blood into an open drain in the floor. "Looks like Niles was working with your rivals, the Vitreomancers. Did you know?"

"No!" She hissed and disappeared from sight leaving behind a hint of ozone and burning sulfur. Steel gasped and turned quickly. None of the flies remained active. He didn't have much time before more of the demon drones reappeared.

Birdsong burst from the stall and rushed over to Steel. "You okay?"

"No. You heard all of that?"

"Yes. And that thing! Seven I take it?"

Dr. Merchant opened the stall door and stepped out slowly. "What have I gotten myself into?"

"The supernatural." Steel said. "I'm sorry you got pulled into this thing."

Birdsong stooped down and studied the body. "So, this fellow's a Vitreomancer?"

"Yeah. Shutendoji sent him to keep an eye on me and she had no idea he was keeping an eye on her. I'm betting Shutendoji didn't know he was a Vitromancer."

Birdsong stood up. "Shutendoji is seven?"

"Seven what?" Merchant asked. He was shaking.

"Seventh demon." Birdsong said. "Out of twelve."

"Seven, six, and five together. They didn't waste any time. They have Josh. He's sick. And I'm being monitored."

"By whom?"

"No whom. What?" He motioned to the inanimate flies. "First Niles who turned out to be a double agent. And demon insect drones and there will be more any minute. We don't have much time to help Josh."

"What's wrong with Josh?" Birdsong asked.

"Guillian Barre' Syndrome. Aftermath of a viral infection." Merchant added. "I wondered what happened to him. I came up to check on you that night after his spinal tap and they said he had been transferred to another hospital."

"You checked on him?" Birdsong said.

"Dr. Merchant is a radiologist in Shreveport. He did a spinal tap on Josh." Steel cleared his throat of the growing emotion.

Birdsong nodded and sighed. "I should have guessed. No coincidences, right? Merchant is right where God needs him, right?"

Merchant looked back and forth between them. "What?"

"Sorry, brother. You've just been drafted into the divine army."

"No!" Steel said. "I'm not putting Jack in danger."

Merchant took off his glasses and wiped his eyes. "I have no idea what is going on."

"They gave it to him, Jack." Steel said. "Some kind of virus that makes him paralyzed unless he gets treatment. Only they have the cure."

"They?" Merchant said.

"Three demons, this time. The unholy triad. And now we know their sworn enemies, the Vitreomancers, are working against them. Oh, and they are working with Hampton."

Birdsong raised an eyebrow. "The British dude Monty took the crates to?"

"That would be him. Never met the man, but he knew me, and he knew Josh. Josh went with Monty to see the museum while I was with Raven."

Birdsong nodded. "How's she?"

Steel felt more emotion grip him. "Dr. Monarch tried to neutralize her implants and bring back her memory. Instead, she erased everything."

"What? Erased? You mean like?"

"Reformatted the hard drive. Max has taken her to retrain her and care for her." Steel said.

Merchant stepped over the dead body as he took off his glasses and wiped the moisture from them on his shirtsleeve. "Look, I have no idea what is going on here. But I've looked evil in the face before." For a moment, his eyes filled with emotion. "I lost people I love because of the evil of mankind. I haven't met any of your demons, but I don't doubt there is a struggle going on between good and evil. Powers and principalities, the Bible says."

Merchant nodded and swallowed. "Of course, it has never been *this* real. A woman teleporting like she just beamed up to the Enterprise. Flies as spies. A man with no pupils in his eyes. I'm going to have to try and digest all of this." He looked up as Steel. "But I know one thing. I promised I would help. If there is one guiding principle for my life it is to help those in need."

"A helper in the time of need. Yes, I remember you said that. Why?"

"One day, I'll tell you the stories. One day, assuming I don't lose my mind with all this supernatural insanity, we'll sit down with a cup of coffee," He paused and raised his hands in defense, "Decaffeinated, of course. And I'll tell you everything." Merchant put his hands down. "For now, I will do whatever it takes to help Josh. After all, he's still MY patient."

Steel nodded and glanced at Birdsong. "Okay, so I am a demon buster, you might say. God pulled me into this business. There is a Council of Darkness with 12 demons on it."

"Not anymore." Birdsong said proudly. "Jonathan has taken out six of them."

"And the rival group call themselves Vitreomancers. Has something to do with the white eyes. Raven was an assassin hired to kill me, but she became a woman of faith and renounced her ways."

"And now Raven is a blank slate." Birdsong said quietly.

"I have amnesia, Jack. It's a long story but my father had surgery performed on my brain to erase my past. He did the same thing to Raven."

Merchant crossed his arms. "Okay, so this sounds very, very complicated. It sounds bizarre and wild. But that woman materialized out of thin air. I saw her through the crack at the edge of the stall. And she turned into that hideous creature. Then, she just disappeared."

"Some powerful demons have mastery over space and other dimensions. It takes its toll on the human host but what do they care? Satan will use up anyone he needs until they're a husk of a living being wishing nothing more than to die and go on to hell." Steel wiped his mouth. "There's more but I don't have time."

Merchant reached out and placed a hand on Steel's arm. "Jonathan, what can I do to help Josh?"

Steel nodded and swallowed. "Jack, Josh is in a private clinic north of Dallas. Very exclusive. Dr. Hampton is in charge and security is tight. I doubt anyone could get in and even if you did, they are watching."

"They have no idea you have a partner, right?" Birdsong said.

"You're right."

"And I'm an assistant medical examiner following up on a potentially deadly virus. I could easily say I'm working with the CDC and use my credentials to get through the door. I could at least check on him for you, Jonathan. Because it sounds like you have a flight to catch."

"Or Josh misses his next dose of medication." Steel said.

"And shouldn't a medical examiner have accompanying law enforcement?" Birdsong said to Merchant.

"Of course. We could pull this off."

Steel froze. "No, I don't want to endanger your lives. This is my burden to bear. I made a deal with the devil. Not you."

Birdsong put a hand on Steel's shoulder. "You had my back in Jerusalem and Numinocity. I'll always have yours, Jonathan."

"Jerusalem? Numinosity?" Merchant said.

"Catch him up on everything, Jason." Steel said and then he looked at Merchant. "You don't have to do this. Your life would be in danger."

"Won't be the first or the last." Merchant said. "Now, you need to get to the airport. You don't have much time. We'll check on Josh and we'll call you. Now, Jason, right? You need to help me eliminate any evidence that would link us to the body."

"Really?" Birdsong said.

Merchant smiled for the first time. "I'm an assistant medical examiner, remember? I know how to bury all the skeletons."

12

Steel's seat was much roomier and far more comfortable on this flight to Zurich than the last flight he had been on. But then, that flight had crashed killing hundreds. This time, he had a seat in first class and his little cubicle effectively isolated him from other passengers. He felt a movement in his shirt pocket and glanced down to see one of the demon drone spiders stick its legs out of the pocket. He was still under surveillance! What about human surveillance?

His closest neighbor was a woman swathed in a headdress with a surgical mask covering her lower face. She only glanced at him once and then leaned her seat back into the reclining position for sleep. Was she one of the unholy triad's observers?

He leaned his seat back partially and propped up his feet, but sleep was far from his mind. He powered up his phone and stared at the icon for a Bible app. Since the events in London, he wanted to make it a priority to read his Bible. The supernatural experience the night before had not quite seeped in because of his anger. Steel had to remind himself what he experienced in Numinocity. After seeing how powerful the Word of God had been in the hands of anyone brandishing the "whole armor of God", perhaps it was time to arm himself. His mind kept coming back to Josh. Was his disease a real thing? Jack had seen changes in Josh's brain on his MRI. But now, could what Josh was experiencing be at the hands of demonic power? Josh was a Christian. He could not be possessed by a demon.

Once connected to the airplane wi-fi, he put in search words for demon and began to sift through the encounters between Jesus Christ and demonically possessed victims. Specifically, he wanted to understand the relationship between demonic possession and physical illness. Josh's illness seemed mysterious and out of the ordinary if Dr. Hampton and the unholy triad were the only cure. His Internet search yielded over ten million results! Most topics dealt with the perceived relationship between demons and mental illness. Steel was looking for information on physical illness. He opened the Bible app and searched for demon. He read every scripture in the New Testament about demon possession. Almost all cases were obviously insanity, seizures, mute, or blindness. And one could argue these could all be the manifestations of mental illness.

His eyes blurred and he realized he was exhausted. He hadn't slept well the past four nights since Josh had gotten sick immediately after they returned from London. He laid his seat all the way back and shoved the small pillow under his head. He tried to close his eyes but found them filled with moisture. He had cried more in the past few weeks than in his entire remembered life. His hand throbbed and the light glimmered from his palm. He was somewhere else.

THE 7TH DEMON

The anger came out of nowhere. Clay was huddled in the corner of the "Tank", the youth building at Community Church. Clay's face was too close to the face of his girlfriend.

"Why are you just sitting there?" He heard the voice whisper in his ear. He glanced over at his backpack. Hidden inside was the photo album. He had explored most of the photos inside. Pictures of his grandfather filled every photograph from locations all over South America and Mexico. Grandfather stood at the base of Aztec pyramids. He posed alongside the ruins of Machu Picchu. He stood at the mouth of a cave and the caption read, "Patagonia". Grandfather sat in a boat on the Amazon. He found the photos mesmerizing and the voice that continued to whisper to him troubled him less. He was just thinking out loud, wasn't he?

He stood up, fists clenched as the anger took him and he stormed across the room toward his best friend, his betrayer, Clay.

A short, dumpy man with a bare scalp stepped in front of him. "Hey, dude, what's up?"

He slid to a halt and looked into the smiling face of his youth pastor, Kevin. He drew a deep breath and tried to step around him. Kevin stepped to the side.

"Hey, man, you look like someone on a mission. And not a good mission. Why don't you sit down and cool off before you do something you'll regret?"

He glared at Kevin. "Clay is supposed to be my best friend." He pointed over Kevin's shoulder. "He's moving in on my girlfriend."

Kevin nodded. "It happens. Who is your girlfriend?"

"Penelope."

Kevin pointed to a couch in the huge room. "Dude, Clay's talking to Alexis."

He froze and glanced again over Kevin's shoulder. The girl moved so that her face was illuminated by light. It was Alexis. Not Penelope. He blinked and unclenched his fists. He whirled and slumped onto the couch.

Kevin sat beside him. "Man, you gotta chill. JJ, where's all this anger coming from?"

He glanced over his shoulder at his backpack. "It's a long story. My Dad is gone all the time. My grandfather was crazy. You wouldn't understand."

Kevin nodded and pulled up his shirt exposing his chest. "See that?" He pointed to a long pink scar that ran across his chest and onto his back. "Want to know where that came from?"

JJ drew a deep breath and fought for calm. "I don't care."

"My stepfather chased me for three blocks with his belt in hand. That belt had a buckle on it the size of a cell phone. When he finally caught up to me, he hit me so hard the buckle tore through my shirt and ripped open my chest." He lowered his shirt. "He would have killed me if someone passing by had not stopped him and called the police. You see, my stepfather beat me every day. Then, he would beat my mother. If you could see my X-rays you see that I've got several healed broken bones."

JJ studied Kevin's intense gaze. "I'm sorry."

"I planned on killing him. Had it all laid out. I didn't care if I went to jail. It was better than living in that hell. I bought a gun from a gang member in my high school and waited for my stepfather to come home from the bar. I sat in the living room with no lights on and waited with the gun resting on the couch pointed at the door. Someone opened the door, and I couldn't pull the trigger."

Kevin looked away and a tear leaked from his eye. "It's a good thing. It wasn't my stepfather. It was our pastor. I say, our pastor, but I hardly went to church. Mother did. She prayed every day for my stepfather to stop. I prayed for him to die."

Kevin looked back at him. "Where was God in all of this? I asked myself that question over and over. Sometimes, God gives us over to our reprobate minds and the results are deadly. My stepfather was hit by a car while leaving the bar. He was killed instantly. Our hell was over, dude. The pastor was coming to tell us."

"God answered your prayer." JJ said.

Kevin lifted an eyebrow. "No, I don't think so. Not then. But later God did answer my prayer and gave me something worth living for. He changed my heart. I gave my life to him. You can do that, too. It will give you peace."

"Kill him!" The voice was suddenly whispering in his ear. He froze and glanced back at the backpack. "Kill him! He's the enemy! He hates you!"

"Dude, you okay?"

JJ glanced once at Kevin and bolted up from the couch, snaring his backpack as he ran from the Tank.

"MY, BUT YOUR EYES ARE VERY STRIKING." STEEL HEARD someone say in a Middle Eastern accent.

Steel blinked away the memory and looked up into the eyes of the woman in the next seat. "What did you say?"

She leaned over the divider between them. Her mouth and nose were hidden behind the surgical mask and only her dark, brown eyes were visible. "They are like jewels of turquoise. My husband is a jeweler in New Mexico and he collects that beautiful gem. I'm sorry to have interrupted your rest but I heard you talking in your sleep."

"Bad dream. I'm okay. I'm just missing my son." He managed hoarsely.

The woman nodded. "Family is important. I hope you have some good rest." She disappeared and Steel massaged his eyes. He had to be get control. He couldn't afford to be emotional right now. Too much rested on his ability to fulfill the requests of the unholy triad and at the same time thwart their ultimate goals. But, how to do that? He glanced at his hand and the glimmer of light faded. More memories of the photo album. The whispers? Was he hearing voices back then? Could that have been the earliest symptoms of a mental illness? Schizophrenia? Multiple personalities?

When he was in Numinocity in the beach house he had met his "other" self, an echo of the person he used to be before his amnesia. That version of himself had suggested he was once possessed by a demon. But what if he had inherited his grandfather's mental instability? He couldn't think any further on this right now. He other more pressing concerns.

Right now, he was headed to Zurich to meet with Max, a powerful and wealthy individual with an extensive enterprise in doing exactly that – thwarting the evil machinations of the Council of Darkness. Thwart? Sounded like scripture. Reading his Bible was beginning to sink in.

How then could he deceive Max? He touched the medallion hanging around his neck. It had a twin hanging around Max's neck and when the two were put together, it would be a key to open a deposit box with Raven's deepest secrets. Like a record of Faust hiring her to take out his enemies. But he couldn't tell Max any of this. To do so would be to doom Josh.

Raven. His mind drifted to her. The last he had seen of her was when Dr. Monarch had attempted to return Raven's memory. Unfortunately, Monarch had erased everything in Raven's mind. Raven had become a blank slate, an adult infant. Max was supposed to have taken in Raven to begin her re-education.

He wondered what had happened to Dr. Monarch and her daughter, Olivia and her son, Steven. Josh had never made it back to school, so he had no idea if Olivia was back in school, too. Monarch may have stayed in London with her recuperating son.

And, thinking of London, he wondered if Dr. Montana Holmes had returned to the states yet? Should he tell Monty that his "mentor", Dr. Hampton was working with the Council of Darkness!

Steel needed to talk to Dr. Montana Holmes as soon as possible. The spider wriggled in his pocket. Steel tried to ignore the woman sitting in the seat next to him. But he was aware of being surveilled by the spider in his pocket. He couldn't sleep and he had to learn what he could about demons and physical illness from someone who was an expert in Christian apologetics, Montana Holmes. Josh had equipped him with a MacBook pro laptop and an iPad Pro to keep in touch with Josh. Right now, he would give anything to talk to Josh.

He took out the iPad Pro and logged onto the airplane Wi-Fi. He sent a text message to Dr. Montana Holmes. He had first met 'Monty' in Jerusalem during the encounter with the ninth demon and they had become fast friends. And it had been Monty who led Steel to embrace the 'whole armor of God' in Numinocity that led to their victory over the eighth demon. The last time he had seen Monty, he was at Dr. Hampton's museum. He received a reply from Monty.

"I'm awake. Barely. It's 530 in the morning in London but I just got back from a short run. What's up?"

"Can we FaceTime?" Steel replied.

"If you don't mind my appearance."

Steel opened up the FaceTime app and dialed up Monty. He took out a set of AirPods and put them in his ears, glancing once more at the woman beside him. Her eyes were closed in sleep. He felt the spider writhe in his pocket and realized he had to be discreet. How could he tell Monty about Hampton?

Montana Holmes' face appeared on the screen. His dark hair was plastered to his face, and he wiped away sweat with a hand towel. "Jonathan! Sorry I'm rather indisposed. It's a good thing you can't smell me!"

"Hey, Monty. How are you?" Steel felt his heart skip a beat

at the sight of his friend. How he wanted to tell Monty all that had happened. But, he couldn't.

"I'm okay. Trudging my way through Dr. Lawrence's crates. Matching the manifest with the object and then guaranteeing each artifact is genuine and in pristine condition. It's slow and methodical." Monty swept his hair away from his face and drank water from a bottle. "How's Josh?"

Steel froze. "He's resting up. Jet lag."

"Where are you?" Monty asked.

"On a flight to Switzerland. I need to finish up my business with Max."

Monty nodded. "She's something else! Tell her I'm thankful for helping us out in Numinocity. Speaking of which, how are you?"

Steel shrugged. "On to the next thing, Monty."

Monty froze. "You mean?"

"That's why I called you. I need to pick your brain."

Monty drank more water and in the background a tea kettle whistled. "Let me get some caffeine in me first. Go ahead and talk while I'm preparing this 'proper' tea. Dr. Hampton showed me how to make it the 'right' way, not the American way. I can hear you." Monty walked away from his device toward a small stove in an equally small and compact kitchen.

"Are you in an apartment?"

"No. Hampton has some living quarters in his museum. Creepy, but convenient." Monty began preparing his tea. He wore a sweat soaked tee shirt and athletic pants.

"Have you seen him lately?"

Monty shook his head. "No, he's on a trip somewhere. Don't know when he'll be back. What can I do for you?"

Steel sighed and the spider crawled out of his pocket, down his arm and perched on the top of his table. Steel's face grew warm with anger. The spider listened and its green eyes glowed. He couldn't talk anymore about Hampton. The unholy triad was seeing to that!

"I need to understand the connection between demons and physical illness." Steel said.

Monty returned to his device with a steaming mug in hand. "Okay." He sipped the tea and grimaced. "What I wouldn't give for a coffee pot. All Hampton has around here is tea. Now, demons and physical illness?"

"Yes, Monty. I've read the scriptures. Jesus cast out demons constantly but most of those cases seemed to involve some kind of mental illness." Steel said.

"I'm sending you a link to J. Warner Wallace's excellent discussion of this from his website, Cold Case Christianity." Monty tapped at a keyboard and Steel opened the link from his text message while Monty talked in the background.

"Wallace establishes that angels were originally created to love God but some rejected God, as we both well know. The basic desire of demons who have rejected God is to daily oppose the spiritual understanding of God's truth by humans. How do they do this?"

Monty's face appeared in a smaller window. "First, they attack the mind's ability to understand and comprehend God's truth. In the scriptures, we see many instances where demons have impaired human's abilities to see and hear the truth of God's word by creating sensory disabilities. That would be a very physical attack and would be understood in more modern terms of blindness, deafness or aphasia. Those are NOT mental illnesses, Jonathan."

"Got it." Steel said. The woman stirred in the seat beside him. The spider scurried back up his arm and into his pocket well out of sight of the tablet camera. Steel glanced at her as she opened her eyes. Her gaze passed over the iPad screen for a moment and she yawned and then turned away from him back into sleep.

"Second, they attack the body's ability to act on God's truth. Epilepsy, paralysis, inability to walk are just some of the examples. Again, these are not necessarily mental illness." Monty said. "They are very physical."

"Finally, they attack the body's ability to show others the Image of God, the Imago Dei. There are accounts in the New Testament of men who would not wear clothing or live in a normal situation like living in a graveyard."

Monty sipped more tea. "Now, it is wrong, Jonathan, to attribute all physical illness to demons but the scriptures will sometimes mention two afflictions in the same person. There is an entire movement to blame every negative thing a person experiences to a specific demon such as demon of gluttony, depression, anxiety, etc. Some religious groups have a 'demon trial' to determine if the person is afflicted by a demon. They practice deliverance ministry. Personally, I think demons can afflict or oppress a Christian but they can never possess them. And we give them far more power than they actually have."

Monty pointed to his screen. "Here is a quote from Wallace's website that kind of some up what I agree with:

> *'Christians do not attribute all illnesses to demon possession, but it is clear demons are continually doing what they can to keep God's chosen from a relationship with Him, and this often takes the form of some sort of bodily attack. Demons are focused. They are trying to stop God's work, stop the growth of the Kingdom, and stop men and women from hearing the Good News. One thing is certain, however. Those of us who have already placed our trust in Christ (and have been filled with God's Spirit) cannot be demon possessed. Demons are mere creations of God, and as such, they do not possess His power.'*

"Thanks, Monty. This helps me a lot." Steel said and he felt the spider squirm in his pocket.

Monty glanced at his watch. "Hey, Jonathan, I need to get

cleaned up. I'm meeting Cassie for breakfast pretty soon. Why don't you call us when you get to Switzerland?"

"Cassie?"

Monty froze and cleared his throat. "Yeah, she stayed in London. She's working on her new show, you know and is doing some research here while helping me go through Dr. Lawrence's artifacts."

"I see." Steel smiled. At least something good was happening right before his eyes. "Tell her I said hello, Monty. I'll try and call you later today. Don't spend too much time in those crates. Enjoy the city. With Cassie."

"Sounds good. Godspeed, Jonathan. I'll take a break from the crates." Monty laughed and ended the call.

"The crates." He hissed. Hampton had wanted three of Cephas Lawrence's crates filled with arcane antiquities. Why? Hampton's motives had to be more than just putting these objects in his museum! If Hampton was in league with three demons, then there must have been something in those crates.

Wait a minute! What had Josh said about his brief visit to see the crates while in Hampton's museum? They had just settled onto the flight back to the states and he had pointed to a puncture on his finger. And, he had mentioned it at the clinic.

Dr. Cephas Lawrence had specialized in collecting artifacts pointing to good and evil. And some of those artifacts were in the crates sent to Hampton. A puncture from an artifact in a collection of ancient evil objects! Was that how Josh had gotten sick? If so, he had to find Monty as soon as possible. Steel froze and looked around the cabin. The lights were down and almost everyone was asleep in their cocoons. Except for the woman next to him. He glanced over his shoulder, and she was sitting up in her seat reading a book. She could be one of the triad's operatives. If they were indeed keeping an eye on him then he had to be careful how he communicated to his friends.

Steel slumped back onto the bed in despair. Why was it that everyone he cared about was always in danger for their very lives? Would there ever be a respite? There was another big word for him. Respite. He definitely needed a respite. He closed his eyes and breathed a silent prayer for sleep. Mercifully, it came.

13

Josh tried to roll over in his hospital bed but his legs would not cooperate. He opened his eyes to total darkness. His stomach growled with hunger. Where was his nurse?

"Hello. Is anyone there?" He said weakly. A flickering orange light played across the ceiling above him. Instead of square ceiling tiles, above him were thick wooden beams with a thatch roof across them. He tried to sit up and his head swam with dizziness. "Hey, where am I?"

The light came from a candle sitting on a roughhewn wooden table to his left. The table sat in the center of a room with stone walls and hand made chairs. A counter against the far wall had a stone top and upon it sat various clay and metal receptacles of various styles.

A figure appeared from the corner obscured in shadows. The figure approached swathed in an all-encompassing white cloak. The hood hid the person's face in shadow. The figure paused. It threw back the hood and the woman from earlier shook out her long, reddish hair and shrugged out of the cloak to reveal a flowing gown that fell to cover her feet. She ran her hands through her hair and blinked her turquoise eyes as she drew a deep breath.

"Now, Josh, here's the deal." She said in a husky, raspy voice. "I've played around with you long enough. I let your brain produce these images so that we could make progress, but I've grown impatient."

Josh swallowed. "How can you be in my head? I'm a follower of Christ."

She raised an eyebrow and crossed her slim arms across her ample chest. "I am not a demon, Josh. I am Pandora."

"Then, how?"

"You might call it genetic memory. I'm not a modern scientist. I did dabble with alchemy and some of the darker arts before I was killed in the urn."

"Urn?"

She laughed. "Surely you've heard of Pandora's box! See, it wasn't actually a box. It was more like an urn. With a lid." She pointed a finger at him. "An apprentice is no greater than her teacher. My teacher called herself a sorcerer. But she was nothing more than a chemist and, unknown to her, a geneticist. You know, if you play around with dangerous forces long enough, you might stumble across something truly world ending!"

Pandora pulled up a stool and sat on it. Her skin was pale with fine red freckles. She licked her lips and closed one eye in thought. "I had learned so much and she wouldn't listen. I tried to tell her she was going too far. But she did listen to one thing. She sealed her latest concoction into an urn. She had finished her work, Josh. She claimed to have turned a pig into something that was a cross between a pig and a goat. Would you like to see?" Before he could protest, she touched his forehead with her finger.

THE 7TH DEMON

"Maria, here are the herbs you requested."

Maria glanced up from the bubbling, seething apparatus on the table before her. "Pandora, you startled me! These ministrations are very delicate."

Pandora stepped around the heavy-set robed woman whose her head was covered with a squatty bonnet. "Of course, they are. I have learned so much from you."

Maria sighed. "You may be a quick learner, Pandora, but you do not have the right spirit to be involved in my alchemy."

Pandora rolled her eyes. "Not again!"

Maria turned to face her. "My goal is to understand creation. And, on understanding creation, the Creator." Maria's gaze grew flinty. "But you, my dear are more interested in the power of the Creator, not the person of the Creator."

Pandora pursed her lips. "You mistake me for my namesake."

"Yes, created by Zeus to afflict mankind. I am familiar with the myth. And Pandora opened the urn containing all of the world's woes and unleashed evil on the world leaving behind only one element in the urn."

"Hope. Yes, I am familiar with the story as well."

Maria crossed her laboratory and motioned to a large stone urn. She lifted the top ever so carefully. "Inside this urn are the combined elixirs of centuries of alchemy, the Elixir of Life! It was passed to me by my teacher."

"And, one day it will be mine!" Pandora said.

Maria placed the lid on an adjacent table. "That is yet to be decided, Pandora. Come. See what is inside."

Pandora hurried across the room and the odor from the urn made her nose wrinkle. She held her nose and leaned over to look into the urn. Dark, viscous liquid filled half the urn. Its surface moved with a shifting iridescence. "What is that smell?"

"A vital and living combination of multiple contributions from all over the world. This urn has been passed back and forth among alchemists for over five hundred years. Each alchemist has added his

or her secret ingredients to this liquid. Always, it is half full. Always it moves and glitters with life. And, I have taken a small quantity of the Elixir of Life and placed it in my special apparatus."

Maria motioned to a stack of hissing and steaming pots stacked atop each other. "Gentle heating is necessary to preserve the delicate biology of the elixir. Unlike the threat of death, chaos, and destruction, Pandora, here is hope. Only by understanding the world as it is, will we gather an image of the mind of God. Paul wrote of this in his letter to the Romans."

A gently susurration came from the hissing contraption. Three arms of metal dripped fluid into bowls. Something rattled within the large container. Maria's eyes widened. "This may be it!"

Maria snuffed out the flame beneath the main vessel and used a metal tong to unseal the central chamber. She lifted it and Pandora peered anxiously over her shoulder.

"What is it?"

A red and gray stone with bright golden veins across its surface gleamed and glittered from the vessel. Maria lifted the stone into the meager light coming in from a lone window in the wall of her home. "I have converted part of a simple stone into gold!" Maria placed the stone on the tabletop. "Imagine by wedding two substances I have created a third that is, in itself a blending of the two not unlike the man and woman coming together to become one flesh thanks to the Elixir of Life."

Pandora's heart raced. If she could learn how to turn any ordinary object into gold! She would be wealthy. She would be powerful! She reached for the object and grabbed it before Maria could stop her.

The pain was intense, burning and searing through her palm and up her arm. She tried to release the stone without success. Her hand was in spasm around the gold laced object and now her skin began to turn an ugly green and black. Pandora fell backward, stumbling as the transformation reached her shoulder.

"What have I done?" Maria gasped.

"Stop it!" Pandora screamed. "Make it stop!"

Maria pointed to the urn. "Immerse yourself in the elixir. Now!"

Pandora hurried across the room as the green and black scales grew across her chest and up her neck. She climbed feet first into the urn and felt the cold elixir around her knees.

"All the way, Pandora. It is the only hope for you. The liquid is filled with the secret of life. It will heal you. Now immerse yourself quickly before the stone converts you to rock."

Pandora collapsed into the cold, viscous liquid and her arm remained outside the urn. The scales continued to grow across to her other arm and down her chest. She could no longer feel her right arm. It looked like green and black flinty rock and as she tried to pull it into the urn with the rest of her, her arm cracked and splintered and the forearm and hand fell away.

Pandora screamed in agony and Maria's face appeared above the rim of the urn. "I am sorry, Pandora. I know not what you have unleashed but I must contain it in this vessel. Forgive me." She dropped Pandora's broken arm pieces into the urn. The stone lid to the urn slid into place sealing Pandora in darkness.

Josh's vision cleared and Pandora sat before him. She held up her right arm. Only then did he notice it was made of gleaming gold.

"Whatever was in that elixir combined with the effects initiated by the stone and I found myself melting into the urn. But rather than dying, I lived on as an embodied mind, trapped within the fluid in the urn. It truly was the Elixier of Life! Others were added over time. Their essence, their minds were mine to absorb. Over time, the sealed urn was lost to antiquity until followers of the Hermetic way during the Renaissance found it."

"By then, only a small concentrated amount of liquid

remained of my substance. It was transferred to a box, and I was sealed within for centuries. Imagine being denied the outside world? Imagine your mind trapped within darkness. But I can still sense the outside world. You hear. You learn. In time, I pieced together the growing knowledge of the centuries of learning. I learned of DNA and I finally understood. After all, DNA is just information, right? That is what I am. Concentrated information no doubt stored within the shell of protein inside a viral agent. With each infection, I grow more powerful. I learn more."

"The box in Uncle Cephas' crate?"

Pandora shrugged. "Well, sort of. The old man actually put my essence into a syringe. I'm not really sure what box I came from. You know, the needle that pricked your finger. And now I am feeding on your DNA, your proteins, your mind." She held up her golden hand and smiled.

"You're not real, then." Josh whispered. "You're in my mind."

"Of course, I'm real!" Pandora shrieked. Her face reddened and she stood up straight and smoothed down her dress. "I am manifested in your mind, but I am real. I am independent as any viral or bacterial infection can become."

"Why are you doing this?"

Pandora reached over and put a cold hand on his cheek. "You are so young. You have so many special memories of supernatural and trans-dimensional events. In time, my mind will supplant yours. I will become you and you will go away into darkness and then I will be free."

"And do what?" Josh asked.

Pandora shook her head slightly and crossed her arms again. "Oh, many things. Revenge for one. Kill as many troublesome humans as I can. Cleanse the earth. And eventually pass myself on to millions. I will *become* the world, Josh. I am not hope. I am hopelessness. I am despair."

Josh tried to pull away from her hand. "I will stop you. I won't let you take me. Thirteen tried and I defeated him."

Pandora shrugged. "There is one caveat. You have to give me permission to use your mind and your memories. I can only intrude so far."

"Then why would I ever let you take over my mind? I've been there done that."

Pandora grinned. "Because if you do not, then the ones you love will perish. They will die a painful death. I will unleash untold pestilence upon them. They will beg someone to kill them." She smiled. "Like your Dad? Jonathan?"

"No!" Josh screamed as feeling began to return to his chest down.

Pandora jerked away her hand and frowned. She looked around her as the room began to disappear. "How are you doing this?"

Josh smiled. "I'm receiving another treatment."

Pandora held her hands before her, and the flesh of her normal arm filled with red streaks. Blisters and boils broke out on her face, and she screamed in agony.

"Looks like you're the one begging to die." Josh hissed. Pandora and her laboratory vanished from his awareness, and he opened his eyes. Faye Murphy stood over him.

"Hey, calm down, Josh. You okay?"

Josh blinked sleep from his eyes. "Where's Pandora?"

"You mean the planet in that movie?" Faye said.

Josh focused on her. "No. A woman. In my head. In my dreams."

Faye nodded. "Nightmares. Sorry about that. The meds along with the residual swelling in your brain will give you very vivid and disturbing nightmares. It should pass with treatment, Josh."

"I want to talk to my Dad." Josh whispered. "It's important."

Faye fiddled with the IV machine. "I'm afraid Dr. Shutendoji has taken away your talking privileges. Doesn't want to get you too upset, she said." She was frowning when she looked back at Josh. "But I understand. You feel alone. Abandoned. Hopeless. But you don't have to. I'm here to watch over you Josh. I will not let anything happen to you. I promise."

Josh stared into her eyes and felt fatigue come over him. He tried to move his hand and he felt nothing from the chest down. "I can't feel my hands!"

Faye checked his hand with a pin prick. Josh felt nothing.

"Your paralysis comes and goes, Josh. The medicine we just started will reverse that. Just relax."

Josh studied her face. She was far from relaxed. "I'm scared, Faye. There's more going on here than just a virus. Look in the drawers over there. Please I have to find the Bloodstone."

Faye started for the drawers and then stopped. She pulled up a chair and sat down with her face level with Josh's. Josh felt his heart rate quicken. At least he could still feel that.

"Now, Josh. Listen carefully. This clinic is a very special medical facility. The Board of Directors are composed of several oil tycoons with millions. They set this clinic up to provide a place for patients with the most bizarre and unusual illnesses to get cutting edge treatment free of charge. We have access to thousands of experimental protocols from all over the world. When you become a patient here, you are entered into these trials. There is no place on the face of this planet where you will get better care than here." She patted his arm and Josh gasped.

"I can feel that!"

"See, the infusion is working already. These dreams and delusions you are having are a common symptom of altered mental function. You have to realize that and come to grips with the fact that some of what you believe is a lie."

He held up his finger with the small red wound. "Is this a lie? That is thanks to Dr. Hampton and Jonathan said he brought me here."

Faye sat back and nodded. "Josh, there is no Dr. Hampton on staff here. And all visitors have to come through security. Maybe you confused someone else with this Dr. Hampton."

"No! He's from London. He had Pandora's box and I pricked my finger."

Faye raised an eyebrow. "Pandora's box? Pricked your finger?"

"I did. Dr. Hampton has a laboratory in London. Check it out on the internet. He's real and he was here. He did something to me, Faye. I swear. All of this is an experiment on me. It's not part of one of your clinical trials. You have to believe me?"

Faye stood up and glanced at her watch. "I just got notice of someone asking for you up front."

"Jonathan?" Josh said hopefully.

"I'll have to see. Now, just calm down and I'll be back in a minute."

14

When Steel walked out of the off ramp from the airplane into the terminal at the airport in Zurich, two people were waiting for him. He stopped before they saw him. Inspector Swarsin and Inspector Goudreaux stood deep in conversation next to a trash receptacle. Both of them had been in pursuit of Steel for the crash of Flight 1145 in Bern. Steel stepped aside and let the other passengers pass him by. A fly buzzed by his head. It was bad enough to be constantly surveilled by a demonic insect and now, he had to contend with two legal authorities from his past who had sworn to have him arrested. He felt a hand close on his arm. Before he could pull away a voice whispered.

"Mr. Steel, it is Ishido. Come this way quickly."

Steel glanced over his shoulder at the dark eyes of his friend and Max's protector, Ishido. Like Raven, Ishido had been an assassin until Max had taken him in and allowed him a chance for reform. Ishido wore a security uniform and pulled Steel back down the walkway toward the airplane. He paused at a door through which carry-on luggage was being unloaded. Ishido led him past the waiting passengers and through the door. He smiled at the baggage handler, and they passed by him down a flight of stairs onto the tarmac. Ishido pointed to a door leading into the baggage area.

"This way. Max has cleared the way for us."

"What about my luggage?" Steel said.

"I'll have it delivered to Max's chalet."

The air was frigid as Steel followed Ishido beneath the undercarriage of the big jet and into the dark storage area beneath the terminal. Ishido led him through piles of baggage to an outside entrance and into a small parking area. Ishido pointed to a small truck, and they climbed in. Snow was falling around them in the morning air and Steel shivered. He had brought only a light jacket over his flannel shirt and jeans.

"It's cold." He said through chattering teeth. The fly landed on the top of his head.

"November, Mr. Steel. Two weeks ago, it was a little warmer but now the real snows begin." Ishido drove out of the airport and toward the outskirts of Zurich. Snowcapped mountains gleamed in the morning sun. Snow covered a frozen lake. Before on his trip, he had been confined to a safe house and had left in the darkness of night. But the sights and sounds of Zurich were enchanting and for a moment pulled his thoughts away from Josh.

"Max was surprised to hear about your swift return." Ishido said.

"I wanted to finish Raven's business." Steel said, looking out the window. "And check on her. How is she?"

"I must let Max tell you more." Ishido said.

Lake Zurich spread out below them, austere and gray surrounded by the far distant Alps shrouded in snow. Ishido drove along the lake side beside picturesque buildings and avenues. Clouds blotted out the blue sky and snow swirled in the air like tiny ghosts. Ishido pulled into the circular driveway of a three-story mansion on the slopes of the lake. He stopped the car and opened Steel's door.

Ishido ushered him up snow covered stone steps to an immense front door. Ishido placed his palm on a copper plate beside the door and the lock clicked. The fly landed on a sconce just outside the door. It jerked and fell off the sconce onto the pavement. What had just happened? Ishido opened the door and motioned Steel in before him.

Steel stepped into an immense foyer filled with fresh cut flowers and classical paintings. Before him, the foyer led to a large staircase that split halfway up the wall and circled around the outer edges of the foyer. Little had changed since his last visit just a week or so before.

"This way, Mr. Steel." Ishido directed him toward a double set of rich, mahogany doors. They slid aside to reveal the library packed with shelves and books. In the center of the library, a half dozen leather couches surrounded a low-lying table piled with ancient books.

"Max will be with you in a moment. You can warm up beside the fire. Would you like something warm to drink? Coffee? Tea?"

Steel shivered again. "Tea would be fine." He walked over to a roaring fire in the fireplace and let the warmth soak into his tired body.

Ishido left the library, sliding the doors shut behind him. Steel walked around the room, studying the shelves and listening for the buzz of insects. Nothing. Quiet except for the ticking of a clock. The room reached upward to the top of the second story. A walkway circled the room ten feet above him giving access to a second level of books. Two rolling ladders gave access to the lower bookshelves and a spiral staircase led to the second level.

"I love books."

Steel turned as Max walked into the room. She was tall and willowy with silvery hair carefully brushed around her stern, aristocratic face. She smiled and opened her arms. Steel crossed the room and embraced her. He inhaled her faint perfume and for a moment almost gave in to his sorrow. Could he tell her why he was here? How could Shutendoji and her ilk possibly eavesdrop on him here? But, then Goudreaux had managed to spy on him in the safe house. No, it was best to keep Max out of the loop for her own protection. He pushed away gently and smiled at her.

"It is so good to see you, Max. Thank you for all you did for us in London."

Max motioned to a sofa and settled onto the rich fabric. "My dear, it was difficult but necessary."

Steel sat beside her and Ishido appeared with a tray of cups and a teapot. "Have you had breakfast, Mr. Steel?"

"No." He took a cup of tea and sipped the hot, spicy liquid. It tasted wonderful and he wasn't a tea person.

"Then, Ishido must set another place at the table. Come join us." Max stood up and motioned to a far door. Steel followed her into a dining room surrounded by windows that looked out over a snow covered back yard. Sculptures softened by snow dotted the area. Before, he had never noticed these touches of beauty. He had been preoccupied with the accusation of being a terrorist and then being arrested by Goudreaux.

"I hope you're hungry." Max motioned to the dining room table replete with fragrant dishes of food. Steel's stomach growled and he slid into a seat to her right and placed his tea beside the plate.

"I am very hungry." Ishido appeared with a platter of some kind of steaming meat, scrambled eggs, and pastries. He placed a piece on his plate.

"I hope you enjoy my pastries." Max said as she dished a

small portion of eggs onto her plate. "I made them myself. Baking is my escape."

Steel filled his place and bit into the eggs and sausage. The bear claw was delicious. He washed them down with the spicy tea. "Thank you. I haven't eaten since yesterday. I think."

"Why is that, Jonathan?" Max sipped at her tea.

"A lot has happened since I got back to the states."

Max studied him with a strange expression on her face. She placed her cup in a gold rimmed saucer. "When were you going to tell me about Josh?"

Steel froze. "What do you mean?"

"His illness."

Steel cleared his throat. "He's doing well in a private clinic in Texas. It will take a couple of weeks of treatment so I thought I would try and get Raven's business out of the way before the holidays."

A muscle twitched at the corner of one of Max's eyes. She regarded him with a blank expression. "Very well. I will accept that for now."

She sipped more of her tea. Steel glanced at Ishido whose eyes were hooded and averted. "How's Raven?" Steel asked.

Max lifted an eyebrow and her cheeks reddened. "Dr. Monarch should have waited until I had my experts confirm her methods. Raven is safely hidden away in a private school for mentally challenged individuals."

"I saw her yesterday." Ishido said. "She's learning quickly."

Steel reached into his shirt and pulled out the medallion. "Then we need to proceed with her final requests."

Max nodded. "Yes. The sooner the better." She pulled her own medallion from her blouse. "These are no ordinary medallions. Each is a key with a tiny circuit that is linked to our biometric imprint. When Raven passed it to you, you became the default owner of the medallion. And my medallion is the second key to a safety deposit box in one of the most secure banks in Switzerland. Together, these medallions give us access to the contents."

"And remind me again what is in that box?" Steel asked as if he didn't remember.

"A record of every assassination Raven has ever been paid for." Max tucked the medallion out of sight. "I need access to those records because Raven made me promise in the event she died, I was to take her assets and make reparations to the families of those she had killed."

"She's not dead." Steel said.

Max glared at him. "She might as well be."

Steel ate some more breakfast and now acid boiled in his stomach at the thought of what he was about to do. "Can we take care of that today? I really want to get back to Josh if I can't see Raven."

Max placed her utensils carefully beside her plate. "I thought you had two weeks, Mr. Steel." She said with formality.

"Yes. But the more I think about being away from Josh, the quicker I want to get back to him."

Max nodded. "Well, your luggage has yet to be delivered but Ishido has taken the liberty of securing you a warm jacket if you are to wander down the streets of Zurich in falling snow. I suggest you take a short nap to recover from your jet lag and then this afternoon we will head to the bank."

She stood up abruptly and motioned to Ishido. "Ishido, show Mr. Steel to his room."

Steel stood up quickly and Max had turned and walked away before he could respond. He swallowed down bile. This was not getting any easier.

Steel awoke as he hit the floor, pain lancing throughout his body. He opened his eyes and looked around the room. Sunlight streamed in through a window illuminating a four poster bed. He pulled himself up in the tangled covers and blinked the sleep out of his eyes.

"Mr. Steel, are you awake?"

Steel turned and Ishido stood in the door of his bedroom. Baroque era furniture and paintings adorned the room. It looked like something out of a museum. "I fell out of bed."

Ishido crossed the room and helped Steel untangle himself from the covers. "I have laundered your clothes. I hope the pajamas were warm."

Steel nodded as he looked down at the silk pajamas. "How long was I asleep?"

"Six hours. It is now two o'clock in the afternoon. The bank closes at 4 so you must get dressed. I have a hot bath drawn for you with special herbs to rejuvenate you. You'll find your clothes in the bathroom."

Ishido led him across the carpeted floor to the bathroom. The bathtub was ornately tiled with gold and marble. Ishido motioned to the foaming water in the tub.

Steel looked at the soothing waters in the tub and smelled the fragrant herbal aroma of the steam that arose from the surface. Steel watched the door close. He stripped and stepped into the water. As far as he could remember, he had never had a bubble bath!

But the waters were not bubbly. They felt heavenly as he lowered himself into the tingly water. His muscles instantly began to relax and uncoil. Ishido had worked magic after all. But he tensed at the sound of a tapping. He glanced up at the stained-glass window above the tub. Three flies were trying their best to break through the glass!

After a quick late lunch of cold cut meats, cheese, and bread they loaded up in Max's size-able Mercedes and pulled out of the chalet garage. Three flies landed on his window and clung to it as they pulled out of the driveway. He ignored them. He hadn't told Max the real reason he was here. But did the triplets suspect he had? Had the flies been unable to hear them? Well, now they could conduct their surveillance even through a window. Nestled in the back seat next to Max, Steel tried to ignore the flies and found a folded map in the pocket of the front seat.

"A map? Isn't that archaic?"

Max sniffed. "What's wrong with being a little archaic?"

Steel opened the map. It showed Zurich with the lake and river bisecting the city. The map had sections marked in highlighted colors with interesting titles. "Hipster Socialists? Organic Food? Best Spot to Hang out in the summer? Weed smoking hipsters?" He glanced at Max.

"That map belongs to Alpha, one of my young proteges." She said.

Steel nodded. "And, of course, you live in this section labeled 'Rich People'."

Max glanced at the map. "Right at the edge with the 'Golden Coast Rich People' area."

"I would think anyone living in Zurich would qualify as a rich person. Just look at the cars and the bikes and street life. I didn't get to see much of Zurich before. Once I arrived I was essentially under house arrest. Speaking of which, have you heard from Goudreaux?" Steel asked as he tucked the map back into the pocket. Max tapped her fingers against the well-polished wood of her ever-present walking cane.

"She showed up while you were napping along with your luggage. It seems they want to question you some more."

"I had nothing to do with the airplane disaster." Steel said.

"I have provided the authorities above her with ample evidence to that effect. I had to be careful." Max smiled. "I don't want her to know the entire extent of my covert abilities. I sent her away demanding what you in the states would call a search warrant."

Max looked out the window at the passing buildings along the lake. "I don't like her. She has an agenda that extends beyond her investigation."

"How do you know that?"

Max frowned as she looked at Steel. "Intuition, perhaps? Years of experience dealing with people who are intimately involved in evil affairs? Having developed the ability to read between the lines? I believe is the spiritual gift of discernment. I can easily see through someones, shall we say, BS." Her eyes narrowed as she studied Steel. "Any idea what might be going on, Jonathan?"

Steel avoided her gaze and studied her cane. "With Goudreaux? No idea, Max." *Unless she's a spy for the holy triad!* He had to change the subject. "Your cane? You seem quite spry without it. Is there more to this cane than meets the eye?"

Max regarded him silently as the car moved smoothly along the streets of Zurich. She nodded. "Very well, then." She lifted the cane's tip into view. The shining metal of a knife blade thrust itself into view with a loud click. "I was a fan of Doc Savage, a pulp fiction book written back in the 1930's. One of the characters carried a sword cane. I have found it to be useful on many occasions. But the tip is not deadly. It carries a dose of heavy sedative that can incapacitate an enemy, not kill." The blade receded with a click and Max put the cane aside.

"The Crimson Snake had such a walking cane." Steel looked away avoiding Max's gaze. "But the tip contained a deadly poison. Ishido and I were lucky she didn't kill us on the train to London."

Ishido pulled into a parking garage off a huge open square. Steel climbed out of the car and followed Max and Ishido out of the parking garage. He faintly heard the buzzing of the flies. They were still following him. The street before him was packed with pedestrians. The blue and white trams that traversed Zurich moved down the center of the street with their upswept power arms gliding along the six hundred volt power wires strung above the street.

"Where are we?"

Max had donned a long, white woolen coat and a gray knitted cap over her hair. She pointed with her cane down the long avenue before them. "Bahnhofstrasse is Zurich's main downtown street and one of the world's most expensive and exclusive shopping avenues."

Steel followed her as they moved deftly through the crowd. The air was cold and filled with a fine, powdery snow. Ishido stayed behind him, his gaze shifting back and forth in anticipation. Did the man ever relax? Probably not. They passed retail stores tucked into gray, stone buildings that defied aging. Jonathan stopped in front of the Apple Store. He swallowed hard and fought down emotion. Josh would have loved to go in there.

Max paused and motioned to him. "We need to keep moving, Jonathan. I chose this route so that we would disappear into the crowd. We want to avoid Goudreaux's prying eyes."

"Where are we headed?" He said as he followed her past the Apple Store.

"To Paradeplatz. It is a square just ahead in downtown Zurich. The bank is there. It is one of the most expensive pieces of real estate in Switzerland and has become synonymous with wealth and the Swiss banks."

Steel wore a long, dark coat and had covered his bare head with a fedora supplied by Ishido. "To keep the cameras busy." Ishido had said. Ishido wore a thin, dark blue long coat and a knit cap. A messenger bag was slung across his chest. His hands, like Max's hands, were covered in leather gloves. Steel shoved his hands into the pockets of his coat and tried to keep them warm. Beneath his shirt, he felt the medallion tingle against his skin, a lump of cold metal.

The Paradeplatz was a large, open square and the trams moved around the center tram station. On one side, a five-story building squatted in grayish splendor. "Credit Suisse" glowed almost subtly from the top floor corner.

"Are we headed there?" Steel pointed to Credit Suisse.

"Oh, no." Max led him down the walkway away from the building. "Too conspicuous for Raven. We are headed to a smaller, quieter bank."

The Paradeplatz was a bustling city square and tram junction in the Bahnhofstrasse. Around the odd shaped "square" were banks and the Savoy Hotel. Seven tramlines converge at the Paradeplatz, and as Steel tried to keep up with Max, the square was abuzz with streams of business people, workers and shoppers. A massive clock looked down upon them.

"That is Türler-Clock in the Türler shop." Max said. "And, if we have time, we might stop and have some luscious chocolate at the Sprungli Café."

They passed stores featuring top designers such as Armani, Gucci, Rolex and Jimmy Choo. An elongated oval roof covered a squat building in the center of the square. Blue and white trams sliding along their electrical wires suspended above the streets waited for passengers to load and unload at the building. Wooden benches curved around the ends of the small building. A few coffee shops and newsstands filled the small, narrow building.

Steel hurried across the street as a tram swung around the curve behind him and pulled up to the central building. More trams converged from several different directions.

"How do you keep it all straight?" He asked.

Max shrugged. "We are used to it, Mr. Steel. Have you

ever been to New York City? Bumper to bumper taxis. People moving in droves. This square is nothing compared to Times Square. Ah, here we are."

Max paused in front of a nondescript black door in the center of the walkway. She leaned forward and gazed into a tiny peep hole. A light flickered and the door opened quietly. She motioned to the door and Steel followed. Ishido handed the messenger bag to Steel and remained outside, his ever-vigilant gaze pouring over the busy square. Steel glanced once at Ishido and saw a fly land on his shoulder. He closed the door before the fly could enter the building.

The office beyond the door was a simple, small room with a man sitting behind a chrome and glass desk. No phone. No computer. Just the man in an impeccable gray suit and a shiny bald head. Behind the man, dark wooden panels covered the back wall. No doors. No windows.

"We are here to view the contents of Box 8113. I spoke to Klaus earlier." Max said.

"Passport, please." The man stood up and held out his hand.

Max retrieved her passport from her coat and the man held it in front of his watch. A light flickered and he touched his right ear and listened. "You may go in. Klaus said your guest is welcome."

Behind the man, one of the panels slid aside and he motioned to a hallway beyond. With her cane tapping on the tiled floor, Max led Steel down the hallway. It was austere with gray painted walls and a bare concrete floor. Office doors flanked them as Max walked toward a large, corpulent man standing in the distant hallway. His salt and pepper hair was carefully combed back from a high forehead. He wore rimless glasses that magnified his bright, green eyes. His face hovered in a sea of chins. His cheeks glowed redly as he reached forward with both hands.

"Max, my dear friend."

Max offered her gloved hand and he kissed it. "So good of you to come see me." His speech echoed with a faint Germanic accent. "It has been so long since the ski party. When was that?"

"Five years ago, Klaus. You were on your fifth wife, I think."

Klaus chuckled and opened his arms and hands into a gesture of surrender. "What can I say. I am looking for number six. Tell me you are interested."

Max smiled. "Let's not ruin a good friendship. This is my associate, Mr. Jonathan Steel."

Klaus turned his attention to Steel. For a moment, his face slackened, and he put his hand to his chin. "Steel? Jonathan? Sir, have we met?"

Steel felt a tingle of excitement. In the years since he had awakened on a beach in Florida with no memory, he had longed for an encounter with someone who might know him. "I don't know, sir. Do you know me?"

Klaus studied him with his magnified eyes and shook his head. "You look so familiar. I never forget a name. But, sometimes, I am terrible with faces. Your name is foreign to me. But your face. Your eyes. They are so strikingly familiar."

"I hate to interrupt this recollection session," Max said, "But we are getting near to closing time for your bank?"

Klaus shook his head and smiled again as he focused on Max. "Of course. Follow me." He led them into a small, nondescript office and opened what Steel thought was a closet door. There was barely room for all three of them inside. A door slid shut and the floor descended. They were in an elevator.

"Give me a few minutes, Mr. Steel and perhaps I will recall where we have met."

"I have amnesia, Klaus." Steel said hoarsely. "I don't

remember anything past a year or so ago. If you have any inkling of a previous encounter, it might help."

The elevator halted and the door opened allowing bright light to spill into the elevator. Max moved into the hallway beyond, and Klaus followed and led them through an open door into a small room. He motioned to two chairs at a metal table. A large safety deposit box sat on the table. "Have a seat."

Steel studied the box as he sat at the table. His heart began to race. How would he get his hands on the dossier? How would he get it away from Max?

Klaus held out a hand. "I trust the two of you have the medallions?"

Steel reached into his shirt and pulled the necklace over his head. He handed the silver medallion to Max. She took a necklace from around her neck and placed her medallion in her other hand.

"First, you must combine the two medallions to confirm their mutual identity."

Max handed the medallions to Klaus and he placed them on the table lining them up along their matching edges. Something clicked and a tiny green light burned from both medallions.

"Good." He separated the medallions and handed them back to Steel and Max. He motioned to the box. At one end, two gray circles were etched into the white lid of the box. "Place a medallion in each circle on the lid. There is an RFID chip that will be the first step in activating the electronic lock."

Max placed her medallion on a disc and Steel followed suit placing his medallion on the other circle. He heard an electronic whirring. The medallions popped open. Inside each medallion was a small, L shaped piece of metal the size of a tiny memory card. Klaus pointed to the keys inside.

"Now take your keys and place them together. They should fit together like two puzzle pieces. Mr. Steel take your key and Max take yours."

They took their respective keys from the medallion. Steel noticed that his L shaped key when turned properly would fit inside Max's key to form a rectangle. Max held her key toward him and he placed his next to hers. With a metallic snap, they magnetically popped together. Klaus pointed to a slot in the front of the box.

"Now place the completed key into the slot and the box will open."

Max slid the key into the slot until it was almost completely inside. The circles on the lid glowed with an inner light.

"Now, each of you place your thumb on the circle for biometric verification." Klaus smiled.

Steel pressed his thumb to the circle. Max followed suit. The lid of the safety deposit box slid open. Steel stood up and Max leaned over the open box. Klaus retrieved the two medallions and placed them on the tabletop. "Very good. You may examine the contents."

A black spiral notebook sat nonchalantly in the box. It was over two inches thick and bulging from the papers stuffed inside. A wide rubber band held it closed. Max retrieved the notebook from the box. She glanced at Steel and a lone tear ran down her cheek.

"We can make things right, Jonathan. It's all here!"

Steel pulled the messenger bag from around his shoulder and placed it on the table. Max slid the notebook inside and closed the bag. Klaus handed the medallions and the key to Steel. "I hope you have found what you needed."

"We did, Klaus." Max's voice was heavy with emotion. "Thank you again for being so kind. I'm having a dinner party in December, and I want you to come."

Klaus' cheeks reddened. "I would be honored. Perhaps I can meet number six?"

Steel tensed at the mention of the number and tried to relax. He had to figure how to get the notebook from Max. He slid the medallions and the key into his pants pocket and draped the messenger bag strap around his neck and left shoulder. It hung down his left side and he felt the weight of it resting against his leg. The weight of every kill. The weight of every person who had not only hired Raven but every person's family she had destroyed. But, more importantly, the contents of the bag would save the life of Joshua Knight. If, indeed, Dr. Faust records were there. If, indeed, he had hired Raven as Ross suspected.

Ishido waited for them as they exited through the black door. The busy patrons of Paradeplatz had not abated. Max pointed to the Savoy Hotel.

"Let's pause for a coffee and a pastry and let the crowd thin a bit, shall we?" Max said.

15

The woman came out of nowhere clothed in a body hugging white athletic outfit with her hair covered by a white knit cap. Steel saw the cane knife as it flashed in the meager sunlight and instinctively fell back away from the woman. The knife slit the sleeve of his coat. The tip snared the messenger bag's strap and severed it with a quick snap. With a deft movement, the woman caught the falling bag with a copper tinted metallic hand. Steel continued to fall back into the crowd of people behind him as the woman smiled at him. A red tattoo of a snake crawled up her neck.

"Max!" He screamed! The woman continued on into the crowd and Ishido was a black blur of motion as he headed after her. A man caught Steel and pushed him away and Steel shoved his way through the crowd after Ishido and Snake.

He burst through the crowd into the street just as a blue and white tram hurtled toward him. He fell back onto the walkway. To his left, he saw Ishido scurrying through the crowd. A building being refurbished had a section of scaffolding in the front and he spied Snake climbing up the metal work onto the scaffolding.

THE 7TH DEMON

"Up there!" He shouted after Ishido. Ishido didn't hear him and ran under the scaffolding and out of sight. Steel pushed his way through the crowd and started up the scaffolding. Wooden planks made a walkway along the scaffolding and were slick with snow. He heard a shout as Snake collided with a worker ahead on the scaffolding. He ran across the planks and slid to a stop just short of the fallen man. He hopped over him as Snake disappeared around the corner of the building. Steel hurtled around the corner, his feet sliding on the snow slick planks, and something shot out at him. The slippery wood saved his life as he fell backwards, and Snake's blade whistled past his cheek. The plank beneath him tilted down and the other end caught Snake's metal arm. She fell forward onto the tilting plank and Steel slid backwards. He landed hard on a metal surface and Snake followed close behind.

They were on the roof of one of the moving trams! He grabbed a metal edge near the middle of the tram to keep from sliding off. His feet hung over the side, and he looked out over water as the tram made its way along the river. Snake squatted securely just six feet away from him. She held her cane with the blade out toward him and smiled.

"Time to go, Steel." She raised the blade, and it accidentally touched the wires along which the trams moved. Sparks scattered from the blade and Snake swore as she fell forward onto the tram. Steel managed to pull himself up and slid backwards away from Snake's struggling figure.

She looked up at him, her knit cap now gone in the wind and snow swirled into her red hair. A look of murderous rage was on her face. Her mechanical arm hung useless at her side. She retrieved the blade with her good hand and shoved herself with her feet, sliding toward him with the blade pointed right at his abdomen. The tip grazed his leg, and he felt the sting of its cut.

Steel rolled away and fell. He saw the shocked face of a child inside the tram as he plummeted past him. He hit a stone railing with his now numb leg and somersaulted through the snowy air until he hit water. He plunged into freezing water and sunk deep into the river. The shock drove the air out of his lungs and there was a growing numbness crawling up his leg from Snake's wound. The poison!

He swam toward the surface and the current took him down the river until a shadow passed over him and he thudded into stone. The current pushed against his chest, driving what little air was left and he grappled along the stone toward the surface. A hand shot down through the water and grabbed his. Someone pulled him up and up and when his face broke the surface, he gasped for air. Ishido squatted at the base of one of the bridge supports. The river surged around them and Ishido pulled him up onto the ledge. He motioned to someone, and a boat appeared out of the snow. It was a wide, glass topped boat for sightseeing.

Ishido grabbed Stone under his shoulders and pulled him along the ledge just as the boat came even. Ishido jumped and Steel's legs bounced against the side of the boat. He felt no pain. He felt nothing from the chest down.

"Leg. Poison. Snake." He said hoarsely. Ishido placed Steel in a chair under the glass roof of the boat and spoke to the driver. A few scattered tourists stared at Steel. The numbness was growing and now and he was having trouble breathing. As the boat neared a dock along the shore, he glanced up once to see Snake standing on the bridge. Her mechanical arm hung useless at her side. She smiled at him and held up the messenger bag. She stepped back and out of sight as darkness took Steel.

"JJ stop! You're hurting me!"

He glared at Penelope and down at his hand gripped tightly on her arm. What was he doing? He released his grip and stepped back. They stood outside the church youth building. The sun set behind them and the sky was filled with clouds moving in for a spring storm.

"I'm sorry. It's just I don't want to go to a Bible study tonight." JJ said.

She rubbed her arm and looked at him with sadness in her eyes. "I don't know what's going on with you anymore. You're not the person I met on the tennis court a few weeks ago."

JJ stepped back and leaned against his mother's car. He had borrowed it for what he thought was a date to dinner and a movie. He wanted to see the latest Marvel movie complete with nonstop action and lots of violence.

"Go ahead and slap her!" The voice whispered in his ear. "She deserves it. She doesn't care for you!"

JJ closed his eyes and fought off the desire to hurt his girlfriend. He had never hit anyone! "No, I will not hit her." He whispered.

Penelope stepped back. "What did you say?"

He opened his eyes and shook his head. "I'm sorry. I, uh,--"

"You can take your sorry butt and get out of here." She screamed at him. "You were going to hit me? What is wrong with you? I guess you're just as crazy as they say you are."

JJ froze. "Who says I'm crazy?" The anger came, building to a red-hot haze. His arteries pulsed in his temples. His face grew hot.

"Hey, chick, get inside before Vesuvius erupts." A girl said as she stepped through the doors to the Tank. She was short and wiry with a dozen tattoos on her arms. Her hair was cut to the scalp on one side of her head and the rest was swooped over the other ear. It was dyed a bright maroon. Two hoops pierced her nostrils, and one hoop pierced her lip.

Penelope stepped backwards, fear in her eyes and ran through the door into the Tank. The girl sauntered over to him and leaned *against his car. "You really should wear a wife beater undershirt if you're going to hit girls."*

JJ blinked in confusion and tried to relax. "Who are you?"

"Mercedes. Like the car. New girl in town. My mother makes me come to church at least once a week or I have to go back into rehab. I figured the Wednesday night Bible study would be less boring than a Sunday service. So, you like to hit girls?"

He felt his face cool and shook his head. "No! I don't. I don't know what came over me."

"That's easy. Evil." She pulled a vape stick from her jeans pocket and inhaled the white vapor. She blew it out in a large plume of white. "Want a hit?"

JJ stepped back. "No. I don't want a hit."

"Funny, you act like the type. My type."

"What's your type?"

"I don't mind the rough and tumble routine. I'm used to it. Been in four foster homes before my biological mom cleaned up her act and took me back. She's clean now. Sober. Boring." She blew more smoke into the air. "So, what's your story?"

"I don't have a story." He mumbled.

"Course you do. Most guys are jerks, but most guys don't go around hitting their girlfriends. They're all weenies! Afraid we'll hit back. Or, kick back." She kicked out toward his groin, and he recoiled just as she held off the final blow. "Hey, just kidding. Chill out."

She opened the passenger door to his car and slid in. He glared at her. "What are you doing?"

"Taking you for a drive. I need some caffeine at Rhino's coffee. Let's go." She closed the door.

"Go ahead. She's more your style." The voice whispered. JJ swallowed and glanced once more at the door to the Tank. Penelope was visible just inside the door being consoled by two of her friends. He'd show her. He'd drive off into the sunset with the new love of his life.

※

"Mercedes, where do you go to school?"

Mercedes sipped her latte and leaned back in her chair. The sounds and smells of Rhino coffee filled the air thankfully drowning out the voice. "I don't. I'm getting my GED. School is too boring. You?"

JJ told her his school name and sipped his cappuccino. "I'm in the ninth grade. Just got my driver's license."

"You're a baby." She ran a hand through her maroon hair. Each fingernail had a different glittering finish. "Look, I'm probably a couple of years older than you but if we have sex, I'm still young enough not to have abused a minor."

JJ spit coffee and foam onto the table. "Sex?"

She studied him with reptilian eyes. "You a virgin?"

JJ looked away. This was getting far too uncomfortable. "Uh, I, well." Was all he could manage. He took another sip of his cappuccino, and it went down the wrong way. He started coughing and sputtering and he saw spots before his eyes. He stood up and felt dizzy.

"Hey, let me take over." The voice said at the back of his mind. "I can handle this."

※

JJ sat up in complete darkness. His shirt was gone. His pants were gone. He was in his underwear. He looked around him. He was in the parking lot of the church lit by yellow sodium lamps in the night. Somewhere he heard a cell phone warbling. His mother's car sat at an angle in the parking slot nearby.

He crawled across the cold pavement and opened the driver's side door. His cell phone was on the front seat. He picked it up.

"Hey, tiger. Thanks for the ride." Mercedes said. "I had to slide. My mom was waiting for me. We'll chill later."

"Wait! What happened?"

"What happened? If you don't remember what happened, you're deaf, dumb, and blind. Okay, so just lame. Bubbye!"

JJ looked down at himself and panic filled his mind. He looked at the car clock. The last thing he remembered he was having coffee and that had been three hours before. Three hours! He had blacked out. And, he had no memory of what happened. Where were his clothes?

"Oh, God! What is going on?"

"You're having the time of your life." The voice said only this time it came from the back seat; from inside the backpack. He threw open the back door and dug the photo album out of the backpack. A dense swath of thick woods backed up to the church property. He ran barefoot to the edge and hurled the album deep into the woods.

"Hey, what are you doing?"

He whirled. Kevin stood at the front of his car. JJ hurried over to him. "Kevin. I'm in trouble. I did something tonight. Something bad and I don't remember it."

Kevin leaned toward him. "Nice tighty whities. Have you been drinking?"

JJ blinked and cupped his hand. He sampled his breath. Coffee and something else. Incense? "No. I took a ride with this girl and the next thing I know I'm here in my underwear."

"I'd better call the cops. She might have slipped you a roofie and then robbed you."

JJ held up his hand. "No. Wait." He looked in the back seat. His clothes were piled on the floor. He rummaged through his jeans and found his wallet. He looked inside. Everything was there.

"She may have roofied me, but she didn't rob me. Oh, God, what am I doing? Kevin, I'm all out of control. I'm white hot mad one minute and then I've lost time."

Kevin put a hand on his arm. "Hey, calm down. Go home. Get some sleep and then come in and we'll talk. Counseling. You probably need it."

From deep within the forest the voice floated out and was right in his ear again. "You don't need no stinking counseling! You are strong enough without this wimp! Tell him to shove off." He could never tell someone to shove off. Or, could he? He looked down at his hand and he made a fist. The confusion began to abate and a new kind of power filled him. Anger. Fury. Hatred! He felt a surge of courage, of defiance and all his doubts disappeared. He straightened up and slammed the back door. He glared at Kevin, the busybody.

"Kevin, I don't need counseling. I'm not crazy! Get lost." JJ slid into the front seat, started his car and tore off across the parking lot. How quickly things had changed! He had gotten rid of the album and somehow had rediscovered his mojo. He wondered if he would ever see Mercedes again. If not, he'd find someone else.

16

Steel's head pounded with pain as he opened his eyes. He tried to sit up, but dizziness gripped him, and he felt nauseous. Another memory! Before he could even consider what he had just learned about himself someone placed a cool hand on his forehead.

"Mr. Steel, please remain motionless." He glanced at the young woman sitting beside his bed. She had short, black hair and dark skin. She tapped out a text on her cell phone. "I am Gamma, one of Max's students."

Steel looked down at the bandage on his leg. "I was poisoned."

"Merely a sedative." Max said quietly as she stepped through the door to a small, nondescript bedroom with no windows. "Fortunately for you."

Max still wore her long coat. She shrugged out of it and handed it to Gamma. "Thank you for dressing Mr. Steel's wound. Have Alpha contact Ishido and see if preparations are complete. We don't have much time."

Steel swung his legs off the bed and held his pounding head. "Max, Snake has the dossier. Josh!" He blurted out.

Max sat in the chair. "You are safe in this room, Jonathan. Inside my chalet the insect drones would be neutralized."

Steel's mouth fell open. "How did you know?"

"I'm good at what I do, Jonathan. Very good." She held up a glass vial containing a motionless fly. "There is a dampening field around my chalet to forbid any surveillance."

"That is why the spider dropped at the front door when I arrived." Steel said.

"Yes. I knew then you were under surveillance but I did not show my hand. You need not worry. I have made sure even my students don't hear what you have to say. We are quite safe to talk." She placed the vial on the table beside her coat. "Now, you will talk to me."

Steel drew a deep breath. "If they think I neutralized those insects, Josh dies. If I tell you what is going on, Josh could die. If I don't do what they say, Josh will die." He felt emotion surge and pressed a hand to his mouth.

"You are safe." Max patted his arm. "One of my students is feeding a video loop of our meal to the only fly left intact. We have some time before your adversaries realize what is going on."

"Snake took the dossier." Steel said.

"Yes, she did. Do you have any idea why?"

Steel shrugged. "There's a lot of damaging information in that dossier, Max. In the wrong hands it could be used for blackmail."

"Exactly!" Max smiled. "I haven't told you everything, Jonathan. Raven and I planned the storage of her dossier very carefully. The notebook is a fake. It is filled with false information. Raven was always afraid someone would get their hands on it besides me. But she devised a second way to store the data. The safety deposit box itself contains a small storage drive with all the information on it. When we placed the key in the lock, that information was downloaded onto the key and then all of the information was erased from the hidden drive inside the box."

Steel's mouth fell open and he slid his hand gingerly into his pants pocket. The cut on his leg throbbed as he dug around and pulled out the rectangular key. "This?"

"It is a memory card. All of Raven's information was downloaded onto it." Max sat back. "Now, the question is what do you do now? You know I can't let you take the flash drive and risk losing the contents. I made a promise to Raven." She carried a small purse on a golden chain, and it lay on the coat. She picked up the purse and withdrew a small pistol from within. "You could take this away from me and hold me hostage until you leave this building with the card."

Steel studied the pistol and his heart raced. Max stood up and pointed the pistol at Steel. He groaned in agony. "But, Josh?"

"I understand you are an expert marksman, Jonathan. You could take this pistol from me and put a hole through my forehead before I could draw my next breath. What are you going to do?"

Steel looked at the memory card in his hand. "I have to take this with me, Max. If I don't Josh dies." He looked up suddenly. "Can you copy the data from it?"

"No. If you try and copy the data, it erases all files. Another one of Raven's fail safes."

Steel nodded. He moved quickly, so quickly Max never felt him wrench the pistol from her hand. She fell back into the chair with a gasp. Steel held the pistol before him aimed perfectly and motionless at her head. "Max, I have to do this. I have no choice." His voice shook and he felt hot tears on his cheeks. The memory of the 'other' Jonathan from Numinocity flashed in his mind. The man's fierce, hungry stare. The man's evil tinged voice. His most recent memory of an angry young man who was willing to beat up girls. Was Max now seeing the real Steel? He moaned again and dropped his arm. He handed the pistol and the memory card to Max.

"I don't know what to do, anymore, Max. I have to take this, or Josh suffers."

"I deduced as much." Max slowly stood up placing the pistol back in her purse. Her hand trembled slightly. "Jonathan, I have never trusted anyone more in my life than I trusted Cephas Lawrence. When I thought he had betrayed me, it almost destroyed me. It took years to get over the sense of betrayal. I loved the man and thought he was responsible for the death of my daughter." She paced the room and paused, turning to regard him. "Until you told me the truth about my daughter. You strike me as a person who has great difficulty being dishonest. I was hoping you would be reasonable."

"I don't lie very well." Steel stood up. "I will fight for Josh, you have to know that. Even if you try and stop me. He is all I have left."

Max's features softened. "No, Jonathan, he is not all you have left. You are a good man and there is some Godly plan playing out around us. No coincidences Cephas used to say. I am here to help."

Steel glared at her. "Don't you ever get tired of being a pawn in God's games of good versus evil?"

Max lifted an eyebrow and sighed. "Ah, there it is. That famous Steel anger and fury. You think you are the only servant of God to have suffered losses? Jonathan, in the vast give and take between the forces of good and evil, you must have an eternal perspective."

"What?"

She came closer and put a hand on his chest. "I loved my daughter very much. How many years of her life did I miss because I thought she was dead. If I had known she was alive, I would have done anything to recover her."

A tear trickled down one of pale cheeks and her gaze bored into Steel. "You love Josh very much. If all of this is part of some mysterious plan of God, then you must cling to one thing. Faith. Tell me what you know, not what you feel."

Steel blinked. "What I know? I know that Josh is sick, and he was deliberately infected by the unholy triad. I know that they are forcing me to do Satan's bidding to save Josh. How can God forgive me for that?"

Max raised an eyebrow in surprise. "What you say is true. But you have not embraced the whole truth of your situation. Let me show you what I know, not feel." She turned and opened the door and motioned to Gamma. "My Bible."

Gamma peeked in and nodded. Max took Steel's free hand and led him to a chair beside the bed. "Sit for a moment. We don't have much time but there is something I can share with you that may help you with all of this."

"Max, I betrayed God. I betrayed you!"

Gamma appeared and handed a large, blue leather Bible to Max. She opened it and turned through the pages. "Ah, here it is.

'We know that the law is spiritual; but I am unspiritual, sold as a slave to sin. I do not understand what I do. For what I want to do I do not do, but what I hate I do. And if I do what I do not want to do, I agree that the law is good. As it is, it is no longer I myself who do it, but it is sin living in me. For I know that good itself does not dwell in me, that is, in my sinful nature. For I have the desire to do what is good, but I cannot carry it out. For I do not do the good I want to do, but the evil I do not want to do—this I keep on doing. Now if I do what I do not want to do, it is no longer I who do it, but it is sin living in me that does it.

'So I find this law at work: Although I want to do good, evil is right there with me. For in my inner being I delight in God's law; but I see another law at work in me, waging war against the law of my mind and making me a prisoner of the law of sin at work within me. What a wretched man I am! Who will rescue me from this body that is subject to death? Thanks be to God, who delivers me through Jesus Christ our Lord!'

Max closed the book. "Paul wrote that. He killed Christians, Jonathan. He realized that as humans we are slaves to sin; to our inner weaknesses and desires. The inner battle is inevitable. We do the things we do not want to do. And the things we must do we won't do. What you must do, Jonathan, is turn this situation upside down. Do not view this as a command to do evil in order for good to come of it. Look upon this as an opportunity. You can't see the possibility because the enemy has blinded you with their threat against Josh."

Max sat on the bed beside Steel's chair. "If God has allowed Josh to enter into danger, then you must have faith that God will take care of him. Give Josh over to God, Jonathan. And give yourself fully to this task. But find a way to turn it around. How can you gain the upper hand?" She looked away and sighed. "After I left Cephas, convinced my daughter had died I was distraught. I was a victim." She looked back at him. "There was nothing I could do to bring her back. And then I realized I could turn this defeat into a victory. I changed my status, Jonathan. I was no longer a victim, I would be a victor!"

Max took his hand in hers. It was warm and soft. "You are acting as if you are already defeated. Remember, Satan is defeated. He lost the day the stone rolled away from the tomb and the moment he was sure he had won the battle for all eternity. His hubris was and will always be his downfall." Max placed the flash drive in Steel's hand and closed his fist. "You take the drive and do with it what you must. We both have to hope that in the process you will not only save Josh but the information on that disk will return to us in proper time. I have faith in you."

Steel blinked away moisture. "Max, you are unbelievable."

"Yes, I am." Someone knocked on the door behind her. She stood up and opened it and a young man in a three-piece suit stepped into the room. His hair was shoulder length, and he held a tablet.

"Ishido has returned. He was unable to find the woman."

"Not a problem, Beta. Have you arranged for Mr. Steel's departure?"

"Yes. One of our smaller air charter companies will fly him into France and he can catch a passenger jet home." Beta said.

"And it will look like he set it up himself? There can be no hint I aided him." Max said.

"Yes, but he must escape the chalet. Goudreaux is at the front door with a search warrant."

Max picked up the fly drone in the glass vial and glanced at Steel. "I believe Goudreaux is working with these demons."

"We can't be that sure." Steel shook his head. "I'm cerain Snake is working for the Vitreomancers. There was a man from the triplets' service who betrayed them. He had white eyes."

"You are in more danger than I thought." Max froze and drew a deep breath. She handed him the vial. "Take this with you. Once you are on the jet back to the states, release the fly and it will reactivate. By then, you will be beyond the reach of Goudreaux whoever she works for."

Steel took the vial and put it and the key back into his pocket. "This device that dampens any surveillance, you wouldn't happen to have a portable version, would you?"

Max smiled. She took her cane and tapped it three times on the floor. The top of the handle popped up and out slid a fountain pen. She removed it and handed it to Steel. "Fully charged. Giving it to you had not crossed my mind. An old woman is slipping up, Jonathan. There is a USB port to recharge it. Press down on the top to activate. A tiny green light will flash. Press again to turn it off. A tiny red light will glow. It should protect you for about a twenty foot radius."

"Another one of your protege's inventions?"

Max closed the top of her cane. "Heavens no! I made that myself. And, I have more where that came from."

Steel nodded and slid the pen into his shirt pocket. "What do I do now?"

"Beta, take him to the back bedroom on the second floor. Gamma will have a change of clothes for him and all of his valuables." Max turned back to Steel. "Now, hurry while I delay Goudreaux."

Beta led Steel to the same bedroom where he had taken a nap just hours before. Steel took off his wet and muddy shirt and pants in the bathroom and put on another pair of jeans and a warm sweater. He took the key and the vial out of the pocket of his bloody pants and slid them into the pocket of his clean pants. The clothes fit perfectly even over his throbbing leg wound. Max was amazing. He looked at himself in the mirror and took a washcloth and wiped spots of mud from his face and hair.

In the bedroom, Beta sat cross legged on his bed with a large iPad Pro. "I have downloaded the necessary ticket information onto your phone, Mr. Steel. We can get you to France but from there you will be on your own."

"I've done this before." Steel picked up his phone, passport, and wallet. A lightweight wool coat lay on the bed. He shrugged into it. On the bedside table he spied a small pad of paper, envelopes, and a pen. After Max's words and a dozen silent prayers a plan had already formed. He grabbed the paper and envelopes and tucked them into his coat pocket.

Max stepped into his bedroom and closed the door behind her. "I have delayed Goudreaux as long as possible. She is here to arrest you, Mr. Steel."

Steel shook his head. "I can't let them put me in jail, Max."

"I know. That is why you must fight with us and then run." Max grabbed her blouse and ripped the sleeve off her left arm. "Beta, I hate to do this, but I must strike you."

Beta nodded. "Yes, ma'am." He tossed the iPad Pro against the nearby wall and the screen shattered. "We don't want Goudreaux to know about Mr. Steel." Max backhanded Beta with a sudden, powerful slap. Blood poured from Beta's nose, and he fell back onto the bed. Steel gasped in shock. She took the pistol from her purse and fired it at the wall. The explosion was loud in the small room and a mirror shattered on the far wall. "Your fingerprints are on the gun." She explained. She tossed it onto the bed and Beta picked it up and held on.

"We fought and I managed to get the gun from you." Beta said.

The door opened again and Ishido appeared. "I heard a gunshot."

"Change in plans, Ishido. Get Mr. Steel out of here. Take the back window and the alley behind. The only functioning drone is securely stuck to the dining room window. But if Goudreaux is indeed working with the triplets, they will know soon the video loop was a ruse. I can only hope we can buy both Jonathan and Josh some time. Go. You know what to do."

Ishido nodded and picked up a chair and threw it through the massive, beautiful window above Steel's bed. Glass shattered into the dusk. The sound of approaching sirens echoed in the snow filled darkness outside the window.

"Max, thank you." Steel said.

She nodded and motioned to the window. "No time for sentiment. Now go!"

Steel followed Ishido out onto the slippery, snow-covered roof and followed him into the growing darkness.

17

Tristate North Dallas Clinic

"HELLO, I'M DR. JACK MERCHANT. MAY I SPEAK WITH your chief nurse?"

Birdsong looked around the foyer for the Tristate North Dallas Clinic. It was sumptuous to say the least. From the outside, the "clinic" reminded him of a sprawling ranch house surrounded by verdant green grass fields with roaming cows. All that was missing was the theme song.

Paintings of cowboys and outdoor scenes. Leather couches and chairs completed the rustic appearance of the foyer which was bigger than his house. He pulled at the tight collar and desperately wanted to loosen his tie, but he had to look professional, Merchant had said. He represented the Caddo Parish Sheriff's department. Parish? Yeah, Louisiana was weird all right. Parishes instead of counties.

The man sitting behind the information desk stood up. "Do you have an appointment?"

Merchant glanced at his watch and grimaced. "People are dying," he leaned in to look at the man's name tag. "Donald. Unless I speak immediately to the person in charge, we could be blamed for another pandemic worse than COVID."

Donald crossed his arms. "Sir, I have no idea who you are."

Merchant reached into his white coat pocket and pulled out a wallet. He opened it and held it inches from the man's face. "I am a Deputy Medical Examiner from Louisiana investigating a patient with a viral infection of interest to the CDC. I have been tasked with tracking down this patient who was transferred to this facility a few days ago. This individual was an in-patient at one of our local hospitals in northwest Louisiana and his viral infection is of great interest to the CDC. We were unable to complete our viral studies before he was transferred to this facility. You may not be aware of the concentration of COVID-19 cases we had in Louisiana, Donald." Merchant pocketed his wallet. "Louisiana was in the top five states affected by that pandemic, and we will not allow that to happen again because of your bureaucratic self-importance. Now, either you find someone in charge around here or I will have a cadre of CDC and FDA agents descend on this little private clinic within 24 hours." Merchant leaned forward. "Or, worse, I will call for a Medicare inspection."

Donald's face reddened and he stormed off down a hallway behind the reception desk and disappeared into an office.

"Where have you been all this time?" Birdsong whispered.

"What do you mean?"

"Man, with that attitude we could have used you in Jerusalem AND Numinosity."

"I'm still processing all of that information." Merchant said quietly and he cleared his throat. "If I hadn't have seen that woman turn into a red multihorned beast, I would be sending you to my favorite psychiatrist." He had tried his best to process everything Birdsong had told him while they drove from Shreveport to Dallas. Less than two days had passed since the incident in New Orleans, and they had heard nothing from Steel. If what Birdsong told him was true, there were forces mounted against them that used supernatural power unlike anything Merchant had ever heard of.

"I've wanted to see a counselor or two myself. Problem is, if I told them what I told you, I would be committed." Birdsong said. "Looks like Donald found someone."

Donald reappeared and motioned to a heavy-set man in purple scrubs. "This is Travion Jackson, our Charge Nurse."

The man glared at them through squinted eyes. "I don't know who you are, but you don't come into my clinic and talk to my people this way."

Merchant held up his wallet again. "I don't care. We are talking about another possible pandemic, and I need to see this patient now." He handed him an envelope with printouts inside. "Those are a copy of his medical records from Shreveport, Louisiana. I would have brought electronic records, but I wasn't sure how advanced this facility would be."

Travion's eyes filled with fire. "We are one of the most technologically advanced clinics in Texas."

"Sorry. Let's dial it down a bit." Merchant pocketed his wallet. "Look, all I'm asking for is a little cooperation in the interest of national security. If you can't let me see," He glanced down at the envelope again, "Joshua Knight and take a blood sample, then I will have to start an inquiry. I assume you are up to date on your inspections? JCAH? Medicare?"

Travion frowned. He grabbed the envelope and glanced at the papers and then tossed them onto Donald's desk. "Donald, take these gentlemen to hall C. Let Faye escort them to Mr. Knight's room. We can give you thirty minutes max, Dr. Merchant. And you can draw your own blood. I assume you have brought your own equipment?"

Merchant pulled two red top vials from his pocket. "Yes. Donald, after you."

They followed Donald down a corridor. They arrived at a nurse's station configured more like an expensive dining room complete with a large wooden table. A small woman in green scrubs and white coat waited for them. Birdsong gasped as they neared and whispered into Merchant's ear.

"That's the same doctor we saw in the restroom, isn't it?"

The doctor stepped forward and lifted her head in defiance. "I am Dr. Yeosut Gumijo and I do not approve of this interference in my patient's treatment."

"I'm Dr. Merchant and I could care less." Merchant said. "All I need is a few moments alone with Joshua Knight so I can collect blood samples and make a brief assessment. As I told Donald, you don't want the government breathing down your neck any more than they already are. Give me ten minutes and we'll be out of your hair."

Another woman in dark green scrubs and a white coat appeared behind Dr. Gumijo. "Is there a problem?"

Gumijo glanced at her. "These gentlemen are here to see Joshua Knight." Gumijo seemed to see her for the first time. "You are his nurse?"

"Nurse Practitioner." The woman said testily. She glanced at Merchant and Birdsong. "What is your business with Josh?"

"We are with the medical examiner's office in Louisiana where Josh's infection began. We are only following up according to protocol to check on his therapy and to acquire some blood samples for our state department of health." Merchant said.

She locked eyes with him and then her gaze drifted to Birdsong. "And who are you?"

"An officer of the law required to accompany Dr. Merchant on all official business." Birdsong said.

"Dr. Gumijo, I'll take it from here." She said. "My name is Faye Murphy. You can call me Ms. Murphy."

Gumijo nodded. "Make it quick."

Faye nodded and pointed down the hall. "This way."

She led them down the hall and through a wooden door into a spacious room. Birdsong drew a deep breath when he saw Josh obscured by blankets in the middle of a hospital bed. The windows were darkened, and the room was warm and humid.

"Why so dark?" He blurted out.

"Photosensitivity." Faye said.

Birdsong moved close to Josh and noticed the boy's eyes were closed. His chest moved up and down beneath the covers. "Josh?" He said. No response.

"He is awake between infusions. We just started his latest infusion." She pursed her lips. "You called him Josh?"

Birdsong froze. "Uh, short for Joshua?"

"What are his symptoms?" Merchant had moved to the other side of the bed and was examining the intravenous tube attached to Josh's arm. He withdrew blue gloves from his white coat pocket and pulled them on. Morgan turned her attention to him.

"Paroxysmal ascending paralysis. The infusions seem to reverse much of the paralysis but in the interval between, the paralysis returns." Faye said. She crossed her arms. "And each time the paralysis moves higher."

"And why isn't he in isolation?" Merchant asked.

"According to our tests, the virus is gone and, even if it was it is not contagious unless you exchange body fluids." Faye stepped closer. Birdsong watched her features soften.

"He goes in and out of delusions and hallucinations when he is awake. Most of what he is experiencing is a type of auto immune reaction."

Merchant uncovered all of Josh's arm and unhooked the intravenous line from an angiocath in the boy's arm.

"What are you doing?" Faye stiffened.

"It is easier to draw blood from his angiocath than to stick him again." Before she could protest, he removed a syringe from his pocket and aspirated the fluid from the short plastic line leading to the needle in Josh's vein. He laid the syringe aside and then attached another and withdrew ten cubic centimeters of blood. He reattached the intravenous line just as the machine started beeping. "See, less than a minute."

He turned and walked over to a red plastic box sitting in the corner and dropped a syringe into the box. He removed a blunt tipped needle from his pocket and attached it to the blood-filled syringe. He stuck the needle through the red rubber top of each of the two vacuum tubes and filled both with the blood. He dropped the syringe into the red box. He held up the two tubes. "Two vials of blood as I requested."

Dr. Gumijo appeared through the room doorway and her steely gaze played over the room. She eyed Merchant suspiciously and walked over and glanced through the open top of the hazardous material red box. She seemed satisfied and nodded. "Now that you have what you want, please leave."

Merchant had moved over to Josh's side and had leaned over the boy's head. He opened the boy's eyelids and nodded. "Very well." He straightened and stripped the gloves from his hands and tossed them into the red container. He motioned to Birdsong. "We have what we need. Thank you for your cooperation."

Birdsong raised a hand to protest, and Merchant shook his head slightly. They walked out of the room and Birdsong paused to cast one lingering look back at Josh. The boy looked like a prize wrapped in a spider's web waiting for the queen spider to devour him and her name was Gumijo! His heart raced and his face grew warm with anger.

"Jack? We can't just leave him." He tried to keep up with Merchant as they hurried down the hall.

"Nothing we can do here, Jason." Merchant said. "We have to get these samples back to my lab." He removed the syringe from his pocket with the fluid he had aspirated from the angiocath. "I threw away two empty syringes. This contains whatever it is they are treating him with. If I can find out what that is, we can get him out of this hellhole."

Birdsong followed him out of the dark, humid hospital into the parking lot. The bright, November sun almost blinded him. They slid into Merchant's truck. Merchant opened a small ice chest on the front seat and placed the three samples inside. "Jason, I have no idea what is going on here, but it is not good."

"They didn't want us to talk to him." Birdsong said hoarsely. "I can't just leave him here."

Merchant started the engine. "Right now, this place is the only thing keeping him alive. I'm sorry, Jason. I wish things were different." He pulled out of the parking lot and headed east toward Louisiana.

HOURS LATER AFTER HAMPTON LEARNED OF THE VISITING doctor his concern was significant. He arrived at the clinic and immediately bypassed the nurse's station to the conference room. He paused outside the door to the conference room and checked his watch once more. He had a few hours before he had to meet with his significant "other" for dinner. Right now, after the visit by the doctor from Louisiana, he had concerns about his plan. He opened the door to the conference room and walked in unannounced.

The triplets were deep in conversation using a guttural language he understood all too well only he could never let them know that fact. He was especially adept at hiding his relationship with his partner in evil.

Shutendoji stood up and her normally passive features twisted in anger. "You are never to interrupt us, Hampton."

"Forgive my intrusion. I want to know what you plan to do about this doctor who showed up unannounced from Louisiana." Hampton said kindly.

Shutendoji looked at the other two women. Gomijo nodded slightly and glanced at Santelmo. Santelmo reached for a tablet on the table. "We have an associate who is very interested in keeping an eye on this doctor for us."

"Can he be trusted?" Hampton said.

Shutendoji looked like she was chewing on broken glass. "Of course not! But he is very ambitious and there are things he wants. Things only we can give."

Santelmo opened a chat window on the tablet. Hampton tried to move to where he could see the screen, but Shutendoji blocked his way. "The less you know the better."

A man's voice came from the device. "Good evening my dearest." His voice was warm and seductive.

"I am not your dearest." Santelmo said to the tablet. "Have you considered our request from earlier today?"

"Of course. Have you considered my terms?" He said.

"Yes, we have. We agree we will help you achieve your main goal. But only if you complete this task without leaving a trail of bodies."

Maniacal laughter came from the tablet. "I don't leave trails, dearest."

"Stop calling me that!" Santelmo's face flashed red with flames for a second. "I will text you the information. The doctor is from Shreveport, Louisiana so there should be no problem with your anklet."

"I am allowed to travel to neighboring states so no one should be alerted." The man said. "Let me get this straight. I can't kill the doctor?"

"That would raise too many questions. The man is part of the medical examiner's department." Santelmo said. "We need subtlety. Keep an eye on him and find out what he learned from the samples he obtained from Mr. Knight."

"Too bad." The man said calmly. "I'm craving seared brain."

Hampton felt a chill run down his spine. It was not from fear or revulsion. It was from the recognition of someone with whom he shared certain 'tastes'. "Can I not meet this man?"

Shutendoji shook her head. "No."

Hampton ignored her and moved to the end of the table. For a second, he saw the man's face. He had perfectly combed black hair and an exceedingly handsome face. But his most striking feature were his eyes. Each one was of a different color. Santelmo turned the tablet face down.

"Out! Now!" Shutendoji intercepted him. "This business does not concern you."

"On the contrary, Dr. Shutendoji. The Elixir of Life infusing young Mr. Knight is mine. I developed it. Keeping Mr. Knight subdued and on the brink of death is absolutely essential for you to complete your plan. Any kink, as you Yanks say, would interfere with my plans as well as yours."

"Let me talk to the good Dr. Hampton." The man's voice came from the tablet speaker. Santelmo glanced once at Shutendoji and she nodded. Santelmo handed the tablet to Hampton. The man's eyes seemed to almost come out of the tablet as he studied Hampton's features. "I see. Interesting. Hampton's Museum of the Weird? I understand there is a furnace in the basement level behind the dissection room that was once used for cremations. How often have you used it lately?"

Hampton paled and he swallowed nervously. How did this man know these things? "I do not discuss my business with a man I do not know."

"Drake is my last name. That's all you need to know." The man said. "I have a bothersome attorney who has managed to have me confined to limited travel with an anklet and I have this fantasy of watching her roast alive. Your furnace would be perfect."

Again, the mixed feelings came over Hampton: revulsion and respect. He cleared his throat. "I thought you agreed to keep a low profile."

The man shrugged. "I have lots of time. Maybe one day I will visit London. Now hand me back to the pink one so I can close the deal."

Hampton slid the tablet back onto the table and quickly left the conference room. For the first time in years another human being had scared him half to death and the thrill was almost more than he could stand!

18

Ishido pulled his truck into the parking lot of a snow-covered airport terminal outside the city of Zurich. So far, not a single insect drone had shown up.

"What are you looking for? Snake is long gone with the messenger bag."

"When she realizes it is a fake, she'll be back." Steel said. "I'm looking for demonic flies and spiders!" His face grew hot with fury. "And, assassins with metal arms! White eye goons battling humans in league with their demons! Ishido, I am getting sick and tired of the whole thing! I am tired of letting things happen to me."

"Perhaps it is time for you to stop being a victim and go on the offensive, Mr. Steel." Ishido said.

"That is Max said." Steel glanced up at the man's dark eyes. "But with Josh the victim, I can't afford to stray from their demands."

"Yes, Mr. Steel. However, once you have what they seek you must assume the driver's seat and not the passenger's seat. You now have something they want."

"I reluctantly have come to that conclusion, Ishido. And

that is precisely what I am going to do. It is risky. They have a bargaining chip in Josh. I have a bargaining chip in what they want." Steel let his anger die and slowed his breathing. Tell me what you know, not what you feel Max had said.

"What they have underestimated, Mr. Steel, are your friends and companions who are willing to help you battle this great evil." Ishido said.

Steel looked out the frosted window and felt the guilt grip him. "I betrayed Max. I lied to her. I had planned on taking the dossier without her knowledge. I don't think she will ever trust me again."

Silence filled the cab and Ishido sighed. "Max is quite familiar with betrayal. For years she expected it of everyone. Not because she considered them evil or unreliable. But because in the end, each individual will do what is best for themselves. To expect this outcome is never to be disappointed but to always be surprised when they do not. Her betrayal by Cephas Lawrence could have made her bitter. Instead, the death of her daughter at the hands of demons inspired her to turn that bitterness into resolve."

"Cephas didn't betray her." Steel said. "Her daughter did not die at the hands of demons."

"My point exactly. Mr. Steel when you brought this news to Max you restored her respect for people. You tempered her suspicious nature. You have no idea how much she values you, Jonathan."

Steel glanced at Ishido. "Then it is time I earned that respect." He had composed the note on the pad from Max's bedroom and tucked everything into an envelope. "I hope this is the right thing to do. What's next?"

Darkness was falling and Ishido sat back in the seat of his truck as snow continued to fall outside. "Mr. Steel, your passage to France is taken care of on a small regional jet. When you reach France, you are on your own. I suggest you talk to no one and sleep on the short flight to Paris." He held out a mud-streaked hand and shook his head. "I have not yet even washed my hands after pulling you from the river, but it has been a pleasure working with you."

Steel shook his hand. "Ishido, you saved my life. I owe you a life debt. But, right now, I need your help again. I have one small task only you can perform. But you must not let Max, or anyone, know you have done this for me. You will be doing this for Josh. I need to make a video recording on your phone and then I need you to do something with it. Then you can pass it on with this." He handed the envelope to Ishido. "This has to be between us only. I don't want to endanger anyone's life, but I must ask you to take this risk. And I need some privacy."

"Of course. Please hurry, Mr. Steel." Ishido handed him his phone, stepped out of the truck and shut the door. Steel took the phone and recorded his video message. Ishido's phone was secure thanks to Max.

Steel tapped on the window and Ishido got back inside. "Ishido, I hate for you to once again risk your life for my life and Josh's life. I need you to take a trip to somewhere you do not want to go. Can you do that for me?"

Ishido brushed snow from his shoulders and his dark eyes focused on Steel. "I cannot return to the chalet for a while. With Goudreaux watching everything it will be best if I lay low."

Steel handed him the envelope. "Good. Guard this with your life. I no longer have my secure phone so your phone contains a video to the recipient of this envelope, and I need you to deliver it in person."

"Who am I delivering it to?"

Steel drew something on the envelope and Ishido raised an eyebrow in alarm. His face paled and he swallowed. He nodded. "I can do this, and I will help you save the ones you love. I did not have that opportunity with my loved ones."

Steel got out of the truck and entered the front doors of the small air terminal. In his reflection in the glass doors, he saw the spider drop from the edge of the building and land on his shoulder. "I was wondering where you were." He whispered. Now, if only the spider would eat the fly in the vial in his pocket!

Once Steel arrived in Paris, he contacted Shutendoji and she arranged a flight back to Dallas. He was not in first class but did have a more comfortable seat in business class. It wasn't exactly a full bed but rather like a cocoon that leaned back part of the way. He was shocked to find the same woman from his first flight seated right next to him. She was asleep when he took his seat and never stirred during takeoff.

Steel leaned back in his seat and tried to sleep. With all the traveling, his metabolism was so screwed up! And all he wanted to do was to speak to Josh.

"You are a very smart man."

He opened his eyes and looked into the gaze of the woman in the seat next to him. She wore the headdress and the face mask. She lowered the face mask and the contours of her face fell into a familiar pattern.

"Snake!" Steel tried to stand up and the seat belt confined him. He reached for the flight attendant button and Snake snared his arm with the hard grip of her artificial hand.

"Calm down, Mr. Steel. I am not here to hurt you. And as you can see my arm has recovered its full function."

"How do you get past security with an arm that becomes a deadly weapon."

"I know who to blackmail and who to bribe." She slammed her mechanical hand against his chest and he felt the spider drone shatter in his pocket. The blow drove the air out of his lungs. She pulled the spider drone out and searched his other shirt pocket until she found the vial with the fly. The fly was motionless within. "Hello, sweetheart. Come back to Momma." She kissed the vial and then put the vial in her pocket. Steel gasped for breath and Snake smiled.

"You sent the fly?"

"No. But I know all about those creatures." She tapped the pocket of her robe with her metal hand. "You see, I helped Cobalt design them. There's so much you don't know about me."

"You're not working for the unholy triad. That I had already decided." Steel rubbed his sore chest. "What will they do when they realize it isn't working? I have Josh to think about."

"They will assume it malfunctioned due to the flight mechanics. Not that they would worry. Where would you go on this flight? There will be more waiting for you in Dallas." She smiled. Snake peeled off the headdress unleashing her unkempt curly red hair. She shook it out and drew a deep breath. "Ah, freedom at last. How do they do it?"

Steel swallowed and his heart raced. "Will you kill me now?"

Snake giggled. "If I wanted you dead, yadda, yadda, yadda. I used a sedative, didn't I? Not my usual poison but I have a new boss. He's a bit more cautious than Thakkar was. Too many dead bodies raised unnecessary attention. In fact, I'm in a bit of trouble with him."

"You took the dossier. They had given *me* that job."

Snake shrugged. "You assume our bosses are the same people. Or maybe it's just that a girl has to play her own game."

"This isn't a game! My son is sick and without that dossier, they will let him die." Steel hissed.

Snake studied him with an amusing smile on her face. "Really? You are so bad at being deceitful. I know the dossier was a fake. I discarded it safely. Seven will never know. All she will know is that you have the memory card with all the information on it. But you did something with it, didn't you?"

Steel blinked. "I'm not telling you anything. Unless you plan on torturing me on a flight filled with hundreds of people. Or are you going to kill them too?"

Snake looked away. "My other operation was a bit of an overkill. Pardon the pun. I tend to over plan."

Steel fought for control of his anger. "Hundreds died, Snake. Innocent people."

"There are no innocent people, Steel!" She hissed. "You have no idea what my life has been like!" She fell silent. "Are you familiar with a man named Lucas?"

Lucas was one of Satan's personal operatives, sort of his right hand man. Lucas housed dozens of demons which he passed on to unwitting victims. "The pale devil! Yes."

"Let me tell you what life is like with that creature."

Snake sat atop a gargoyle just underneath the overhang of the castle. Inside the decaying building, the Council of Darkness was meeting. Again. The man appeared out of the rain, his pale skin illuminated by a flash of lightning.

"She is in there with them." Snake said.

Lucas paused and studied her face. "How do you like your new prosthesis?"

Snake glanced at the mechanical apparatus where once had been an arm. "I'm getting used to it."

"And to whom do you owe your thanks?" Lucas stepped closer.

Snake leaned back. "You. Of course you're the reason I lost the arm to begin with."

"I was not responsible for Cobalt's space station blowing up. Vivian was!" Lucas glared at her. "When you worked for Cobalt, you could have killed Vivian before she betrayed us all!"

"I served Cobalt at the time. Not you."

Lucas stepped closer and grabbed her by the throat. His tattoos writhed across his skin. "I am the head of the Church of the Enochians. I saved you from the remnants of that exploding space station. You owe your life to me!"

Snake gasped for breath, and he released her allowing her to tumble off the gargoyle to the ground. "Yes."

"Yes, what?" Lucas glared at her.

"Yes, master."

Lucas smiled. "That's better. Now that you have kept an eye on Vivian, I am through with you. Go to the new rendezvous point in England. We have a new wave of slaves coming in that need to be processed. Oversee that and then wait for my instructions."

"From whom? Who are you working with now?"

Lucas glared at her. "Number Eight and I have plans. You will be part of those plans."

Snake rubbed her neck with her good hand. "And what of Vivian?"

"I am about to end her demonic career!" Lucas walked past her into the tunnel leading into the castle.

Snake swore and stretched her neck. The rain had ceased, and she looked down at her artificial arm. It was bulky and heavy and not at all as agile as her native arm.

"I can help you with that."

Snake flinched and looked up into the face of a very handsome man. Where had he come from? He had short, dark hair shot with streaks of gray. His face was ageless with an aristocratic nose and high cheekbones. He wore a white suit. His eyes glowed with the pale blue of the ice from a crumbling glacier and those smoldering eyes filled her with excitement. His face was gorgeous! Something about the man oozed charisma and power.

"Where did you come from?" She whispered.

He looked up at the sky. "From somewhere else. Somewhen else. Certainly not this unwieldy broken reality."

Snake stepped back as a powerful wave of evil broke against her like a tidal wave. She gasped for breath. He reached out and touched her artificial arm. The ugly, ungainly metal began to reshape itself into something more elegant and graceful. The harsh dull metal gleamed a copper rose in the moonlight that broke through the dissipating rain clouds.

"How?"

"There are many things I can accomplish, my dear. I have plans for you. I want you to continue to work for whoever pleases you. But one day you must return to Lucas. I am about to break him, but I will not kill him. He still amuses me and in the near future, he will think he still has mastery of his miserable kingdom. That is where you will come in when the time is right. Now go before my wrath is unleashed or you may be caught in the backlash."

"Yes, Master!" And this time she meant it. He was the true Master of the demons! Snake hugged her new arm to her chest and nodded. She ran down the battered, broken main street of the abandoned amusement park toward the distant forest as if the devil himself were on her tail. Because he was.

"You spoke to Satan?" Steel asked.

"Right before he punished Lucas. Took away his demons and made him a broken man."

"So, you still work for Lucas?"

"If it amuses me, yes."

"And you are waiting for Satan to call in his debt." He pointed to her arm.

"I suppose so."

Steel looked away and shook his head. "How could you be a part of all of this?"

"My soul is already damned, Steel." She said. "Growing up in that church with Cobalt was not a picnic. I was his favorite concubine. And not willingly. I was only sixteen when he recruited me. I was duped, brainwashed by the teachings of that cult. Now, I am free to do whatever pleases me."

"Better to reign in hell that serve in heaven?" Steel asked.

Snake laughed. "Look at you all innocent. It didn't take you long to make the decision to serve the Council of Darkness."

Steel's face heated with anger. "They have Josh!"

Snake shrugged. "We all have our rationalizations. Mine is to finally see Lucas come to an end. I understand you have amnesia." She looked at him with a slight smile on her lips. "What evil have you done in the past? How do you know you did not serve the plans of the Master?"

Steel opened his mouth to speak and fell silent again. "I don't. And, frankly, I don't care. There's only one thing I know for sure. The memory card is safe, and I will make sure it gets to Seven for only one reason, to save Josh."

Snake rolled her eyes. "Well, then there is only one thing to do." She held up her good hand and pointed to her fingernails. "I don't need my ceramic sword. These will do."

Before he could react, she plunged the fingernail of her index finger into the flesh of the back of his hand. He swore and pulled away but already he could feel something warm coursing through his veins, pulling him down into a blanket of sleep.

"Don't worry. It's just a sedative, sweetheart." Snake said quietly. "This way neither one of us had to put up with the other all the way home. Nighty night."

19

"What happened on the airplane?" Shutendoji said.

Steel was still groggy and confused. He glared at the doctor wearing her ever present pink scrubs. A security guard from the hospital had been waiting for him when he got off the airplane. He was escorted outside, into a waiting car and taken directly to the clinic. "I want to see Josh. Now."

"You are in no position to make demands." Shutendoji said. They were standing outside the entrance to the clinic in Dallas.

"Someone else wants the dossier." Steel said. "She sedated me on the flight and searched my things. She didn't find it."

Shutendoji studied him as if he were an insect of great interest. "Where is the dossier?"

"Josh. Now." Steel growled rubbing his throbbing head. Thankfully the air was cool outside, and a fine mist was falling. He glanced at his watch. It was two in the afternoon. "You're wasting time, Seven."

Shutendoji frowned and led them into the clinic and

down the hallway. Steel hurried after her and beat her to the door to Josh's room. When he pushed through the door, he was shocked. Josh lay back on his bed. His skin was pale, and he had lost weight. A woman with long, black hair stood beside his bed checking his IV. She looked up and for a moment, her lips turned into a frown.

"You must be Dad." She said.

Steel ignored her and focused on Josh. "Josh, it's me, Jonathan."

Josh did not stir. His eyes were closed, and his chest rose and fell with each ragged breath. Steel whirled on Shutendoji.

"You said he would be better."

"He's just received an infusion." The woman said. Steel glanced at her.

"And you are?" Didn't they talk earlier?

"Faye Morgan, nurse practitioner. Josh has talked quite a bit about you." She crossed her arms.

Steel tensed at the tone in her voice and his anger surged. "Hey, don't cop an attitude with me! You have something to say, say it."

"Okay, fine. I was adopted. One of six kids. The oldest. My father and mother were not perfect, but they never abandoned me when I was sick." Faye said.

Steel froze. "Josh thinks that?"

"No. I think that."

Steel looked down at Josh and then back at Shutendoji. The woman had no idea what was really going on here. Steel turned back to her and drew a deep, calming breath. "I'm sorry you don't understand why I had to leave. It was a matter of life or death. Josh will understand that, once I can explain everything to him." He glared at Shutendoji. "But, for now I have no other choice."

"We always have choices, Mr. Steel." Faye said.

"Nurse, you are getting close to being out of line." Dr.

Shutendoji said quietly. "Please leave us until you can regain your composure."

Faye blinked and reached out and pulled Josh's blanket up around his shoulders. "No matter what happens, Mr. Steel. I will take care of Josh."

Steel swallowed and felt moisture at the corner of his eyes. "Please take care of him. No matter what happens."

Faye's face slackened and her brow wrinkled in confusion. She nodded and left the room. Steel turned back to Shutendoji.

"Why is he no better?"

Shutendoji smiled. "As I said, he just received an infusion. Each infusion causes him to sleep."

"He's wasting away."

"Then perhaps you should speed things up."

"The notebook was a fake. But you probably already know that."

"What?" Shutendoji said. She frowned. Either she was a good actor, or she did not know about the notebook.

"But there was a small memory chip that contains all of the information. It can be transferred one time. Try and copy it and it will automatically erase. One time access to the information. And, it is in a safe place, Seven. Safe from you and safe from the assassin who stole the notebook."

Shutendoji stepped back. "Assassin?"

"You have competition, Seven. You didn't tell me about that. Or did you not know about that? First, Niles turns against you and then, the Crimson Snake tries to kill me in Zurich." He stepped closer to Shutendoji and she moved away. "Now, here's what you are going to do. You are going to continue to give Josh his next dose. You are going to let the two of us have time together without your vile presence. Once I am satisfied then I will take on task number two.

And, when I've finished all three of your profane tasks, I will give you the memory card."

Shutendoji glared at him. Something foreign and alien crossed her face. "You are playing a dangerous game, Steel."

"And you never told me there were other parties after the dossier. You placed my life and Josh's life at risk." He moved toward her quickly again and she stepped back. "I know your type. I've taken out six of you so far. I know that when the going gets rough, you will forget about your devotion to the other demons. You will take care of number one. It's your nature. So, if I give you the drive now knowing that Vitreomancers and who knows what else are involved in this, you will abandon your sisters. And, Josh. So, to keep Josh safe, you will do what I tell you to do. I gave you my word and I will deliver when I am confident Josh's life is no longer in danger. Do you understand?"

Shutendoji stiffened and her face darkened as the demon inside warred with the ambitious human host. Finally, she bowed slightly. "Very well. Josh will awaken within the half hour. I will leave you alone."

She turned and stormed out of the room. Steel collapsed into a chair and glanced skyward. "Lord, forgive me. Just take care of Josh as I wage battle with these demons."

20

Pandora ran a finger along Josh's cheek. She leaned over him, and her hair brushed his face. "You are such a lovely boy, Josh."

Josh tried to pull away from her touch, but his head would not move. The paralysis had reached his neck. What was next? His breathing center at the base of his brain?

"I know you are not real. I know that I am hallucinating."

Pandora stood up and put her hands on her hips. "You only hallucinate when you are awake, Josh. There is a term for what you are experiencing." Pandora put a finger to her lips. "Lucid dreaming. That's what you call it. You heard that term once in a high school psychology class." She smiled back at him and motioned around her. The ancient lab was now a more modern version. In fact, it matched Dr. Monarch's lab exactly. Pandora was accessing his memories. "You see, I can move all around the modern world."

"With access to my memories?" Josh said. Could he block some of those memories? Or possibly fake them?

"There is a term you are familiar with. Something to do with your girlfriend, Olivia. Something about her brain.

Neuroplasticity?" Pandora moved a stool over by Josh's bed. "You will tell me all about that."

Josh tried to hide the word. Tried to hide his meager knowledge of the subject. But, in his time with Olivia, he had discussed the subject extensively. Olivia was hoping to have better control of her epilepsy through neuroplasticity.

Josh gasped. "Olivia is just a friend."

Pandora grinned. "You can't lie to me, Josh. I sense how you feel about her. Now, neuroplasticity."

Josh tried not to think about it. Tried not to consider the reality that the brain was a living, changing organ of the body that had the capability of rerouting neurons and rewiring itself. The brain could change itself physically through selective stimuli. He closed his eyes and tried to sing a song.

"Ah, the brain is pliable. Thank you, Josh. You've already told me about DNA and RNA. You've already told me about information in those molecules. Well, I am a very independent strand of such information and given the proper amount of time, I will reformat your brain to become mine." She leaned forward and he felt her cold breath on his face. "Through the process of neuroplasticity. We will be very happy together."

She straightened and turned to the lab bench. A flame came from a Bunsen burner. She took the burner and studied the flame. She reached down and took Josh's hand.

"Can you feel that?"

Josh gasped and his eyes flew open. He could feel her touch. He glanced at the flame. "No."

"Good."

Pandora lifted his hand and he tried in vain to pull it away. She placed his index finger into the flame. The pain lanced along his arm, and he screamed in agony. Pandora dropped his hand and put the burner back on the bench.

"There's another term I've learned from your memory.

Hypersensitivity. I can dial up your pain receptors to ten times what you would normally feel."

Josh fought to control his breath and sweat popped out on his forehead. "What do you want from me besides my mind?"

Pandora shrugged. "Pretty simple. Don't tell anyone about me. Not Hampton. Not Jonathan Steel. Not that nosey nurse practitioner. This is our little secret, Josh." She leaned forward and brushed the sweat from his forehead with her hand. "Just you and me. Together. Forever."

Pandora straightened and frowned as her world began to fade. "More treatment? This has got to stop, Josh. You have to get out of here. I'll take care of your body and brain. I will restore your strength, but these treatments must stop." Along with her lab, she faded from view.

JOSH SWALLOWED A BITE OF PUDDING. "BRO, AS BAD AS THIS tastes, I want more." He whispered. It took only ten minutes after Shutendoji left the room for him to wake up and then another ten minutes to sit up in bed.

"Take it easy." Steel said. "Don't want you to get sick."

Josh finished the pudding cup. "Look at me. Dude, I'm wasting away! I mean, I don't work out but I'm losing all my muscle mass."

"What little you had." Steel took the cup and dropped it in a trash can. He glanced over his shoulder at Dr. Shutendoji who had returned with the meal tray. "Privacy, remember?"

Shutendoji stood with crossed arms. "I wanted to make sure Mr. Knight kept down three cups of pudding."

Josh wiped his mouth. "So far, so good. I won't eat any more right now. Promise."

Shutendoji glanced at her watch. "Ten minutes then Mr. Knight will need to rest."

"I've done nothing but rest." Josh said testily.

"I'm talking about your brain." Dr. Shutendoji said. "After talking, you will be weary. And then, Mr. Steel and my colleagues and I will have a conference concerning your future treatments."

"Yeah, about that." Josh yawned. "How much longer?"

"About ten days." Dr. Shutendoji turned and left the room.

Josh started to protest and then shook his head. "I just want to get well." He straightened himself in the bed. "So, what's the real story?"

"Real story?"

Steel touched his ear with his right hand and mouthed. "Listening."

Josh stared at him, and his eyes shifted back and forth in thought. "I've had seven visitors lately." He opened his eyes wide. "But recently there were two visitors. I think. I was in and out and wasn't awake enough to speak to them. One was a doctor from Louisiana. The other was a policeman." Josh glanced at the closed door. "Sort of the doctor's WING man."

Steel drew a deep breath. "When?"

"Yesterday? Maybe? Last night? I'm not sure. I was in and out of it. That doctor and Dr. Shutendoji didn't get along. He was checking on me. Said he was from back home and had to follow up on my infection." Josh blinked and yawned. "No! I'm not sleepy yet." He said as if talking to someone else.

Steel wanted to blurt out the question? Had it been Merchant? Had Jason Birdsong been the policeman?

"Josh, this is the only place you can get this treatment." Steel said carefully. "If you leave this place, you will not recover. You have no idea what I had to do to get you in here for treatment. I'm sure the state health department is merely following up this viral infection. They don't want another pandemic."

Josh's eyes widened. He nodded. "Yeah, no one wants a Pandora." His eyes widened and he stared right at Steel. "I mean, a pandemic. I just wish you were here when I wake up every time. But I'm sure you have some business to attend to. Faye thinks you abandoned me. Maybe you did."

Steel looked away. This was a dangerous game Josh was playing. Pretending to hate him. "I know you hate me for leaving."

"Dude, we've always had a love hate thing going on. I'm trying to understand, but it's hard. You walk out of here and get a break from all the misery. I get it. But I'm stuck right here in the thick of things. I'm *boxed* in." He raised his eyes again and Steel wrinkled his forehead. Josh was trying to tell him something.

"Hey, Jonathan, I don't hate you." Josh said. "Look, when we were in Lakeside in the church basement. That thing had taken over my mind and body. It was controlling me. Bro, I fought as hard as I could to stop it from doing damage to you or my mom. I couldn't control the situation."

"I understand."

Josh's eyes filled with tears, and he yawned again. "Not now! Just another minute." He said to the air above him. His eyes focused on Steel. "No, you don't understand. Bro, I never talked to you about the guilt. What I had to live with after it was all over. I had to face the fact that my choices led to someone being hurt. If I could have made a difficult choice to help someone instead of giving in to them, I would have paid anything. Anything. Any cost. Doing good costs us something. Sometimes our lives."

Steel looked away. "Stop it. Don't say that. You're a teenager. You're not supposed to be this—"

"Wise?" Josh's grip tightened. "Dude, it ain't the years. It's the mileage. We've been through a lot. And I understand something that Paul once said. For me to live is Christ and for me to die is gain. I know where I'm going. Don't do something you will have to wallow in guilt for just to save me." The look on Josh's face said it all. He knew. Somehow, he knew the demons were holding him hostage to control Jonathan Steel. And now, he was volunteering to just go ahead and die rather than give the demons any satisfaction.

Steel gripped Josh's hand. "Don't say that! I know what I'm doing. We will get through this. There is something else Jesus once said. Be as wise as serpents and as harmless as doves. You have to think like a serpent to defeat a serpent."

Josh's grip weakened. "Just don't become one." He slumped even more into the covers of the bed. "Shutendoji was right. Bro, I'm crashing."

Steel bent over him and leaned close to his ear. "Hang in there. There's more to this than you think! I need you to be strong." He pulled back and his gaze focused on Josh's face. "I love you."

Josh pulled away and the tears poured down his cheeks. "I love you, too, Jonathan. Be careful."

Steel stood up and fought back emotion. "One thing for sure, Josh. I will not be harmless."

STEEL STOOD AT THE HEAD OF THE CONFERENCE TABLE AND crossed his arms. "What's next?"

Seven, Six, and Five sat around the table. "We have agreed we will allow you to keep the memory card. The fact someone wanted to take it from you is alarming. Perhaps if they think you have given it to us, they will try to move against us instead of you and this will reveal who they are and what their motives are. You are sure the card is safe?"

"Yes. In the best of hands." Steel said. He looked at Six. "Let's get on with it. Time is wasting."

"Your enthusiasm is refreshing." Gumijo stood up. She wore pale blue scrubs and a blue scarf around her neck. "There are some artifacts that were not in two of Dr. Lawrence's crates. The third crate will not open for us. We believe it will only open for you. You will go to London and try and open that crate. Your companion, Dr. Holmes is still there."

Dr. Montana Holmes had remained in London to catalog the contents of the three crates loaned to Dr. Hampton by Dr. Lawrence. Steel did not want to drag his friend into this if he could avoid it.

"If, when you open the crate, the items we are searching for are within, then your task will have been very easy. However, we suspect the objects are not in that crate." Gumijo walked around the table until she stood by Steel looking up at him with her haunting eyes. "However, if our sources are accurate, you may have already had access to the possible location of these items."

"What are these items?" Steel stood his ground against the cold wave of evil emanating from the woman.

"The staff of Moses and the Bronze Serpent and the Urim and Thummim." Gumijo said.

Steel's brow furrowed. "What?"

"Read your Bible, Mr. Steel. If the rod is not in the crate, it may be elsewhere. The two stones are mentioned in the Old Testament. Did Dr. Lawrence have a hidden cache of artifacts? If so, you should know where to find them. Or perhaps the objects are stored in an ancient ark? There were two such arks you have been around in the past year. The Ark of Chaos." Gumijo stepped back dramatically. "And the Ark of the Covenant."

Steel opened his mouth to respond and then closed it. He didn't know what to say. "I have no idea where the Ark of Chaos is."

"It was in the possession of Vivian Darbonne for a time. Then, the thirteenth demon."

"Vivian has disappeared." Steel said.

"Then, if the items are not in the crate, find Lawrence's hidden cache. Or start with the most likely source. The Ark of the Covenant."

Steel looked away. "I don't know where the Ark is located."

Gumijo laughed. "You are a terrible liar. There is someone in your past who has a passion for locating the Ark. In fact, she was with you on your journey to Africa."

"Dr. Sebastian?"

"The Artifact Hunter is in London as we speak. Now, you have two sources to help you." Gumijo said. "You will leave in two hours for London. Open the crate and if the objects are not there, then find Dr. Sebastian and look in the Ark of the Covenant. We have good information she is in London to meet your friend, Dr. Holmes. And we are fairly certain the objects are in the crate. Do not return without them, Mr. Steel. You saw how quickly Mr. Knight returned to his weakened state. Each time he awakens, his sessions of awareness will grow incrementally shorter. Don't dawdle. I believe you demanded we 'get on with it'? Then do so."

Gumijo nodded to her sisters and the three of them left him standing helplessly in the conference room. He pulled his cell phone out of his pocket and started to dial Jason Birdsong but thought better of it. If they were monitoring his calls, it would give Birdsong away. It sounded like Jason and Dr.

Merchant had already started working on Josh's illness. It was best to fly under the radar for now. One task down two to go. And for the moment he had the advantage. Weariness gripped him and he could not remember the last time he ate. Another flight to London? Right about now was when he wished had the ability to teleport. But the price to pay was too much!

He went back to Josh's room and stood over Josh. The boy's chest moved erratically and his eyes roved beneath the lids in dream. What was he dreaming? What was he hearing and seeing? The spider crawled across Josh's face. Steel's anger burned within him. He grabbed the spider and tossed it on the floor and squashed it. He looked up at the ceiling.

"No more surveillance! You hear me? I am in charge for now and I will do your bidding but I will not have one of your vile creatures touch Josh again? You understand? There is no need to keep an eye on me. Instead, you should be looking for the Crimson Snake."

Josh groaned in his sleep and Steel gasped. He squatted beside the bed and put a hand on Josh's forehead. It was cold and clammy and covered with sweat.

"Sorry, Josh. I will take care of this. I will rescue from these servants of Satan if I have to march into hell myself!" He leaned forward and in a most foreign but suddenly comfortable act kissed Josh on the forehead. "I love you, son." He stood up, gripped his fists and stormed out of the room.

21

Josh awoke and touched his forehead. Someone had touched him but the room was empty. At least he was away from Pandora. Someone opened the door to his room and he closed his eyes. He heard his footsteps across the tiled floor of his room.

"Jonathan is that you?" He said quietly. No answer. He opened his eyes. "Who is there?"

"A friend." A man stood across the room in the shadows.

"Do I know you?" Josh whispered weakly.

"I knew your Great Uncle."

"Uncle Cephas?" Josh tried to focus on the man standing in the corner of the room.

Dr. Nigel Hampton walked out of the shadows. He paused and regarded Josh with an upswept eyebrow. "Ah, yes. Dr. Cephas Lawrence. Hmmm? Very well, let me tell you a story." He pulled a chair up beside Josh's bed. Josh tied to pull away from the man, but he was so weak. He could hardly move. Dr. Hampton wore a brown tweed jacket and a brown bowler sat on top of his head. He took the bowler from his head and placed it on the bedside table. "You need not worry about interruptions. I saw to it that you and I would have some private time together."

"No!" Josh said hoarsely. "You did this to me!"

"Now, Josh, remain calm. You wouldn't want to upset your neurochemical balance. Just lie there quietly and I will tell you all about meeting your Uncle Cephas. Of all places, I met your Great Uncle here in Texas. In a town called Canton. You see, long ago a tradition called First Monday began in Canton only an hour's drive east of Dallas along I-20. The event was the first rumblings of what became a typical American phenomenon. A few junk dealers and those who called themselves antique dealers set up shop in an open pasture the weekend before the first Monday of every month. Now, First Monday is a huge, sprawling enterprise. Ah, but back then, it was small and intimate and filled with treasures no one anticipated. Especially the dealers. I was in Dallas planning and building this private clinic. I ran across a brochure for one of the dealers at First Monday." He frowned.

"I would not call it a real brochure. It was handmade and poorly designed and printed on a low-resolution inkjet printer." Hampton leaned toward him. "But, my boy, there was an object described in the brochure that piqued my interest. And so, I rented a car and chancing my ability to drive on the wrong side of the road headed east along the interstate highway for Canton, Texas."

Dr. Hampton parked his rental car in a dusty, bumpy area of open pasture marked off with yellow crime tape. An attendant in a Gulf cap and a sweaty tee shirt accosted him as he climbed out of his car.

"Hey, buddy, that'll be ten dollars."

Hampton sniffed at the odor of the man. "I beg your pardon."

"Ten dollars for parking. You don't pay, you get towed."

Hampton rummaged in the inner pocket of his tweed jacket and pulled out his passport wallet. He examined the green bills inside and found a ten. "Will this suffice?" He handed the bill to the attendant.

The man smiled revealing stubby, yellow teeth half of which were missing. "Pleasure to do business with you." He winked. "Matey."

"I'm not from Australia." Hampton stiffened as the man handed him a roughly cut piece of red paper with a number on it.

"On the dashboard there, matey. I love your chicken on the barbie at Outback." He tipped his cap and walked toward the next car pulling into the makeshift carpark. Hampton tossed the paper on the dash of his car.

"Matey, indeed!" He straightened his jacket and glanced around the field. It was early October and he had to admit the orange and red leaves of many of the trees were beautiful. Fiery waves of color undulated with the wind. He glanced up at the sky. From the west, a dark gray cloud lay across the horizon. Perhaps it would be wise to leave. He did not look forward to experiencing one of the famous Texas tornados. Ten dollars, however. He pulled the brochure out of his jacket pocket and placed his wallet back safely in an inner pocket.

The "booths" as they were called ranged from seedy metal and blue tarp topped tents to elegant gazebos. Most booths held nothing but old junk, ancient roadside signs, dented scratched furniture advertised as antiques from England. He was certain most would have a "Made in Vietnam" sticker on the bottom somewhere.

The men and women at the booths ranged in appearance from the typical "redneck" as he had learned: portly man or woman in tee shirts and cutoff jeans with John Deere caps and Dallas Cowboy caps to men dressed frankly as cowboys with wide brimmed hats and boots. String ties and huge belt buckles advertising what he learned were wrestling clubs, hung at their enormous bellies. They laughed and drank from beer cans and did the most despicable spectacle of spitting oral tobacco juice into empty beer cans. He couldn't wait to return to the more genteel and civilized world of London.

There was no map to guide one around this circus. Over one hundred such booths filled the huge pasture. The grass had been worn down to red clay dirt and he hated to think about what a travesty would occur with the coming rain. A cool wind picked up and he heard the distant rumble of thunder. The ruffians were oblivious.

At the back expanse of the pasture along the tree line were several motor homes with their wares displayed under outstretched awnings. One motor home looked quite expensive and even from a distance, Hampton could tell this "booth" was different. He made his way through the milling throngs of men, women and children "chowing down" on funnel cakes and fried Twinkies and other such life ending fare.

Hampton arrived at the motor home and one man leaned over a table. He was short and had black and white hair that blossomed from his head. He wore tiny gold reading glasses, and he examined a brass object shaped like a serpent.

"No, I don't think so." He mumbled to himself.

"Excuse me, are you the proprietor?" Hampton asked.

The man looked up at him, peering over his reading glasses. A huge mustache hid his lips, and a seedy jacket covered a flannel shirt. He looked like a relative of Albert Einstein. "Proprietor?" He took off his glasses and squinted at Hampton.

Hampton held out the brochure. "The brochure photo has this motor home in the background and I'm looking for this artifact."

The man took the brochure and put his reading glasses on. "Brochure? I had no idea there was a brochure. Would have saved me hours. Yes, yes. This is exactly what I'm looking for."

At that moment the door to the motor home opened. A woman climbed down the stairs. Hampton gasped. She was the most exotic woman he had ever seen. Her skin was the color of milk chocolate and her long, braided lustrous black hair hung across her shoulder. She wore a sarong of sapphire with a gold and silver belt. Her hands glistened with rings. Her eyes were a dark brown and were filled with excitement as she came to the other man.

"Dr. Lawrence, I have been waiting to meet with you. I have the object inside." She spoke with an accent from somewhere in the region of India or Pakistan.

Hampton cleared his throat. *"Here, here! My good man, you did not tell me you were not the proprietor."*

Lawrence glanced at Hampton. *"You didn't give me a chance. I'm Doctor Cephas Lawrence."* He held out a stubby hand and Hampton shook it.

"Dr. Nigel Hampton."

Lawrence's eyes widened and he pulled off his glasses. *"The Museum of the Weird? I visited there once when I was in London."* He chuckled. *"There's a sucker born every minute."*

Hampton gasped. *"Sucker?"*

Lawrence gestured with his glasses. *"Come, come, Hampton. Most of the items in your exhibit are fake. Where did you get the yeti carcass?"*

Hampton blinked. *"I bought it from a documentary filmmaker in London."*

The woman laughed. *"David MacDonald?"*

Hampton glared at here. *"I'm sorry, we were not introduced."*

"Indira Sno, Dr. Hampton. You actually bought the yeti carcass from MacDonald?"

"Well, he said it was more like a bigfoot type creature from the mountains in Arkansas."

Sno smiled and glanced at Lawrence. *"Dr. Hampton, I am only here because my aunt living here in the states passed away and left me with an attic full of what she called 'arcane artifacts'. She was an archeology professor at UT Austin. I'm on my way to Dallas to finish up a local seminar on the future of climate change and I thought I could unload some of her 'artifacts' here at this rural event."*

"I was wondering what you were doing here in this aboriginal backwater junk show. Ahem, so how do you know so much about this carcass of which you speak?"

Sno smiled. "You will not believe this but it belonged to my aunt. She bought it for fifty dollars from a farmer in Arkansas. He was charging five dollars a person to view it in his barn." She smiled and glanced at Lawrence. *"She had the local coroner examine it and he said it was the carcass of a mountain lion that populates those mountains in Arkansas. A film student at UT Austin wanted the carcass for an experimental film. Turns out he sold it to a filmmaker in Shreveport who passed it off as the Fouke Monster, a local bigfoot legend. MacDonald contacted his fellow filmmaker and bought the carcass for his documentary in England."* She walked toward him, a twinkle in her eyes. For a moment they seemed uneven and then returned to their right appearance. *"You see, MacDonald went to the same coroner and convinced him to state that he could not rule out that the carcass was some kind of monster. He told the coroner he would be in the documentary film but it would only be shown in Europe. What one won't do for fifteen minutes of fame. He reasoned no one in England would be the wiser and would buy the legend, as they say here in the states, hook, line, and sinker. After all, you did!"* Sno and Lawrence laughed.

Hampton felt his face heat up and he jerked the brochure from Lawrence's hand. "While the two of you have a laugh at my expense, I remain stoically professional. I believe this chest in the brochure is an object I have been searching for."

Lawrence stopped laughing. "I am sorry, Dr. Hampton. You have to admit that some of the artifacts in your Museum of Weird would fit right in here." He gestured around him. "But I understand. The titillating objects attract visitors and their money fuels your serious research, right? Which is what exactly?"

Hampton's face began to cool as the wind picked up. "I am searching for ancient artifacts that manifest a power beyond our space time continuum."

Sno raised an eyebrow. "You are speaking of the supernatural."

"A word that carries a great deal of emotional heft, madame. I assure you my interests are academic in nature." He frowned. "Dr.

Lawrence you are correct about some objects in my Museum of the Weird. I have to compete with that hideous wax museum!"

Hampton jumped as lightning lit up the forest behind them and the thunder crashed against the motor home canopy rustling it with great force. Sno motioned to the table. *"If you two gentlemen will help me push my display case close to the side of the motor home, I must let down the canopy or the wind will rip it away. Afterwards, you can join me inside for a proper cup of tea and we will discuss this object at length."*

They had just finished when the rain fell in a deluge from the sky. Hampton followed them into the motor home. The walls and floor shifted with the wind.

"Is this one of your tornados, Lawrence?"

Lawrence shook his head. "I wouldn't know. I live in New York City. I flew into Dallas to attend the same seminar at which Dr. Sno spoke. I heard about First Monday and thought there might be some serious artifacts hidden in the rubble."

"What does climate change have to do with your collection of artifacts?" Hampton asked.

"Ever heard of a divining rod? It's used to find water. Believe it or not, sometimes it actually works."

Sno made tea and they sat around her small table tucked up against a U-shaped couch. *"Now, gentlemen, in the back bedroom are dozens of objects collected by my aunt. This chest is one of them and I have no idea of its value or its significance."*

"I think I know." Dr. Lawrence said quietly. "Have you ever heard of the Ark of the Demon Rose?"

Something crossed Sno's face and for a moment she froze. Then, her smile returned. *"I have heard of such a legend. It is just that. Legend."*

Hampton leaned over his teacup. *"I haven't."*

Lawrence glanced at Hampton. *"Oh, it's nothing really. What did you think it was?"*

Hampton's gaze shifted between the two. *"Pandora's Box."*

Sno raised an eyebrow. Lawrence smiled. "Another legend, it would seem. No matter what the chest truly is, I was here first Dr. Sno. I should have right of first refusal."

Sno nodded. "Of course."

"I beg to disagree. I can meet any price you offer, Lawrence."

"It's not about price." Sno said quietly. Her gaze shifted to Lawrence and she sipped more tea as she studied his face. "I think Dr. Lawrence is destined to have this chest if he wants it."

She stood up and Lawrence slid out of his seat to allow her past. She disappeared into the rear of the motor home.

"You Philistine!" Hampton's cup clattered in his saucer. "This is not some random competition." The motor home shook as thunder rolled outside.

"I was here first, Hampton. Get over it." Lawrence massaged his mustache. "If I don't think it's worthy of my attention or of becoming part of my collection, then you can have it."

Sno emerged from the back room. She carried an object wrapped in a quilt. She placed the object on the table and unwrapped the quilt. A dark wooden chest sat before them. Intricate filigrees of gold and silver etched the edges. Etched in gold, an image of a woman sitting before an ancient urn covered the top. Vapors seemed to come from the open urn and formed hideous demon faces.

"That looks like Pandora to me." Hampton said.

"Have you opened it?" Lawrence asked.

Sno leaned over the table. "Absolutely not. I have no idea what is within. I have no paperwork of the origin of this piece. I can only assume the image on the lid would make one suspect Pandora's Box. Although, as you both should know, the original legend spoke of an urn, not a box."

"Then, it is not genuine." Hampton sighed. "Looks like you will be disappointed Lawrence."

Dr. Lawrence ignored both of them as his eyes focused on the box. He put on his reading glasses and leaned close to the surface. He traced a circle around the lid. Hampton had to admit there was a faint circular line of discoloration of the wood on the lid as if something large and circular had once sat on it.

"It will take it, Dr. Sno." Lawrence sat back. "It is wise you did not open it."

Hampton growled and slid out of his seat. "Very well, Lawrence. You win."

Lawrence glanced up at Hampton. He sat back. "I tell you what, Dr. Hampton. Stay in touch with me. Maybe one day, if your Museum of the Weird garners more professional status, I will loan some of my artifacts to you for a season. You can display them for the viewing public. And I will make sure this chest is in that manifest. Does that soothe some of your ruffled feathers?"

"Ruffled feathers indeed!" *Hampton stomped out of the motor home and paused as he ran full on into the pouring rain. He swore loudly and he heard the door open behind him. Sno rushed up to him and held an umbrella over his head.*

"Dr. Hampton, forgive me for not giving you the opportunity to own the chest."

He looked into her fierce, dark eyes. Once again they seemed to shift with the blinking of her eyes. "Madame, you are not to blame. That outrageous man!"

"I'd take him up on the offer." *Sno held the umbrella over them. She stood close to him and he felt the warmth of her flow between them. There was something foreign, exotic, enticing about the woman. His heart raced.*

"Thank you for your kindness."

Sno held up a small, wooden box. "This will probably fit in well with your display. It's no doubt a fake but my aunt labeled it the 'Philosopher's Stone'. Take it as a token of my professional respect."

Hampton frowned. "There's just been a book published about this supposed stone. A children's book."

Sno shrugged. "Very well, then I wish you well on your trip back to your homeland."

Something happened then. It was inexplicable. It was

otherworldly. It was, for want of a better word, supernatural. Hampton felt a wave of energy pulsate from the small box. For a moment he thought a golden light shown from the cracks of the box. He looked up at Sno and she was unaffected by the phenomenon.

"Take me." A quiet voice whispered in his ear.

He whirled and there was no one behind him. He looked back at Sno. "Did you hear that?"

Sno wore a bemused expression. "Just the wind, Dr. Hampton. Take your prize." She placed the box in his hand and he felt a bolt of electricity tingle up his arm. He almost dropped the box. Was it a trick? Was it a magician's illusion?"

"How much do I owe you?"

Sno only smiled. "I'll come to collect from you someday. Just don't forget where you got it." She left him with the umbrella and the box and hurried back into the motor home.

JOSH LISTENED TO THE STORY WITH GROWING DREAD. He knew all too well of Pandora's plans. Josh licked dry, scaling lips. "What did you do to me?"

"What did I do to you? Why nothing." Hampton smiled.

"The box. You made me pick it up. It stuck my finger."

"Oh, that." Hampton crossed his legs and leaned back in his chair. "What an unfortunate event."

Josh tried to sit up, but he was numb from the chest down. "You planned this. Why?"

Hampton stared off into the distance. He glanced over his shoulder at the door to Josh's room. "Of course, I am working in tandem with the unholy triad, as Mr. Steel refers to them. But their agenda is far different from mine."

"A new pandemic?" Josh said hoarsely.

Hampton raised an eyebrow. "Well, the last one was quite effective for people of my persuasion. Chaos. Death.

Destruction. Despair. Hopelessness. Hatred. Violence. Elimination of certain freedoms. But pandemics are short lived." He leaned forward and whispered conspiratorially. "But the triplets think that is what this is all about. And I shall keep it that way." He leaned back and chuckled. "No, Josh, my plans are much longer in execution. The members of the Council of Darkness are too ambitious. They try to do great and horrendous deeds on the world stage. Vampire armies? The Ark of Chaos? Portals to other worlds? Time travel to change all of history? And how did Thakkar possibly think she could control millions of minds? No, my dear boy, the Council will always fail. They are not patient. I have seen the big picture. I am patient. At least my patron is patient." He frowned and something foreign crossed his features twisting his face temporarily.

"If you are not with the Council, then who?"

"Enough about me. What do you know about epigenetics?" Hampton ignored the question.

Josh blinked and tried to clear the grogginess from his mind. "What?"

"External environmental influences that alter genetic expression." Hampton nodded. "Yes, suppose your great great grandfather survived the potato famine in Ireland. Almost starving to death changes the way in which his genes are expressed. His body turns on certain metabolic forces to maximize fat storage for purposes of survival." Hampton pointed a perfectly manicured fingernail at Josh. "And then, a couple of generations later, those same genes are now turned on and you can't seem to keep the fat off. You are overweight and no matter how hard you try, you remain overweight."

"Why are you telling me this?" Josh mumbled.

"Because you, my young friend, have had extraordinary epigenetic influences already in your life. Let's see, demon possession by the most powerful demon short of the Master himself. That was number thirteen, as you designated him. Combine that with an extrasensory perception through dreaming -- "

"Wait? What?" Josh tried to sit up again.

"Your dreams." Hampton opened his hands. "You have extraordinary dreams and if they were cultivated, you would have true prescience. You could predict the future." Hampton stared at him. "Never mind. There's more. You were infected with a very nasty genetically altered prion that changed the neuronal architecture of your mind. Neuroplasticity."

Hampton put his feet on the floor and leaned forward. "Dark DNA, my boy. Ever heard of it? Well, less than 10% of the human genome has no known function. Imagine if we could turn those codes on?" He winked at Josh. "After all, your own father had his DNA altered by an encounter with an evil spirit and look what that produced! The Nephilim! Children with extraordinary abilities."

Hampton stood up paced excitedly. "And you were in outer space among Cobalt's genetically altered children! Who knows what you might have absorbed in their presence? So, infecting you with a nasty retroviral agent from the dim, dark past when our own forces were trying to inbreed some of these characteristics seemed like the perfect storm. You're not just infected, Josh. You are a petri dish! From you I will extract the perfect pathogen that will not just make a person ill but will alter their genetic expression to suit my goals."

Josh was breathing quickly, his heart racing. "What goals?"

Hampton's eyes gleamed with malice. "For one thing, did you know the human brain is hard wired to believe in God? It's a very pesky characteristic that we have tried for millennia to eliminate. Why are there so many atheists angry? If they don't believe in God, why not just leave it alone and let religion die a natural death? But no, they have to stir things up and get Christians all excited and committed! It's because they are at war with their own brains!"

Hampton stood up and paced around Josh's bed. "Imagine if, through the process of neuroplasticity, we could eliminate that center of the brain? Imagine if, through a combination of epigenetics and neuroplasticity we could alter a generation or two of humanity to truly abandon religion. To truly forget God! What a triumph that would be! And it's already begun. The 'nones' are growing in number."

"Nones?"

"People with no religious affiliation. They just don't care! It's fantastical, my dear boy! We are seeing the development of a generation of apatheists! Not atheists but those who just don't care one way or the other. So, you see the effects are already beginning but the brains are not being altered. They are still persuadable and that is where you come in." He paused and gripped the end of Josh's bed. "You, my young man, are the key to this. I am harvesting altered viral particles and free strands of DNA and RNA from you at a furious rate! You will change the world, Josh. You will eliminate God for good!" His eyes fairly glowed with excitement. "And, there is more!"

Josh shook his head. "I'll never help you do that." He glanced across the room as his clothes folded neatly on a nearby counter. If he could just get up enough strength. Hampton raised an eyebrow and followed Josh's gaze.

"Ah, you are considering escape." He chuckled. "My good boy, your legs will not work. What will you do? Crawl down the corridor? I am afraid you are totally and completely under my control."

Josh swallowed hard. It wasn't his clothing he was looking for. It was the necklace made from a shard of the bloodstone his father had used to defeat the eleventh demon. He had worn the bloodstone shard in London, and it had helped him escape Numinocity. If he could just get his hands on it!

Hampton stepped into his view and his hand rested on the bedside table. "Stones, Josh."

Josh froze. How had Hampton read his mind? Or had Hampton had already found the Bloodstone shard.

"Human history is littered with mythical and magical stones. Unfortunately, they are just inanimate objects. Their only magical power comes from the arcane source of the spirits." Hampton opened the top drawer of the bedside table and removed something wrapped in a purple cloth. How long had that been in his bedside drawer?

"I'd like to show you something, my young boy."

Hampton held the object before Josh's eyes. "I have been in the business of finding and locating these supposedly magical objects my entire career. The only person who has been more successful than I have was your late great-uncle Dr. Lawrence." Hampton chuckled again. "I still do not know how I managed to fool him into leaving me at least three crates of his collection. Imagine, he traded a useless wooden chest that carried the image of Pandora for the this." Hampton placed the object on the table beside Josh. He carefully unwrapped the purple cloth. Sitting in the center of the cloth was a simple, red tinged stone covered in veins of gold. "Behold the Philosopher's Stone. It is a famous stone over which alchemists slaved for centuries. One such alchemist succeeded in turning an ordinary lump of stone into gold and imbued this rock with certain abilities."

Josh drew a sudden breath at the memory of Pandora's death. "Maria?" It wasn't the Philosopher's Stone. It was Pandora's stone.

Hampton froze. "Well, her real name was Mary, the Jewess. Or, possibly Maria, the Jewess. How do you know such things?"

"I studied mythology in high school." I also have Pandora stuck in my head!

Hampton shook his head. "Oh, she was not a myth. Maria lived between the first and third centuries in Alexandria. She was one of the first alchemical writers and is credited with the invention of several kinds of chemical apparatus. She is considered to be the first true alchemist of the Western World. If you have ever enjoyed gourmet cooking, you must have heard of bain-marie. Mary's bath, as it was called, limits the maximum temperature of a container and its contents to the boiling point of a separate liquid. Essentially a double boiler."

"She discovered this stone." Hampton calmed down and his wicked smile returned. "Now, the stone will be your constant companion." He placed the stone inside the bedside table drawer again. He closed it carefully. "When you sleep during infusions, do you dream?"

Josh clenched his jaw. "Yes, I dream about Pandora. She is planning on taking over my mind. You may be out of luck."

Hampton stiffened. "What is this nonsense?"

"Pandora. She's in my head when I sleep. Isn't that part of your plan?"

Hampton slowly smiled. "Oh, my! Such delicious irony. The death of God and the birth of the Goddess! And who controls the stone, controls Pandora!" He looked at Josh with wild eyes. "My good boy, this is no longer the Philosopher's Stone. It is now the Pandora Stone!"

Hampton rubbed his hands together in eager anticipation as if he was about to partake of a tasty meal. "Yes, when you sleep and when you dream, my boy, the spirit of Pandora will seep into your mind. There are secrets hidden deep within the substance of her Stone, secrets that will be revealed to you. The stone will connect with you, an extraordinary young man who will help shape the future of this world in ways you cannot imagine."

Hampton put out a hand and patted Josh's shoulder. Josh tried to pull away and realized his body would not move from the neck down. His eyes widened. "What is happening?"

Hampton patted his shoulder. "Your next dose is coming and when you sleep, you will see what is happening, Josh. You will see. And now I must return to my homeland for a short trip while the Pandora Stone changes your mind." He chuckled. "A crude pun indeed."

Hampton doffed his bowler and bowed to Josh as the paralysis crept higher. In the recesses of his troubled and darkening mind he heard Pandora's laughter.

22

Jason Birdsong sipped at his coffee and leaned back in the folding chair. The sun set over Cross Lake painting the November sky in breathtaking brushstrokes of red, yellow and orange. The breeze off the lake was cool but he didn't care. He enjoyed the cool air that was such a departure from the arid, hot climate of Tucson. He ached to be in Texas where poor Josh was at the mercy of demons. But Dr. Merchant had been right. They had to determine what was really happening to Josh and then formulate a plan. The demonic forces in play did not know he was Jonathan's partner, and they had no idea who Dr. Merchant was, or they would have reacted when the two of them had been in the clinic. He knew from surveillance work and undercover work that patience was of utmost importance. Gather the facts. Analyze the information. Then formulate a plan. Right now, he was safe at Steel's lake house.

He stood up and attended to the steaks sizzling on the grill behind him and felt the boat dock shudder as someone walked toward him. He peeked around the outdoor kitchen.

Dr. Jack Merchant hurried toward him dressed in blue scrubs and a fleece jacket.

"It's too cold to be out here on the lake, Jason." Merchant wrapped his arms around himself. "Sorry I'm running late. I had a last minute dialysis catheter to put in an elderly man with a potassium of eight."

"I don't know what that means." Birdsong said.

"Without dialysis, the man would be dead in a few hours. What are you cooking?" Merchant rubbed his hands together and his breath steamed in the evening air.

"The steaks are almost done, and we can go inside. I was just enjoying the view."

Merchant looked around at the lake. "I don't have a view like this. Some of my new partners live on the lake. Houses north of two million. I guess they didn't have gambling debts to repay."

Birdsong placed the two steaks on a platter and covered them with foil. "Let's get inside. The baked potatoes should be ready."

They walked across the yard to the lake house and through the sliding doors to the dining room table. Birdsong had put together a salad and rolls. He set the steaks on the table and went into the kitchen to retrieve the baked potatoes wrapped in foil.

"I guess your cholesterol is normal." Merchant shrugged out of his jacket and sat at the table.

"110. Is that good?" Birdsong placed the plate of foil wrapped potatoes on the table.

"110? I hate you." Merchant put a steak on his plate and glared at his salad.

Birdsong retrieved a bowl of salad from the counter and slid it in front of Merchant. ""I guess the salad is for you, then."

Merchant glared at him and grunted. "So this is where Steel lives?"

"Yeah." Birdsong sat at his plate and cut into the steak. "He never told me the full story. Turns out the thirteenth demon's host owned this place and then Dr. Cephas Lawrence ended up buying it without knowing it."

Merchant tilted his head toward the living room. "What's with the stick above the fireplace?" A walking stick with the head of a lion carved into the handle hung above the mantle.

"Dr. Elizabeth Washington. Dr. Washington helped them out in the early days of the demons. She's a linguist and a snake expert, Jonathan told me. Jonathan said an African chieftain gave her that stick in exchange for marriage. She refused but he let her keep it anyway. Turns out, she's away for the semester teaching but she'll be back for Thanksgiving holiday and then for Christmas. Josh calls her his grandmother."

"Any word from Jonathan?" Merchant asked.

Birdsong sighed. "Not yet. I hope he's okay."

"We need to focus on Josh then."

"Okay, what do you have?"

Merchant pushed his gold rimmed glasses back onto his nose and reached into the inner pocket of his jacket hanging on the chair and took out a small tablet. He chewed his steak as he moved through images on the tablet. "I had the lab isolate this virus from Josh's blood work from my ER." He held up the tablet. The images showed an image that looked like a spider built out of an old erector set.

"What am I looking at?"

"A virus we can't classify. At least, not so far. I could send it on to the CDC but then there would be questions. As long as Josh's life is in the hands of your demon buddies, I can't go much farther." Merchant ate some salad.

"Where did it come from?"

"Not sure." Merchant said. "But we need to find out. If this thing gets loose, it could cause an epidemic. It's not airborne so it has to be ingested or, like HIV, transmitted through body fluids. I have a friend at LSU Medical Center and I had him play around with it. He infected some rats and they died within hours of status epilepticus. That's unending seizures. The post showed the brain had turned to mush."

Birdsong froze and sat back. "Please tell me that won't happen to Josh."

Merchant put down his fork and sighed. "Well, according to the doctors in Dallas, his virus is gone and now he is in a post viral autoimmune type disease. He's no longer infectious. I have some preliminary results on the blood I took from Josh in the clinic. No viral particles."

"Then we are out of the woods." Birdsong started eating again but the acid churned in his stomach.

"Not necessarily." Merchant pointed at him with his fork. "Josh was very fortunate he didn't die on the airplane."

"Why didn't others get it?" Birdsong asked.

"Body fluids, Jason. Thank God it's not an airborne virus like COVID. The only conclusion I can draw is that this mysterious treatment given at the clinic killed the virus. Or Josh's own immune system may have killed it."

"We are safe from a pandemic, then?"

"I think so. What this means is the virus is very virulent and moves rapidly but kills the patient before it can be passed on to very many people. Sort of like Ebola virus. Very virulent and kills fast. Most breakouts are small and self-limited because the virus kills the hosts before it can be spread to very many people."

Birdsong guzzled some water and shook his head. "What has Steel gotten himself into?"

Merchant leaned over his plate and steepled his hands. "I don't know, Jason. But we can't sit on this. I can't let this virus get loose. We have to do something."

"Like what?" Birdsong said.

"Normally, as part of the medical examiner's office I would call in representatives of the CDC." Merchant looked up at Birdsong and leaned back. "But tell them what? I have discovered a viral agent that was deliberately given to a young man by a trio of demon possessed doctors?"

"I understand. I still have trouble wrapping my brain around this supernatural stuff." He finished his meal and pushed his plate away. "Jack, I grew up hearing lots of stories from my grandmother of the spiritual and supernatural mythology of our people. I thought it was all mumbo jumbo until I met Jonathan Steel. These forces of evil are truly insidious. They hide in plain sight. They cover themselves in the invisible shield of rational thinking and scientific methodology. How do you defeat an enemy that no thinking person believes exists?"

"I don't know, Jason. I was hoping you would tell me. After all, you're the one who had been back in time and battled demons on some virtual reality plane of existence. Clearly, we have passed beyond the realms of scientific knowledge."

Birdsong nodded. "Okay, so let's look at facts. These creatures exist and they are just as subject to the laws of nature as we are. So what about the I.V. fluid?"

"A witch's brew of vitamins and minerals." Merchant said. He tapped the table with a finger. "But there is a substance I can't identify. I didn't have enough of the fluid to be sure what this chemical is. It's large and some kind of peptide. Maybe a protein? One thing I am certain of is there are no medications in the fluid you would normally give someone with an autoimmune disease. Bottom line: I need more of the treatment fluid to be sure."

Merchant finished his glass of tea and swallowed. "Jason, I

can't allow this to go on much longer without alerting the authorities. If this virus gets out and people start having the same symptoms as Josh we will need that treatment."

Birdsong nodded and leaned back in his chair. It creaked under his massive frame. "Unfortunately, we can't contact Steel without giving away we know about his predicament. You heard that doctor in New Orleans. If Steel tells anyone, Josh dies."

"I could pay another visit and get more fluid." Merchant said.

Birdsong shook his head. "No, Jack. You've done your part. Now, it's my turn to do what I know best. I'll get into the clinic and get more of the fluid for you."

"How are you going to do that?"

"I did a stent as an undercover policeman for about six months on the force before I went back to patrol. Didn't like having to become something I'm not. But I think I can work myself into the clinic somehow."

"Well, we have to move quickly, Jason. I came here to talk because I can't let anyone at the hospital or the coroner's office know what I'm involved in. The longer we wait, the more likely my investigations will be discovered. And the more likely this virus will get loose and make COVID look like the sniffles."

23

London, England

"Mom, I'm fine. Can we please go home?"

Dr. Monarch looked up from her phone at her son lying in the hospital bed. "When you are better."

Steven Monarch pushed his hair out of his face and held up both hands. "Hands, good as new. Mind, good as new." He pounded his chest. "Stamina, well better." He motioned to the hospital bed. "Hospital bed, overkill."

Monarch smiled. She could not explain the transition in Steven's hands. Prior to her son going under for the virtual trip into "Numinocity", his hands were a wreck from wounds sustained in the shooting of her husband. In fact, there were many things she could not explain; things that smacked of supernatural forces she had denied most of her life.

"You are home." She said.

Stephen looked around the room. "Your laboratory is not my home. I want to go back to the states."

Monarch's phone chimed and she looked away from the hospital bed she had brought to her hidden laboratory in London. Steven had been transferred to a London hospital and then she had taken him into hiding until she could make sure Dr. Sultana Thakkar's Numinocity project was indeed dead. She studied the text message on the screen.

"What is it?" Steven asked.

"Your sister. She's upstairs with an old friend."

Steven slid out of the bed and then wobbled for a second. His tall figure overshadowed her. He wore a tee shirt and a pair of pajama pants. It was good to see him healthier again. During his time under the influence of Thakkar, he had lots weight and almost died. In just a few days, he had already started putting the weight back on. Of course, he had almost eaten her out of house and home. Steven motioned to the door. "I'm good, Mom. I'm also starving. Let's go."

Monarch sighed and led her son up a flight of stairs to her laboratory. She had purchased a riverfront warehouse on the Thames and then put it up for sale under the guise of remodeling. She had never returned the inquiries and had kept the place a secret from her many enemies. When Monarch stepped into her laboratory she gasped. Olivia, her daughter perched on a lab console talking to Max's ninja assistant, Ishido.

"Ishido?" Monarch said. She hurried to the small man and embraced him. He groaned a little.

"I am still not yet well, Dr. Monarch. But I am healing."

"I'm Steven." Steven held out a hand.

Ishido studied it for a second and then shook it. "I understand your hands are back to normal. God has indeed given you a special gift, young man."

Steven opened his mouth to say something and then

glanced at Olivia. "Well, the jury is still out on that. At least for me. I give the nanomemes the credit."

Ishido turned back to Olivia. "You are healing well."

Olivia was much shorter than her brother and wore a sweat shirt and matching sweatpants. He bright eyes glittered with excitement and she and touched the red welts on her face. "Fortunately, only second-degree burns. Hopefully, no scarring by the time it all heals." She had decided to let her hair grow out beyond her usual inch short length but her Mom could still see the scars from her injuries and the subsequent surgeries. Olivia had an implanted device that stimulated her brain whenever she was about to experience a seizure. The seizures were a leftover effect of the bullet that had driven through her brain when Monarch's husband had been shot. She swallowed back the swell of emotion. Both of her children were now safe and here with her. Unfortunately, Ishido had intruded on their solitude and it was not necessarily a good thing.

"So, Ishiso why are you here?" Monarch asked.

Ishido reached into his jacket and pulled out an envelope. "You know I would not risk returning to London unless it was important. Jonathan Steel asked me to bring this to you."

Monarch looked at the envelope warily. "From Jonathan. Not Max? I know she's still mad at me for what happened to Raven."

Ishido shrugged. "That is between the two of you. This is from Jonathan."

"Before I take it, are there any dangers involved?" Monarch said. "I just got my son back in one piece."

Ishido drew a deep breath and thoughtfully considered something. "I will tell you Jonathan was attacked by the Crimson Snake. She made off with something of great importance. Only, what she took was a fake. This envelope contains the real thing. Jonathan merely wants you to put it somewhere safe."

Monarch shook her head and put up her hands. "I don't think so. The last thing I need is the Snake coming after me again."

Olivia slid off the counter. "Mom, it's Jonathan Steel. He saved us from Numinocity."

Monarch's eyes flared with anger. "Steven saved us with his computer virus."

"No, Olivia is right, Mom." Steven said. He shook his head in dismay. "All of that 'whole armor of God' business is what saved us. I hate to admit it because, of course, it smacks of the supernatural."

"I saw the eighth demon." Olivia said.

"You saw what I saw, a computerized construct. CGI." Steven said.

Oilivia pushed Steven away. "Yes, I saw what the program created, Steven. But don't forget my real body was in the warehouse on a slab right next to the slab on which Dr. Thakkar's real body lay. I was there. I saw what happened in the real world."

Thakkar looked back at the slab as the image of Olivia changed, fading into the image of a dark-haired teenage boy. In his hands, the boy held the blue stone. "I'm sorry, Olivia. I am near death now. I cannot hold the illusion much longer."

Thakkar reached over and pulled the mask from the other figure's face. Olivia stared back at her. "Fooled you."

"What?" Thakkar said. She snatched the blue stone from Steven's hands. "It doesn't matter. I now have the nanomemes." Olivia stood up, shakily. "You have no control over me, Thakkar. I entered Numinocity on my own. Your faulty nanomemes have filled the

warehouse, and they interfaced with my brain stimulator. I had a few absence seizures while pretending to be Steven, but the bottom line is you cannot control me. I didn't even feel a flicker of that pleasure you boasted of. Just acting."

"That doesn't matter." Thakkar held up the blue stone. "This is what I came for."

"Really?" Olivia said and motioned with her hand. The air seemed to shudder, and the image of New Stonehenge grew translucent again. Thakkar turned and studied her body, lying on the other slab. "What is this?"

The Crimson Snake stepped from behind a monolith. She walked over and looked down at the sleeping figure of Olivia. She then walked over to Thakkar and reached to her back and pulled out her walking cane. She pressed a button, and the ceramic blade popped out.

"Good, Snake," Thakkar said and looked back at Olivia. "End her."

"No!" Steel tried to stand up and collapsed again in weakness.

Snake laughed and looked back across the ethereal air from her real world into the virtual reality of Numinocity. "I've already had a little conversation with the girl, Thakkar. And, someone else! I have a new boss, Thakkar."

Snake raised the cane's blade and plunged it into Thakkar's neck.

"No!" She screeched as her real body spasmed on the slab. Blood poured onto the slab, and the virtual Thakkar convulsed. She seemed to expand, to swell as her virtual image recoiled from the dying embers of her real mind. Thakkar's body moved again, and then the chest ceased to move. Snake wiped the blood from her cane.

"Snake, this was not what I agreed on." Olivia whispered.

Snake smiled and wiped the blade clean of blood against the hem of Thakkar's garment. "Like I said, I have a new boss."

Thakkar's image almost faded. Her face twisted in concentration, and her lips moved as she spoke aloud a language only machines could understand. Bits and bytes and zeroes and ones spewed from her lips and disappeared in the air. Her fading image stabilized. Her features grew clearer.

Thakkar laughed out loud, and her laughter cascaded throughout Numinocity. "I did it! I have ascended! I am no longer confined to that body." She whirled, and her eyes grew crimson. "I am more than mortal. I am more than spiritual. I am human 6.66! The world will bow before me. Numinocity will replace your reality. With this." She held up the blue stone, and it pulsed once and then opened like the petals of a flower. Tiny blue particles floated into the air.

"Yes, my new nanomemes. Flow into the life blood of Numinocity! Ignite the flame that destroys the real world!" A particle landed on the third eye and burst into flame. Thakkar looked at it cross-eyed and screamed as the flame spread across her skin. "What is this?" More particles landed on her skin and ignited it. She tried to drop the stone, but it melted into the palm of her hand. She screamed again as fire bubbled her skin.

"My final revenge." Steven opened his eyes and said tiredly from the slab. "A virus that will destroy your creation. You will be deleted." He gasped in pain and faded from view.

Olivia screamed and threw herself onto the empty slab, where now her real body seemed to float ghost-like back in the warehouse. Thakkar was aflame, and her screams were inhuman, the screech of machine language and shattering diodes. The monoliths in the real warehouse burst into flame around Snake.

OLIVIA RECOUNTED THE MEMORY. "SO, HOW DO YOU explain Thakkar's ability to leave her body and enter into her avatar? Her solid, real-world avatar? I saw it up close with my very eyes. It had nothing to do with Numinocity. It was her soul, her spirit, Steven."

"So, sister, are you going to become a Christian?" Steven said hotly.

"Maybe. I don't know. It's all so confusing. Look, I just want to go home."

"That we agree on. I want to get back to school and show off my hands." Steven said quietly. "Back to the states."

Monarch raised her hands to silence them. "All right, let's just calm down. Maybe if I knew what you're holding, Ishido, I might consider it. Assuming we are truly safe from Thakkar's lingering organization."

"Max has assured me that Thakkar's influence has been truly nullified, Dr. Monarch." Ishido took out his cell phone and opened Steel's video. He placed the phone on the counter. "This message is intended for you alone, Dr. Monarch. I shall retreat to the stairs."

Ishido hurried to the stairs leading to the lower level and closed the door behind him. Monarch looked at the phone.

"Both of you. With Ishido. Now."

"Mom!" Olivia crossed her arms. "We deserve to see it. It might be about Josh."

Monarch pointed to the door. "No! I can't endanger your lives again. If I think it's okay for you to hear this message, I'll play if for you. Just let me protect you, Olivia. And you, too, Steven."

Steven groaned and took his sister by the arm. "Come on, sis." They joined Ishido in the stairwell. Monarch pressed the play button. The face of Jonathan Steel appeared in the video. His turquoise eyes gleamed with reflected light.

"Okay. Dr. Monarch. This is Jonathan Steel. I need your help. Josh is in danger, and I must cooperate with a trio of demons, or he dies. I have obtained Raven's dossier and it is loaded onto the enclosed memory card. I'm looking for information to disrupt an organization known as the Penticle. That was more than I should have told you. Forget I said that. Dr. Monarch, I need you to hide this away for me as these demons know nothing of your involvement. It is my only bargaining chip for Josh's life. If you access the information without authorization, the contents will be erased. This is our only copy of the dossier. So, please, don't try and access the information. Please. Josh's life depends on it. Thanks. When it's safe, I'll be in touch but right now I am under constant surveillance." The video ended. Monarch picked up the envelope Ishido had placed beside the phone.

She glanced inside the envelope and poured the contents into her hand. A small silver rectangle sat in the center of her palm, a fingernail sized memory card. Her heart raced. If this was the dossier from Raven containing a record of her assassinations, then here was the answer to all her questions! Her son, Steven, had entered Numinocity with the express purpose of finding out who had paid to have his father assassinated. Here was the answer. On this drive would be the name of the person who hired Raven to kill her. She gasped and glanced at the stairwell door. She had not shared with her children the revelation that the assassination attempt was not meant for her husband but had been meant for her. And Steel was telling her she couldn't access the information.

Steven shuffled out of the stairwell. "Mom, we have to look at the contents of that card. This is the information I've been looking for."

Monarch closed her fist around the memory card. "I told you to stay in the stairwell."

"Where we heard everything." Olivia said following close behind her brother.

"I almost died looking for the answers that are on this memory card." Steven pointed to her fist.

Ishido appeared quietly behind Steven as Steven reached for his mother's closed hand. Ishido moved quickly and in a flash had closed both hands around Monarch's fist. "If you will not keep it safe, then I will take on that responsibility."

"Ishido, Steven is right. We must see what is on that memory chip." Monarch said. She grimaced at Ishido's painful grip.

Ishido's grip did not lessen as he used one hand to retrieve something from the inner fold of his jacket. He pulled out a dagger. He offered it to Steven. "Then, send your son to the states with this knife and have him plunge it into Joshua Knight's heart. Because that is essentially what you will be doing if you access the dossier." He shoved the hilt of the dagger into Steven's hand. "Now that God has given you back your life why don't you take another? You have full use of your hands now."

Steven glared at Ishido and rolled his eyes. "Really?"

Monarch took the dagger from Steven with her free hand. "We get your point, Ishido. All three of us owe a debt to Jonathan Steel."

"And Josh!" Olivia said quietly. "Mom, just keep it safe. We have to trust that they have a plan and eventually we can find out who killed father. But I'm not going to let Josh suffer because of us."

Steven swore loudly and stalked off. Monarch handed the dagger back to Ishido. His dark eyes glittered with unleashed malice. She nodded. "I promise I will hide the memory card."

Ishido slid the dagger out of sight. "We are all trusting you now, Dr. Monarch."

24

"Jonathan!"

Steel turned around shouldering his backpack and pulling his carry on behind him. Against the hazy afternoon light coming in through the windows at Heathrow airport a familiar figure moved toward him.

"Cassie?" He smiled. He actually smiled! How long had it been since he felt like smiling?

Cassie stood as tall as he with long blonde hair. She grabbed him in a hug, and he tried to return it but his backpack and carry on prevented it.

"You got my message." Steel said as he pulled back from the hug.

"No, I was driving by and saw a tall, handsome man with turquoise eyes and a perplexed look on his face and thought I'd give him a ride." She laughed. "Come on. I'll take you to your hotel. I assume you've got a hotel?"

Steel lifted his phone and consulted his travel app. "The Coventry?"

Cassie motioned to a cab. "I could have let you take the

cab alone but I couldn't resist." The cabbie was a tall, lanky bloke who tipped his hat at Steel.

"She insisted we wait! I was wondering what kind of mate she was waiting for. Let me put your things in the boot. Where to?"

"The Coventry." Steel said.

They climbed into the cab and for a moment, just a small moment, Steel almost felt like the world was normal again. He was riding in a cab with one of his newest friends, Dr. Cassandra Sebastian.

"So, I got your message and decided I would meet your flight. Hungry?" Cassie asked.

Steel's stomach growled. "Actually, I'm starved."

"There's a nice pizza place across from the Coventry." The cabbie said. "Best pizza in London." He glanced at them in the rearview mirror. "Of course, that's not saying much, mind you!" He laughed.

They arrived at the restaurant and the fragrance of cooked dough made Steel salivate. The pizza was indeed better than he had expected. He didn't often eat such heavy meals, but the pizza had a light, thin crust and was loaded with vegetables and cheese. He studied Cassie as she nibbled at her pizza.

"Cassie, you look good." He paused with his mouth half open. "I mean you look so healthy. You know what I mean."

Cassie held out her hands out in front of her. "Not a tremor in sight. It has been amazing, Jonathan. I was healed by my Savior! Jesus! In Jerusalem from 2000 years ago! How many people can claim that?"

"And what have you been doing?"

"Changing everything." She leaned forward. "I've revamped my show and we launch in January. I'm still the 'Artifact Hunter' but we will be discussing religious artifacts. I'll use that foundation to promote my own devotion to Christ. We will explore the real archeological and scientific evidence for the reality of Jesus of Nazareth. No more flashy sensationalism. No more putting my guests on the hot seat. Just real, reliable information from 'The Artifact Hunter'." She smiled at him. "Thanks to you, Jonathan, my life has really changed." She nibbled at a piece of pizza. "I'm glad I didn't have to face off against number eight."

Steel glanced around the interior of the small café. A few nondescript people glanced back at him. Could one of them be Gumijo's operative? He had seen no drones on the airplane so maybe they had agreed to no longer surveil him. He reached for the fountain pen surveillance dampener in his pocket and decided not to use it just yet. Still, he had to assume that at least human spies might be nearby.

"Why are you here, again?" Cassie brushed crumbs from her hand and drink some of her sparkling water.

"I'm looking for some artifacts."

"Really. You came to the right place."

"I spoke to Monty and found out you were here and that is why I texted you." Steel said.

"What artifacts?"

"Moses' rod and the bronze serpent. And two things. The Urim and the Thummim?"

Cassie raised an eyebrow. "And I thought I was the real artifact hunter! You don't fool around, do you?" She squinted at him. "And why do you think they might be here in London?"

"Monty said you have been helping him catalogue Dr. Lawrence's crates. You know, the ones he loaned to Dr. Nigel Hampton." Steel said.

"That man is creepy, Jonathan. And a charlatan if ever there was one."

"Cassie, one of the crates will not open and there is a

distinct possibility Cephas keyed it to my biometric signature. I need to open that crate and see what is inside."

"To find Moses's rod, the bronze serpent and two stones from the ancient Hebrew priest's chest plate, right?" Cassie said dubiously.

"Oh, that is what the Urim and Thummim are? If so, yes."

Cassie's gaze never left his. She leaned over the table. "Why?"

Steel studied her. "I really can't tell you. Client privilege."

"Oooo! Such mystery, Jonathan." She sat back. "Jonathan, you can't keep this from me. You will tell me eventually. You know you will."

"Well, not just now." He said and ate another bite of pizza. "And not here."

Cassie tapped the table. "So, if you can't open the third crate, then what?"

Steel drank some water. "I don't know." He said sadly.

"Okay, so I'll tell you something I shouldn't." Cassie leaned back into the table and ran a hand through her hair, tossing it back over her shoulder. "Do you remember the time travel guy?"

"Maize? Yeah."

"So, you said that when you and Jason came through the portal, Maize had preprogrammed it for some time in the future and then walked through, right?"

"Yeah. He just disappeared. And good riddance."

Cassie shook her head in dismay. "Jonathan! Do you realize what we could learn from time travel?"

"Been there, done that." Steel said. "And, besides, the machine was powered by supernatural means. The only reason we went back in time is because God allowed us to, and God alone made it happen."

"Maize had access to Anthony Cobalt's Sunstones, didn't he? They were a supernatural source of power." Cassie said.

"What's your point?"

"I've been looking for him and I think I may have found him. Here, near London. That's the real reason I'm here." Cassie said quietly.

"Are you suggesting I got back in time to Moses in the wilderness?" Steel said and for a crazy second he considered the possibility. Then reason prevailed. "I thought maybe you were here to help Monty with the crates?"

Cassie stiffened and her eyes filled with interest. "Well, I was. Eventually. After I found Maize. I mean I am helping Monty. It's just that I feel so weird around Monty."

"Why?"

Cassie's gaze returned to Steel. "I was dying, Jonathan. I was supposed to die a horrible death from my Huntington's Chorea. And even though I did not deserve it, I was healed. By water touched by Jesus Christ." She leaned closer to him, and her eyes glittered with moisture. "I didn't deserve it, Jonathan. The things I have done in my life! And, Monty, the one person on that entire trip who deserved to see Jesus couldn't remember anything! Why was I so blessed, and he wasn't? I just can't face him, Jonathan."

"I have good news for you. Monty remembers everything. All you had to do was ask him."

"Right! Bring up the one thing that would hurt him the most. I couldn't do that to Monty. So far, I avoided the topic with him."

Steel reached over and, in a move so uncharacteristic for him, he thought, he took her hand. "There is so much we don't deserve from God. I used to think it was the assignments, the missions. But now, I realize you can't accept the bad things without realizing he will also bring good things." He glanced around at the restaurant. The other patrons had left. A couple of girls walked in for a to-go order. He leaned forward and said quietly, "And, Cassie, right now, I need a miracle for Josh. He is very sick and I'm on this mission to find a way to heal him."

"You think Moses's rod will help him? What did he do? Open Pandora's Box?"

"I don't know what he did. But I know that if I can find this rod, well, Josh will get better." Steel sat back and hoped no one had heard him.

"Well, you may be looking for the wrong rod."

"What?"

Cassie looked at her phone. "Here, let me read something for you. This is from Numbers chapter 21. The Israelites are wandering about following Moses and they got a bit testy.

'They traveled from Mount Hor along the route to the Red Sea, to go around Edom. But the people grew impatient on the way; they spoke against God and against Moses, and said, "Why have you brought us up out of Egypt to die in the wilderness? There is no bread! There is no water! And we detest this miserable food!"

Then the Lord sent venomous snakes among them; they bit the people and many Israelites died. The people came to Moses and said, "We sinned when we spoke against the Lord and against you. Pray that the Lord will take the snakes away from us." So Moses prayed for the people.

The Lord said to Moses, "Make a snake and put it up on a pole; anyone who is bitten can look at it and live." So Moses made a bronze snake and put it up on a pole. Then when anyone was bitten by a snake and looked at the bronze snake, they lived.'

Cassie looked up at him. "Now, Moses had his staff and so did Aaron. We have no idea what happened to Moses' staff. Maybe what you're looking for is that rod that held the bronze serpent and not Moses' actual staff."

Steel felt his heart race and he nodded. "Do you think this serpent could actually heal someone?" Forget the demons, he thought. If he could get his hands on the serpent and the rod all Josh had to do was look at it! He could be healed!

"Slow down, Jonathan. We may be way out of luck. You see, there were lots of serpent cults in those days particularly in Canaan, the pagan land the Israelites were about to conquer and occupy. Over the centuries, many forms of a serpent have been found in archeological digs around the Middle East. I do know that Moses' serpent survived." She picked up her phone again and tapped the screen.

"Ah, here it is 2 Kings 18:1-4."

"In the third year of Hoshea son of Elah king of Israel, Hezekiah son of Ahaz king of Judah began to reign. He was twenty-five years old when he became king, and he reigned in Jerusalem twenty-nine years. His mother's name was Abijah daughter of Zechariah. He did what was right in the eyes of the Lord, just as his father David had done. He removed the high places, smashed the sacred stones and cut down the Asherah poles. He broke into pieces the bronze snake Moses had made, for up to that time the Israelites had been burning incense to it. (It was called Nehushtan.)"

"What was that last word?" Steel asked.

"Nehushtan means a brazen thing, a mere piece of brass. Scholars believe that over the nearly one thousand years since Moses lifted the serpent up in the desert the image had become a symbol of pagan worship. Israel time and time again returned to idol worship under the kings. Alternating kings always seemed to turn back to idols and then, once Israel was conquered or was in dismay, the nation returned to worship Yahweh. Scholars believe the serpent was left behind by the kings Asa and Joshaphat so that Hezekiah could break it."

"Even if the serpent still existed, it would be in pieces, then." Steel said.

"Jonathan the serpent event took place well over three thousand years ago! I doubt any trace of it still exists." Cassie sat back and drank from her tea. "But I'll wager if anyone could find any remnants of the serpent, it would be Dr. Cephas Lawrence. Now, Moses' rod and Aaron's rod are two different things. There are lots of legends and writings about what happened to them. One of those rods is supposed to be in the Ark of the Covenant."

Cassie fell silent and her eyes widened. "Oh, my gosh! Jonathan, you know where to find the Ark! I could do a story on the Ark!" For a second a fanatical gleam filled her eyes and then she sighed and shook her head. "See, the old me hasn't completely gone away. Look, Jonathan, even if you found this bronze serpent and the rod there's no guarantee it would be effective. The people were healed not by the action of looking on the serpent but by the admission that only God could heal them if they were obedient to his commands. Objects, as we learned in Jerusalem, don't necessarily have power unless God puts that power there."

"Great!" Steel sat back exasperated. "What will I do then?"

"Stick to your plan. See if there is anything in Cephas' crates first. Check with Monty. I had breakfast with him this morning." Cassie said and her cheeks flushed.

"How was breakfast?" Steel said as he smiled.

"Quite agreeable." She said and her smile lit up the morning.

Steel glanced at his watch. "I don't have much time, Cassie. I'm on a tight schedule."

Cassie nodded. "Then let's head to Hampton's Museum of the Weird!"

25

Dr. Jack Merchant showed his I.D. to the security guard at the back door to LSU Medical Center. The guard pushed an old fashioned logbook through the plexiglass divider's opening.

"Sign in, doctor." She said.

Dr. Merchant never ceased to marvel at the mixture of antiquated methods and the high-tech advances at the medical center. He scrawled his name and headed to the elevators. He glanced at his watch. He was late. Again. A call from the hospital right at 5 P.M. had arrived and he had to perform a procedure on call. He had finished up the procedure and had tried to call Dr. Gupta Moshander. His friend had not answered his cell phone. Maybe he had given up and gone home. It had been two hours since they were supposed to meet in Moshander's lab. It was now close to 7 P.M. and Jason Birdsong would be infiltrating the clinic with the night shift. Less security, he had said. He resisted the urge to call Birdsong. He pushed his glasses back on his nose and realized he was sweating. Why was he so nervous? Maybe it was because of the memory of a similar elevator ride in another hospital that had led to an encounter that almost cost him his life.

The elevator doors opened onto a dim hallway on the sixth floor. Few people were present at this late hour. Students were studying from home or in the library on the third floor. He made his way down the dark hallway. Why were the lights at only half illumination? Trying to save money, no doubt. The medical center was constantly in a financial crisis. It had to compete with the medical center in south Louisiana and even though it made more money, the funds were siphoned off to support the "real" medical center close to the famous LSU Tiger stadium.

He stepped in something liquid, and his feet almost slid out from under him. He glanced down at a dark liquid pooling in the hallway. In the dim lighting it appeared crimson, and the unmistakable copper odor of blood wafted up to him. His heart raced and he followed the puddle to the open door of Moshander's lab.

He hurried through the door, sloshing through the blood and gasped at the sight before him. The lab was a shambles. Broken glass and equipment covered the lab tables. Something brushed against his leg, and he jumped as three white rats scurried through the puddle of blood and out the door into the hallway. Merchant took out his cell phone and dialed the security guard.

"Hey, you better get up here. There's blood everywhere and I don't see Dr. Gupta. And, call an ambulance. There's way too much blood."

Merchant stood tentatively in the doorway and pocketed his phone. Should he go in? What if Moshander was hurt? He stepped over the river of blood and followed it around the closest lab counter. The room was filled with shadows from the meager light. He peeked around the edge of the lab counter. Moshander was sprawled in the middle of the aisle. The top of his head was missing exposing brain tissue.

Merchant backed away as nausea gripped him and he stepped on something. He slid backwards and fell into the river of clotting blood. He looked down at his foot. The top of Moshander's skull hung on the toe of his shoes. He kicked it away and back crawled to the door. He made it into the hallway just as the security guard appeared around the corner with two others in tow. She took one look at him and screamed.

26

Birdsong walked down the road toward the clinic. At seven o'clock there would be a change in nursing staff. Already the sun was setting along the horizon and the cool air chilled the sweat from his walk from his hidden car. He wore a pair of blue scrubs and a stethoscope hung around his neck. He pulled his jacket tighter around him against the cold night air. He had parked his truck along the highway and walked toward the parking lot of the clinic. He had been here before so he pulled a bouffant surgical cap over his head and stuffed his hair inside. Then, he took a surgical mask from his pocket and put it over his face. As he was nearing the main driveway, a car pulled up and the window went down.

"Need a ride?" A dark-haired woman looked out the window. She couldn't see him very well for the darkness, but the woman was familiar. Josh's nurse practitioner! And she had just seen him the day before.

"I ran out of gas, and I don't want to be late for work." He said.

"Climb in and I'll give you a ride."

Birdsong climbed in. "Thanks, uh?"

"Faye Murphy." She glanced at his name tag. "Burt Jason. I don't think we've met. Of course, can't tell behind that mask. You know the COVID restrictions are no longer in place."

"I've got the sniffles. Can't be too careful." Birdsong swallowed. He hoped his sudden nervousness didn't torpedo his undercover operation. "I'm a temp. Just for tonight. Filling in for someone on C hall."

"Who?" Faye pulled into the massive parking lot and made her way toward the clinic.

"I have no idea. They just told me to show up and fill their shift. Thanks, Faye. You must be coming on the next shift."

"Well, actually I'm pulling a double shift today. I had to run home and let my dog out." She tried to smile, and it was then Birdsong saw the shadows under her eyes.

"You're working twenty-four hours straight?"

Faye nodded and yawned. "Yep, and then I have a couple of days off. There's a very special patient I just can't get out of my mind. You know what I'm talking about."

"Sure. It's hard to walk away from someone in pain."

As they climbed out of the car Birdsong thanked her and together, they walked through the main entrance along with six other personnel. Faye spoke to the members of the other group as they passed through the front doors. Birdsong glanced briefly at the closest camera. Hopefully he would be lost in the crowd. Security was notoriously slack on the night shift in any location.

Birdsong moved off away from Faye and the rest of the people and made his way down the hallway toward Josh's room. The door to Josh's room opened and one of the doctors stepped out. Birdsong turned immediately into the nearest room and closed the door behind him. The patient in the room was snoring in his bed. Birdsong glanced at the man under the cover and then hurried over to inspect the intravenous lines hanging from poles.

The door opened. "How is Mr. Grapp tonight?"

"Stable." Birdsong said without turning to look at the doctor. The door closed behind him and he began to breathe again. He slowly opened the door and looked out. Usually at shift change, the nurses and doctors would make "rounds" on the patients. If that was so, he would need to lie low for a while. He stepped out into the hallway. A surveillance camera enclosed in a plastic bubble covered the hallway from the center of the ceiling. The camera had swiveled away from Birdsong, and he made his way quietly to the nearest maintenance closet. He opened the door and slipped inside. His phone buzzed in his pocket. He had turned the ringer off. The caller i.d. showed Merchant.

"Jack, now is not a good time." He whispered.

"He's dead, Jason." Merchant was almost shouting.

"Calm down! They'll hear you."

"Who will hear me?"

"The nurses in the hallway. I'm at the clinic. Now, who is dead?"

"Gupta. Dr. Moshander." Merchant said, breathing quickly. "I'm at the police station to give my statement. I'm covered with his blood! They cut the top of his head off, Jason. Who are these people?"

A chill ran down Birdsong's spine and he swallowed back the nausea. It was happening again! "They are creatures in league with Satan, Jack." Birdsong backed into the farthest corner of the closet. "Now, tell me what happened."

Merchant told his side of the story. "The police said everything had been taken. Laptop computers with all of the results from the tests!"

"How do you know?"

"I asked Moshander to keep everything out of the school

system. He put it on his laptop. All of the specimens are gone. They took any evidence of the virus!"

Birdsong sighed. "You aren't safe, Jack. They'll come for you next."

"Well, I have to go by the coroner's office and get my tablet. All the information is backed up on it. I can call the security guard at the coroner's office and have him meet me at the back entrance."

"They'll be coming to your home next."

"What should I do?"

"Get out of town now. Quickly."

Merchant moaned. "I have to work tomorrow. I can't get anyone to cover for me."

"Go to the lake house. They don't know about me and the lake house. You'll be safe there until I can get back."

"Okay." Merchant said quietly. "Better yet, I can stay in a courtesy room at the hospital for the rest of the night and they won't try anything with hospital personnel around. Too many witnesses. Jason, this isn't my first rodeo. I've had to elude people following me before. I've been in dangerous situations before. But this takes the cake."

"If all goes well, I'll have more of the treatment fluid by morning. I can be back in Shreveport before lunch. Stay safe."

Birdsong slid his phone back in his pocket. He turned a mop bucket upside down and sat on it. He leaned back into the corner behind shelves and closed his eyes. What had he gotten himself into? He had agreed to be Jonathan's sometime partner, but the past few weeks had been insane. Time travel to ancient Jerusalem? Check! Almost getting killed in a virtual reality? Check! And now, demonic hosts who cut the top of a person's head off for fun?

"Jonathan, you owe me big time." He whispered.

27

"Deondre?" Merchant stood at the rear entrance to the coroner's office. He shuffled nervously in the cold air while waiting for the security guard to open the back door. A ramp led up onto the slightly elevated platform for gurneys.

"I'm here, Doc." The doors swung open, and Deondre appeared. "Come on in. Things are awfully quiet."

Merchant looked around the rear parking lot. No other cars were in sight. He hurried up the ramp and pocketed his phone. Deondre held the doors open for him.

"Doc, you okay? You're usually not up this hour. Dr. Sam is when there's a body, but you keep daylight hours." Deondre had a totally bald head and skin the color of dark chocolate.

Merchant stepped inside the doors and motioned for Deondre to close them. "Lock the doors and arm the security alarm."

Deondre closed the doors and closed two deadbolt locks. "Doc, you're scaring me, now. Who would want to steal anything from the morgue?"

"Yeah, my question exactly, Deondre. I'll only be a

minute. I have to get something from my office and then I'll get out of your hair." He paused as Deondre chuckled. Deondre ran a hand across his bare scalp.

"That would be a challenge, Doc."

Merchant hurried through the receiving bay and down a darkened hallway to his office. He unlocked his office door and flipped on the light. The room was untouched. No one had messed with the piles of paperwork on his desk. He shuffled through folders. No tablet. Where had he put it? He snapped his fingers. When he came by the office earlier on the way to Moshander's office he had dropped off a folder of forms he had signed. Maybe he had left the tablet with the folders.

He shut the light off in his office and locked the door. He turned and screamed at the sight of Deondre standing in the middle of the hallway.

"Now, Doc. You're spooking me." Deondre slowed his breathing. "What's eating you?"

"A virus, Deondre. A dangerous virus and I have to find my tablet. It has valuable information on it."

Deondre put out a hand. "Just a minute, Doc. You've got blood all over your shoes and scrub pants down there."

Bile surged into Merchant's throat at the memory of Gupta's bloody head. He swallowed and tried to act calm. "Bloody case at the hospital. I think I left my tablet in the autopsy room."

Deondre stepped aside as Merchant pushed past him. Sweat fogged his glasses and he pushed them back up on his nose. He entered the autopsy room. Three bodies lay on gurneys in plastic body bags. He had put the folders in the "in" box by the far door that led to cold storage. He moved around the ends of the three gurneys and paused at the counter. The "in" box contained the folder all right. But where was his tablet? He looked around the entire counter, pushing aside trays of surgical equipment and piles of folded gowns and gloves.

Merchant stopped and fought his growing panic. He had to find that tablet! If everything was gone, then all was lost. He could call Jason and ask him to get more blood while he was with Josh. He fumbled for his phone, and it slipped from his sweaty hands and clattered onto the floor and slid up under the nearest gurney.

Merchant had not turned on the overhead light and only indirect safety lighting directed toward the ceiling gave any help at all. He couldn't see his phone and got down on his hands and knees. He crawled under the first gurney and saw his phone glittering under the second gurney. He retrieved his phone and turned to crawl out from under the gurneys when the first one moved.

"Deondre?" He said. Deondre did not answer, and he heard the unmistakable sound of a zipper opening. He blinked in horror. This could NOT be happening. The first gurney shuddered again, and bare legs suddenly swung into view. He opened his mouth to scream and put his hand to stifle it. The legs plopped down, and the naked body followed. The sagging, aging flesh of an elderly man rippled with movement and the body began shuffling away from the gurney. It moved toward the counter. Merchant was paralyzed with fear.

The man moved zombie like to the counter and with trembling hands lifted the folders he had deposited in the "in" box. The man tossed the folder aside and the papers within scattered across the floor. He watched the shuffling, trembling body of the old man hunch over the counter. A hand moved erratically back into the box and withdrew his tablet.

The man's body jerked and tilted as it turned toward the

gurney. It bent at the waist and the man's face came into view. His eyes were clouded and his mouth drooled blood.

"Looking for this?" The man moaned in a ghostly voice.

Merchant swallowed hard. He glanced at the gurney wheels and slapped off the locks. He grabbed the side of the gurney and shoved it at the man's body. The gurney slammed the man up against the counter. The tablet fell onto the gurney and into the open body bag.

Merchant stood up and reached for the tablet but a cold, wet hand grabbed his. He looked up into the glowing eyes of the dead man now pinned against the counter by the gurney.

"That's mine now." It hissed.

Merchant slapped at the man's hand and dug around in a pool of blood and goo inside the body bag. The man's hands clutched Merchant's hair and pulled him down toward the body bag. Merchant jerked away from the thing's grasp and hair tore out by the roots. This dead man was strong! Supernaturally strong!

"Leave me along you spawn of hell." He screamed. He found the tablet in the folds of the body bag and shoved the gurney against the dead man again.

"You can't hurt the dead." He said as more dark blood poured from his mouth.

"Doc?"

Merchant whirled as Deondre opened the door and flipped the light on. The dead man's body collapsed over the gurney and Merchant stepped back, gasping for breath.

"What the heck?" Deondre froze at the sight of the dead body leaning over the gurney.

Merchant paused and glanced back over his shoulder. "It's the zombie apocalypse, Deondre. I'd go home if I were you." Shaking and trembling, Merchant shoved past him and ran out of the building.

ACKNOWLEDGMENTS

Please check out J. Warner Wallace's website, coldcasechristianity.com for more information regarding demons. While you are there, check out the entire site! Jim Wallace has compiled some of the best information and tools for defending the truthfulness of the Christian faith!

Death By Darwin
The 13th Demon: Altar of the Spiral Eye
The 12th Demon: Mark of the Wolfdragon
The 11th Demon: The Ark of Chaos
The 10th Demon: Children of the Bloodstone
The 9th Demon: Time of the Cross
The 8th Demon: A Wicked Numinosity
The Homecoming Tree
Our Darkness, His Light
With Mark Sutton:
Hope Again: A Lifetime Plan for Conquering Depression
www.brucehennigan.com
www.steelchronicles.com
www.conqueringdepression.com

CPSIA information can be obtained
at www.ICGtesting.com
Printed in the USA
FSHW022256300921
85159FS